Advance praise for Rayo Casablanca and *6 Sick Hipsters*!

"*6 Sick Hipsters* is a wild, poignant, twisted, bitterly funny page turner with dead-on dialogue and a wonderful ensemble cast. Rayo Casablana has written the big novel the hipster generation has been waiting for."
—Jason Starr, author of *The Follower*

"Rayo Casablanca's first novel is thoroughly amusing and utterly demented. It features a killer baboon, sewer diving, men in silly jumpsuits, hipster assassins that will stop at nothing to get what they want, and interesting information about paleontology and knitting. What else do you need to know?"
—Owen King, author of *We're All In This Together*

"*6 Sick Hipsters* is a wild ride of a novel. Something of a magical realist noir that brings a whole new meaning to the fashionable idea of the death of the hipster. It's enough to make one nervous about leaving the house in a Pavement T-shirt."
—Jeff Parker, author of *Ovenman* and *The Back of the Line*

"*6 Sick Hipsters* is a wild ride into the underworld of hip that takes more daring, shocking, bloody turns than *Pulp Fiction*. Rayo Casablanca pulls no punches. Oh, but you'll take 'em . . . and love every jolt."
—Kemble Scott, author of *SoMa*

6 Sick Hipsters

Rayo Casablanca

KENSINGTON BOOKS
http://www.kensingtonbooks.com

KENSINGTON BOOKS are published by

Kensington Publishing Corp.
850 Third Avenue
New York, NY 10022

All Kensington titles, imprints, and distributed lines are available at special quantity discounts for bulk purchases for sales promotion, premiums, fund-raising, and educational, or institutional use.

Special book excerpts or customized printings can also be created to fit specific needs. For details, write or phone the office of the Kensington Special Sales Manager: Attn. Special Sales Department. Kensington Publishing Corp., 850 Third Avenue, New York, NY 10022. Phone: 1-800-221-2647.

Kensington and the K logo Reg. U.S. Pat. & TM Off.

ISBN-13: 978-0-7582-2283-1
ISBN-10: 0-7582-2283-1

First Printing: April 2008
10 9 8 7 6 5 4 3 2 1

Printed in the United States of America

For Sham, Veetros, and Mo.

Acknowledgments

Many thanks to John Scognamiglio and Justin Hocking for making it happen.

A round of applause for my agent, Jessica Regel, for keeping me cool.

A tip of the hat to Yorick, J. Gold, Mr. Mavroudis, and the brothers Rein/Levine.

Cheers to Gary and his machines, Barry and his prehistory, and Andrew and his Avalanche.

To my muse: Keep the TV on.

1

Brittany Worley was pulling into the Getty gas station on Union when she noticed the man in the black Jeep.

He was slender and handsome. His face sharp like he was sucking in his cheeks. Brittany guessed early 30s. Maybe older. He was wearing obnoxiously tight jeans, a denim jacket and a black Iron Maiden T-shirt. The T-shirt had a drawing of a leering zombie in a leather duster smoking a cigarette and brandishing a gun and it said, *Stranger in a Strange Land.*

The man eyed Brittany as she got out of her rented 6 Series.

She found the shirt repulsive. She was sure the guy had that reclining naked chick silhouette on his Jeep's mud flaps. Maybe even a Confederate flag bumper sticker on the rear window and a six-pack of Budweiser in a cheap cooler on the backseat. *Iron Maiden?* Brittany knew that was the cheese-ball metal band Veniss was into. *Ugh.* Veniss even had a tat of that zombie's grinning head on her back. She said it was Eddie, Eddie the Head. *Repulsive.*

Brittany decided to ignore the Iron Maiden guy. This was the first day of her much needed vacation. Two weeks back home.

Two weeks relaxing in the city. Attracting the attention of some heavy metal freak wasn't in the cards but she still watched Eddie the Head fill his Jeep, ready and eager to totally dismiss him. But then he turned to face her and she was immediately struck by how attractive he was. There was something really striking about the bone structure of his face. But his T-shirt was killing it. Cute or not, he had terrible taste in music.

She did a quick self-check, scanning her stretched reflection in the tinted windows of the rental. White faux-fox trimmed leather boots. Hot pink cords. White V-neck sleeveless top. Rose sweater tied around her shoulders. Her hair up in a bun and sunglasses on. She looked as good as she felt. Like Jackie O on holiday in Aspen. Or better, Elizabeth Taylor circa the winter of '66. When the gas pump clicked Brittany skipped into the station to grab a Tab, a Red Bull and a pack of menthols.

On her way across the lot she made the mistake of turning around and looking again at Eddie. He was looking at her and flashed a lopsided smile. Brittany was thrown off guard. His toothy grin was really intriguing. Brittany looked past the shirt, past the stretched skin of the grinning death's head, into this guy's eyes and saw something sweet there. And despite her knowing better, she smiled back. Instinct maybe. She turned back and walked into the station. Something wicked in her hoped Eddie would follow.

He did.

Brittany grabbed the can of Red Bull first and wandered the tight aisles leisurely, eyeing Eddie as he grabbed a bag of peanuts and stopped to flip through a *Weekly World News*. The cover featured a photo of a three-limbed infant with a horn in the middle of its forehead with the caption, *Unicorn Love Child!* A faint shiver of expectation ran up Brittany's spine when she stopped behind Eddie to grab a six-pack of Tab.

"Can't believe how expensive things are these days," he said, eyes still on the newspaper. His voice was calm. Baritone.

Brittany turned to face him and smiled. "I remember coming to this station as a kid and paying forty cents for a can of Tab," she replied.

Eddie looked up, that something sweet still in his eyes. "I remember when it was just a quarter. So, you trying to keep awake?" he asked pointing to the can of Red Bull Brittany was clutching.

"Yeah, late night last night."

"Happens to the best of us. You from Williamsburg?"

"Queens."

"Nothing wrong with that," Eddie smiled. His teeth all jumbled like a fallen fence but shockingly white. They sparkled in the humming fluorescent lights. "You know of anywhere in Queens to have lunch? I'm headed that way. Something spicy. I'm in the mood for spicy."

"Yeah," Brittany blushed and that embarrassed her. "There's a nice place called Loca. It's spicy. Kind of Caribbean-Italian fusion. I've only been there once but it was good."

"That sounds perfect," Eddie said. Something in Brittany fluttered.

"I can show you on a map where it is."

"Do you want to join me?"

Brittany hadn't been out on a date in over six months. And it wasn't for lack of trying. She was a striking woman, voted Most Popular in her senior class at Saint John's. Tall with long golden hair, wide dark eyes and a pug nose. Brittany was a prototypical American girl. A rough mixture of European finery and American mustang sensuality. She was often whistled at by construction workers and that was always a nice gauge. But despite her good looks, she didn't crave the attention. The smiles and roses and whistles were white noise in the background of her demanding life. And that had a lot to do with her being a pop star.

Brittany loved the sound of that. Pop. Star. *Awesome.*

Adored by prepubescent girls across the globe—the most fawning fans for her brand of bubble gum pop were Russian orphans—she was on her way to superstardom. At least her agent said so. Brittany's debut album, *Don't Tell That Girl to Shut Up*, sold 150,000 copies its first month. She knew it wasn't on the same playing field as that other Britney but it was damn good. Great for a college dropout from Astoria. The whole thing was a thrill ride and Brittany loved almost every sugar-coated minute of it. But the tabloids annoyed her. If there weren't rumors in the *National Enquirer* that she was schtupping Brent from The Neon Crusaders in Bucharest or making out with Kool-Loc from the 35 Chambers of Funk, then she didn't exist. If she wasn't being fucked by some star, she wasn't anything. No one wanted to read about how lonely Brittany really was. How bored silly she was with all the slick hangers-on and drunken roadies. Coked out dot com fuckups. Greasy sheiks. Abusive ball players. Brittany tried to just let it roll. She figured that the gossip was just part and parcel of the fame. So long as she didn't get serious, they could never really pin her down. Fact was no one really intrigued Brittany. At least not in years. But there was something different about this Iron Maiden fan. There was something almost *too* intriguing about him.

Brittany fucking hated his shirt, though. She hoped he was an artist or musician. Maybe he was the cute lead singer of that Williamsburg band blowing up in Sweden. Jerry? Jakus? No, this guy seemed too refined. In fact, the more Brittany looked at Eddie the more refined he seemed. And the less repulsive the shirt got. If a B-lister with a mullet had been wearing it she would have wanted to spit in his face. But the fact that this thin, clean and urbane guy was wearing it added a bit of naughtiness. Her agent was always telling her to throw more of that kind of edginess around.

"So," Eddie broke Brittany from her reverie, "you interested?"

"Sure. By the way, I'm Brittany. Brittany Worley."

"Nice to meet you, Brittany. I'm Andy Stare."

That easy, Brittany thought. *I'm on a date.* It was frighteningly simple. Yet it was exactly like her sister had told her, "Let them come to you. Enough sucking dick in stretch Hummers for attention." According to Veniss, Brittany just needed a nice man who felt compelled to walk over and invite her to lunch.

"Why don't you follow me down there?" Brittany suggested.

And Andy did.

Brittany drove slowly. Allowed time for lights to change and traffic to move, without losing sight of the black Jeep in her rearview mirror. A few times she waved back at him. He waved in response. She smiled when he did, a giddy feeling rising and falling like a tide in her stomach. She turned up the radio and bobbed her head along with something that she recognized from a club in Austin. Brittany was a casual music listener, anything so long as it was up-tempo. Mostly country. And whenever she came across one of her songs she'd pump it up and sing along. That always felt a bit strange but she figured there's no fun in making music if you don't listen to it. She lit a cigarette, rolled the mentholated smoke around her mouth, and bobbed her head in time with a twangy song about broken hearts and methamphetamines. Not her kind of lyrics but the chorus was catchy. Brittany didn't have the patience to sing about the world's problems. She left that to the rappers and the cowboys.

Loca's had opened only a month ago but it was early and Brittany was able to find parking easily. She waited, pursing her lips in the rearview and retouching her lip gloss, while Andy parked. They walked into Loca's together. Silently. After they were seated and drinks ordered, they fell into casual but stilted conversation.

"So," Andy said, "tell me what you do."

Brittany told him her rambling story about growing up in Queens. Her time in San Diego with her cousins. Her interest in singing. The thirty second appearance in a Kriss Kross video that got her noticed. Modeling. Signing with her agent. Recording her first single. She told him about the highs and lows of stardom. The limbless Russian orphans. The heart-breaking African kids without cell phones. Travel. Adventure. Drugs. Sex. Loneliness. Most of all she talked about her loneliness. She didn't mention the stretch limo blowjobs.

"To be honest," Andy said, "I haven't heard of you. Sorry."

Brittany admitted she was disappointed. But it also put her mind at ease. She didn't have to impress this guy. "You into metal?" Brittany asked, eyes on Andy's shirt.

"Sure," Andy smiled. "It works."

"Now that you know a bit about me, what do you do?" Brittany asked.

"I'm an artist," Andy replied.

"That's awesome. What kind of stuff?"

"Painting mainly, low brow artwork. Are you familiar with any?"

"No, I don't think so."

"I've been compared to Neckface and David Ellis."

Brittany laughed, "I don't know them."

"Honestly, I don't know if you'd like it."

The waiter came and Brittany ordered the jerk ravioli. Andy had the sausage and bananas.

"You pretty successful with the art thing?"

"I sell a few paintings here and there. I've had some shows in Europe, Australia. I'm actually headed to a gallery opening in Fairfax tomorrow."

"What do your paintings actually look like? You said low brow but that doesn't really mean much to me," Brittany shrugged.

"Like graffiti really. I did a fair amount of bombing as a kid and people just noticed my work. They liked it. I went to the School of Visual Arts here in New York and now I do stuff on canvas. Skulls, cyclopses, skeletons riding tigers fighting minotaurs, you know. I've actually got a kind of trademarked image of a skeleton in a Viking hat. I'm not a huge Iron Maiden fan but I like the Eddie image and people say it reminds them of my work."

Brittany actually relaxed hearing that. "But you like metal . . ."

"Some. I dig some of the thrash metal bands, you know, stuff like Exodus, late-Suicidal Tendencies and Heathen. I don't suppose you listen to metal?"

"No. Not really," Brittany said shaking her head.

They ate and talked more about art. Brittany had taken an art history class at the College of New Jersey before dropping out. She told Andy that she really liked realism. Photo-realism even better. Andy smiled and said that realism was played out. That art brut—raw art, the art of insane, folk art—was the truest art.

"Why? I mean, those people aren't even artists. It's like junk."

"That's the whole point. The art scene is so inundated with quote-unquote artists, people who study their whole lives to become big names and don't really do anything original. The whole outsider movement is about bringing that back to the scene—that sense of wonder and originality."

"But it doesn't sound very pretty."

"Well, not all art is pretty."

Pause.

Andy switched gears, "So, you have any siblings? I've got a brother. He's lazy and ugly. I love him nonetheless."

Brittany was glad to move into more comfortable conversational territory. "Yeah, a sister. She's a filmmaker. But her stuff is really kinda out there. Stuff that . . . Actually you'd probably like her stuff. It's too arty for me, not at all entertaining."

"Amazing, both of you are talented, huh? She sounds interesting. Would I have seen anything she's done?"

"Nah. She made a few independent short films. Nothing big."

"What's her name?"

"Her name is Vanessa but she goes by the name Veniss. With two esses."

"Like *Veniss Underground?*"

"Yeah, like that book. She's always talking how it influenced the look of her films. I didn't read it. Whatever."

Andy blushed, looked down at his hands, "You know, this is

going to seem really funny but I'm actually a big fan of your sister's movies. I've seen all of her shorts and particularly loved her first one, *Technician's Role in Quality Control.* That was sweet and the feature she did . . . What was that called?"

"*Bronchospasm a Go Go.*"

"Yeah, that was amazing. Total DIY filmmaking. She used, like, toy cameras or something. It was surreal and brilliant."

Brittany was chewing her ravioli and didn't look up from the plate. She was annoyed. She didn't like talking about her sister. She wanted to get it across to Andy that she was the one he was talking to and about, not her sis. But at the same time she couldn't fault his interest. Veniss always had been the fascinating creature in the family. Where Brittany wore sun dresses, floral patterned hats and pink sandals, Veniss would turn up in tight, hip hugging kid's jeans. Her pale gaunt legs painfully squeezed into the denim like sausage. A white wifebeater. Chunky black shades. Buffalo skull bandana. Always the attention getter.

Brittany toured Thailand and Veniss would be passed out in a hotel room in Monaco, and there would be no guess about who would get all the press. It wasn't the sibling trying to raise the spirits of the underprivileged. The one smiling with toothless Third World children.

Brittany was the talk of the teen tabloids. Veniss was the talk of the town. Everyone in New York knew her or knew about her. Everyone who mattered in New York and L.A. loved her. Veniss was a cult superstar. She went on frequent binges. Caught spinning around town like Courtney Love but with a fresher face and less elastic thighs. Her arms were usually adorned in permanent marker graffiti. She had her fans write things like "Fuck me, Please!" and "Bitch Goddess" on her forearms. And her boobs were frequently hanging out. Veniss would strut and purr like a punk kitten for all the hipsters that followed her. In the alt press she was seen as some sort of film vixen. A rough-and-tumble artiste both sexy and vulgar. Burping at screenings. Farting at awards ceremonies. Veniss was rock 'n' roll. But Brittany didn't hate her for it. If anything it just made her feel dirty.

"My sister's always been the experimental one. She's even a sex symbol for some really fucked up people."

Andy shook his head, "I don't think of your sister as a sex symbol or anything. Not really my type."

Andy's eyes flashed.

There was indeed something sweet there.

"So, what's the fame like? Dueling famous siblings and all," he asked.

"Sometimes it's fun. Sometimes it's just annoying. My fame's entirely different than Veniss'. She's in a whole other world. We've never really been on the same wavelength."

Andy reached across the table and put his hand on Brittany's. She got a tingling sensation at his touch. A rush of blood to a quiet limb. She knew she should make some sort of reciprocal move. Brittany said, "Do you want to meet her?"

Andy's eyes got wide, "Really?"

"Yeah, she's in town. Just hanging out at my apartment in Long Island City. I bought it to be near my parents but most of my time is in Miami or L.A. Veniss likes to hang there. She usually watches TV and paints her nails and does chick shit that she can't do in public. She saves the farting and puking for public. I don't think she'd mind if we came by, but you should probably not tell her you're a big fan."

"Just a little fan?" Andy said coyly.

"Yeah, a little fan."

It was a quick drive to her place. While Brittany was embarrassed by the sparseness of her apartment, she was very happy she'd cleaned that morning. She had worked hard to make sure the apartment was both neat and playful. The flowering cactus on the kitchen table. The collection of glass koalas on the fireplace. The poster of juggling clowns in the guest bath-room. It was suburban kitsch. Maybe even a bit Veniss without all the drugs and sex and smell.

"I really dig what you've done with the place," Andy said walking in. "It's subtle and clean with pockets of color and life. Does that sound stupid?"

Brittany shook her head. It was cute.

But before she could lean over and kiss Andy, Veniss came out from the bedroom. She was wearing one of her trademark wifebeaters, braless. She stretched, her long pale arms reaching for the ceiling, and her breasts slid out from under her shirt.

"Hi, Veniss," Brittany snapped. A scolding snap, an angry snap.

Veniss paid absolutely no attention to it.

"Who's this guy? I like his shirt."

Veniss sat down at the kitchen table and put her feet up on a chair. She wasn't wearing any underwear beneath her denim skirt. Brittany groaned and pulled Andy to the bedroom to show him around.

"Jealous cunt," she hissed.

Brittany took Andy on a brief tour of the rest of the apart-ment. Really just an excuse to kiss him before she brought him back into the kitchen. On their return, Andy helped himself to beer in the fridge. Then he sat at the table, legs crossed. Brit-tany noticed he didn't look uncomfortable. In fact, he looked entirely at home.

"I said I liked your shirt," Veniss said. "When you walked in, that's what I said."

Andy smiled his jumbled tooth smile, "Thanks. My name is Andy."

"Hi, Andy."

"I've seen a few of your movies."

Brittany had hoped it wouldn't go there so soon, that Andy would play the fan card close.

Veniss closed her eyes and rolled her tongue as though she was bored as shit.

"Yeah, I've got a new flick that's premiering at Cannes in the spring," she droned. "It's kinda hush-hush right now but I think it's going to rock a lot of people's worlds. It's called *Colin Gets the Girl* and it's about this black guy played by Derek Bowles who falls in love with a hip Asian chick. It's got all my trademark style and I even threw in some hardcore penetration shots to shake it up a bit."

"Nice," Brittany spat.

"Yeah, it's gonna cause a ruckus this year."

Andy said, "You like Susan Seidelman? I really think your work is like hers."

Veniss perked up, "Yeah, I fucking love Seidelman . . ."

Andy looked over at Brittany and shrugged his shoulders. *Sorry*, he mouthed.

Brittany just rolled her eyes.

Andy turned back to Veniss, "So you like Vandermeer . . ."

Brittany got up and fled to the bathroom where she applied more makeup and brushed her hair. She sighed as loudly as she could, hoping to deafen conversation in the next room. But it didn't work. She could hear Andy and Veniss chatting like girlfriends until their conversation was interrupted by a bang. The sound of something hitting a hard surface. Or something exploding. A backfire in the kitchen.

Brittany paused. Silence. She shouted, "Everything okay?"

"Yeah," said Andy in reply. "Just a chair fell over."

Brittany went back to brushing her hair and fuming over her sister's behavior. She knew that deep in some forgotten and musty corner of Veniss' damaged DNA was a code for *born to shock*. It was like breathing and eating, if Veniss didn't shock then she didn't exist. Brittany flushed the toilet for effect. Maybe it was a warning shot. Then she waltzed out. "Hope you two aren't getting it on out here," she scoffed.

As she entered the kitchen she slipped in a puddle of blood, crashed on her left hip and let out a shrill cry. It was as much from panic as pain. Veniss was lying on the kitchen floor. Her head was caved in with a meat clever.

Andy was sitting on the kitchen table, blood on his shirt and a gun in his hand.

"Just to tell you, the whole meat clever thing was a bit over the top. A bit too Lizzie Borden for my tastes. I just figured I'd try it out. And guns are so noisy and don't really let you indulge in artistry. I'm sorry you have to see this. Really, I am."

"What the fuck have you done?" Brittany screeched and tried to scuttle across the floor but she kept slipping in the blood and falling.

"Slip and slide," Andy joked and jumped down from the table.

Brittany screamed and shook her head. As though that might clear her vision. Reset the game.

"Let me start by saying, I never planned on using you to get to her. This just kind of fell into place. That was a very good lunch though. Conversation was a bit tired but I'll forgive you that."

Brittany began to cry. Sob uncontrollably.

She curled up. Couldn't move. Could hardly breathe the fear was so strong.

"Don't worry, I'm not going to chop you or shoot you."

Andy put the gun down, got on all fours. He crawled over to where Brittany was shaking in a blood-spattered heap. Smiling the whole time. Eyes glinting with cruel fire. He ran a gory hand through Brittany's hair.

He whispered, "You ever heard of a garrote?"

2

Beth Ann was a sick hipster.

Her knit cap said so. Red with little devil horns outlined on top, the cap had the words "sick hipster" sewn in bold white letters across the brim. She'd knit the cap when the dark spots, the sickness, had almost overwhelmed her. The doctors called it macular degeneration. They used twenty dollar words like drusen. Nonexudative. Metamorphopsia. Beth Ann just called it The Darkness. Or slowly losing her eyesight. But on really shitty days, like most Mondays, it was fucking going blind. The world was fading to black and Beth Ann, celebrated Queen Knitter of Williamsburg, was stepping into the shadows.

The Darkness had been creeping up stealthily for years. First showed up, fittingly, on her sixteenth birthday when the edges of the vanilla cake were amber. The strawberry frosting looked orange like mango. She'd had her period at the time and didn't get any of the gifts she had asked for. It was like the day couldn't get any worse and then the edges of her vision were ragged. The wavy lines appeared in college. Just popped up one morning, wavy lines everywhere. On Cal Pepper's pretty face the morning after they hooked up for the third time. On the budgeting sheets in econ. Wavy lines that began to dance across Chaucer's early English. Wavy lines doing a samba. It was the same way with her dad. Larry Belling saw the lines boogie across his songbooks when he was twenty. Dad said, "You just can't play Roky Erickson's 'You're Gonna Miss Me' when the lines are washing back and forth like seaweed." Beth Ann didn't play guitar but she got the point. Now, a full fourteen years later and The Darkness had a strong foothold. Beth Ann was losing, falling out. Fading.

It was Monday and she was on the L train headed into Manhattan when the redhead with a coy smile sitting across from her started asking questions.

"Having a nice Monday?" the redhead inquired.

Beth Ann didn't answer. She had a terrible headache. She was fucking going blind.

The redhead kept the interrogation up, "It's a lot colder today, huh?"

Beth Ann feigned sleep. Feigned a fear of strangers. Fear of public speaking.

But this redhead, she didn't know when to give up. Her grin was big like a cow's. All teeth and shine. "I do really like that cap. Sick hipster, huh?" she continued.

"Literally," Beth Ann said peeking over the thick frames of her sunglasses.

"Well, it looks really good on you."

Beth Ann wasn't used to compliments. Maybe a mumbled, *She's kinda hot.* A coughed, *Not bad.* She was five foot five and gaunt. Had black hair in a Chelsea cut and deep brown eyes. Deer eyes. Her face was angular. Not punk but union, with freckles that gave away her Irish lineage. Used to have the Betty Page look but she grew tired of all the men drooling. Mainly it was the cheesy pick-up lines.

Always embarrassed by her small breasts and flat behind, Beth Ann draped herself in slack retro housedresses. That way she could appear shapeless beneath loose fitting clothes. That way the mumbles always sounded like questions. The stares more curiosity than boners. And she always wore sunglasses. Though she knew no one could see the slow deterioration in her eyes, she was more comfortable hidden away.

"You knit the cap yourself?" the redhead asked, hands folded on her knees. Pale little hands like hairless lapdogs. She smiled again and let loose a torrent of shine.

Beth Ann smiled back, "Yes. I knit."

Beth Ann was a champion knitter. Queen Knitter of Williamsburg three years in a row. She was, in fact, one of the very best knitters in New York. But The Darkness ensured that she wouldn't be for much longer. Beth Ann wanted to tell the redhead that she was going blind and that in a matter of years—maybe as little as two—she'd see nothing but black. Dull, matte black. But Beth Ann wasn't going to tell her just that. No, she'd also add that she wasn't going to drift into the night without a brawl. *Fuck that,* she'd say. *I knit the cap. I'm knitting my way out of The Darkness.* For Beth Ann, the sick hipster knit cap was indeed her only way out. It was her last ditch attempt. The cap was her Alamo.

If she were going to tell the redhead about it, if she was going to go into detail, she would mention the rats first. Beth Ann saw them clearly now. Before the cap, they were gray blurs or not at all. But now she saw them scatter in the murk as the trains pulled into stations. Now she saw them skittering alongside her in Chinatown. Riding shotgun in trash trucks in Far Rockaway. If she were going to tell the redhead about it, she would mention that when she began knitting the cap a month ago her eyes couldn't penetrate the cowering dimness of the city's armpits. Back then she didn't mind not seeing the Twizzler-tailed rats. The little Brown Jenkinses that flittered about the city like soiled phantoms. But the fact that she could see them now was clear evidence of the miracle of the knit cap.

And that miracle was the stitch. It was like a sip of water from

Lourdes. A hallowed rub of the sacred withered pinky toe of St. Platypus. It was the consecrated mattress stitch. A.K.A. the stockinette stitch. A.K.A. the hardest fucking stitch in the book. The stitch was as tight as Beth Ann had ever gotten it. Normally she didn't pay close attention while she knit. Normally she sat back and watched television and let her hands work silently. On autopilot. But the mattress stitch was different, complex. She needed strategy. Beth Ann couldn't just sit back and watch TV. Her hands couldn't just go on autopilot. Knitting the red sick hipster cap was a trial. A marathon for her eyeballs. But she finished it in three hours and when she was done her eyesight had improved dramatically. She could see the rats under the platforms.

Unfortunately, that was also when the headaches began. Beth Ann figured it was *ying* for *yang*. Maybe *wang* for *chung*. She had the first skull crusher hours after she finished the cap. She was showering when it came on like a wave. Washed over her scalp in ever tightening curls. She had to sleep five hours to relieve it. But then the headaches got worse. Then they were lasting days. Today was no exception. This particular headache had begun Sunday morning.

And the redhead's smile only made it worse.

The redhead's questions made it agony.

"You alright, dear? You look really tired."

Beth Ann learned there were many different approaches to managing headaches. Caffeine cured a stress headache faster than Ibuprofen. Ignatia and Natrum Mur were effective for headaches from grief. Arnica was best for headaches from injuries. Acupuncture was good for migraines. Yoga and meditation couldn't hurt. Her pal Buck, a heavily tattooed pharmacist, had given her a few recommendations as far as prescription meds. Heavy duty shit. She incorporated all of it into what she referred to as her battle plan. Her regimen.

It broke down like this:

Five hours after the headache began she mixed Vicodin and scotch.

After eight bad hours she sat in her shower trying to inhale all the steam through her nose.

After ten excruciating hours she took Arnica (she found it to be more effective than Ignatia and Mur, though the headache was clearly not from an injury).

After fourteen miserable hours, when she was awakened from her sleep, she popped three more Vicodin.

After eighteen numbing hours she watched reruns of *The Avengers*—something about Diana Rigg's eyes that soothed her.

After twenty-one fucking ridiculous hours she dressed and sipped hot tea and took mouse-sized bites of a blueberry scone. Something about processed fruit.

And today, after twenty-three hours of continuous fuck-me-in-the-ass-with-a-chainsaw throbbing, she was on the L sitting across from a talkative redhead and wishing to God she'd stayed at home.

Luckily for Beth Ann and her headache, the redhead exited at 3rd Avenue.

As the train picked up speed and rattled deeper into Manhattan Beth Ann sighed and closed her eyes and prayed to God to make the headache stop. She could keep the blindness at bay. Armed with cable needles and enough yarn, she could manage that much. But she needed a little help from on high with the headaches. When the train pulled into Union Station, she cursed God and headed for the Community Knitting Supply Co. to reload on yarn.

3

Lance thrust Ginger up against the bold portrait of Othniel C. Marsh. She groaned and bit Rex's earlobe, her hands buried in his thick red hair.

"Lance," she gasped, "tell me more about the find at Chester."

"It's the forelimb of an adult Priconodon, *perfectly preserved," he groaned as he slid his Spear of Destiny out from his underpants, turgid with lust, and tickled her pouty, pink . . .*

Harrison stopped typing.

He leaned back in his red leather chair and sighed. It wasn't going. He just knew it was a bad idea to use the *Priconodon*. Hubert at UC-Irvine would have a fucking field day with that reference. Harrison could already see the email.

Found at the Chester dig? You've got to be kidding, Hubert would surely write.

Harrison would reply,

This is fantasy right? This is paleontological porn, not literature. I've included fantastic elements before. There was the one with the knockers rubbing against the "real" Moroccan

special. The Dechenelloides with Tagazella plate structures.
The ménage à trois on the red earth over a full Kenyanthropus
platyops. In South America of all places! You didn't email then.
You saw the fancy in it. But you'll email about the *Priconodon*
being at the Chester dig. You would fucking email about that.

Harrison sighed and got up. He stared out at the snow serpents drifting languidly in the parking lot. That made him sigh
too, because he knew he'd have to leave soon if he was to meet
Amanda on time. And she was such a bitch when it came to
promptness. He actually kind of liked that about her. She was
disciplined. Not the typical Oberlin nerd.

Harrison shut down his computer and was slipping into his
down coat when the phone rang.

"Dr. Gelden?"

"Yeah."

"This is Tom Martin down at receiving. I was told to call you
when a package from UC-Irvine arrived."

Lizzard's *Drotops megalomanicus* no doubt. Harrison was eager
to see the trilobite. Eddie said it was an excessively large speci-
men.

"And there's also something here from . . . Let's see, someone named Dr. Wimmard or Winwood. I can't read the hand-
writing, it might . . ."

"Winward?"

"Yeah."

"What is it?"

"I dunno, let's see . . . The shipment here says 'skull.' That's it."

"I'll be down in a few minutes."

The skull in question turned out to be human and it was
from Harrison's old anthropology professor at the University of
Michigan. Steve Winward had always been fond of Harrison.
Called him "Harry's son" on account of Harrison's resemblance
to pioneering anthropologist Harry Hoijer. When Harrison
began working as a curator at the American Museum of Nat-

ural History, Steve beamed like a doting father. He'd actually gotten Harrison the job. Steve was pals with Gabby Weinberg, the bull dyke on the Museum's board of directors, and Gabby took an instant liking to Harrison. It wasn't because he looked like Harry Hoijer. It was his smile. She liked a man who could smile through a rough beard and look professional.

There was a note affixed to the skull that read:

> *Homo erectus from Georgia, Dmansi dig, thought you might like the transverse torus, oddly elongated don't you think?*
> *Yours, Steve*

Harrison looked at the back of the skull. Indeed, the transverse torus, a protuberance at the junction of the intermaxillary suture and the transverse palatine suture, was longer than he'd seen. Perhaps it was from an injury. Maybe an odd genetic goof. But Harrison's forte was trilobites. Not primitive humans. He appreciated Steve's sending him odd skulls—this one would join several others grinning obscenely on Harrison's already crowded desk—but it remained an idiosyncratic fascination. There would be no publications. No accolades for a weird transverse torus. Certainly no stories.

Harrison took the skull to his desk, turned out the lights in his office and paused again to watch the snow falling in thick clumps. For a brief moment he imagined he was at the bottom of the sea and the falling snow was the "dead fall," the bodies of animals falling from the surface. He had heard that's what it looked like at the bottom of the sea. A constant snow of dead things. Fossilizing as they fell. Gathering calcium nodules like dust.

Like the calcium nodules on the rib cage of the fucking *Priconodon.*

Harrison started stressing out again about the fact that he couldn't finish the goddamned *Priconodon* story. Fucking Hubert was stressing him out. He'd spent the past three weeks trying to come up with a good ending for the story but nothing fit. Lance and Ginger running off to Zaire was silly. Lance dying in a freak accident too maudlin. Ginger going lesbo and disappearing into the bush too *Hustler*. And Hubert was only a few keystrokes away with embarrassing criticism.

"Paleontological porn's for the big boys, Harrison," Hubert's last email had said. "It's not as simple as adding *E. polymera* and some pierced nipples. Not like there's a recipe. You just have to know your art. Well, two arts really—the art of fucking and the art of digging. And in many cases they're the same."

Truth was there wasn't any ending to the *Priconodon* story because Harrison's addiction was overwhelming the science. The whole paleontological porn thing had—in the past few weeks— devolved into an exercise to release sexual tension. Harrison's addiction was getting the better of the bones.

It was funny to Harrison how the root of his interest, the porn that started the ball rolling, was now overshadowing his writing. Overshadowing the very art. Harrison had only recently come to the conclusion that he was a true junkie. Nowadays, he'd surf porn sites every hour on the hour. Watch pornos every evening. Read porn novels on the train in full public view to and from work. He knew it was bad and he was sick of it. Sick and fucking tired of it. Dr. Borgo helped in directing the passion, focusing the energy on stories and writing. And that had been good for a while.

Harrison had always dreamed of being a writer. He had the usual teen fantasies of writing a best-seller about a rogue anthropologist with a hot sidekick but he never had the time to actually write it. It was Borgo's prompting to put pen to paper that helped Harrison avoid the Internet. Avoid the video store. Avoid porn. When he was deep in a story he could actually go days without watching black women gobble down white cocks. Blonde sorority sisters riding buff Mexicans with tattooed asses. Writing became his one true release. Discovering paleontological porn, the two worlds—the pleasure and the pain—melded into one bizarre and sometimes excruciatingly satisfying whole.

It began in grad school. Doing research on *Flexicalymene senaria* in Duck Creek Quarry north of Green Bay led him to a website and a shadowy anthropological publication called *The Mazon Creek Mixopterygium.* The title of the journal was enough to give Harrison pause. All paleontologists know Mazon Creek is a dig site in Illinois famed for its *chondrichthyan* fossils. *Chondrichthyans* were shark-like fish. Fish with cartilage skeletons rather than bone. A *mixopterygium* was the pelvic "clasper" of the male *chondrichthyans,* used exclusively for copulation. Harrison searched the net for any and all information regarding the journal but found nothing save a P.O. box in western Washington state.

He sent a letter requesting information and received a note detailing issue and subscription costs but gave no information about the content of the journal. He paid $8.50 by money order and when his first issue of *The Mazon Creek Mixopterygium* arrived he was astounded to find it contained twenty pages of "fossil erotica" or "paleontological pornography." The last page of the high-brow smut rag listed two other similar publications: *The Serpukhovian Age* and *The Happy Cava.* Harrison ordered issues of both.

The Serpukhovian Age was also paleontological erotica that would appeal only to field geeks. But the material was not as "persuasive" as that in *The Mazon Creek Mixopterygium.* Harrison found it amateurish. Clearly written by students. Lacking entirely in decent character development. *The Happy Cava* was even lower brow. It contained rough sketches rather than full stories and most were quite degrading. Harrison actually felt dirty after reading it.

A few months after receiving *The Mazon Creek Mixopterygium #6,* and having ordered copies of *#1, #2* and *#4* (*#5* was long out of print and traded hands at $300), Harrison wrote his own

paleontological porn story inspired by an erotic poem by Bonersette Holmes titled, "The Tethys Sea Between Her Legs" in *The
Mazon Creek Mixopterygium #2*. He found that it was quite easy
and his first attempt in the genre, "The Affair at Chandler
Bridge," written as Cloverly, was accepted for publication in *The
Mazon Creek Mixopterygium* with little editing. It appeared in #7
and was well received.

Harrison kept writing. Over time he discovered, much to his
chagrin, that many prominent paleontologists and anthropolo-
gists read and wrote for the journals under various pseudo-
nyms. Even scholarly work reeks of personality. Harrison could
sniff most of them out. It was easy to discern that Bonersette
Holmes was really John Liffin out of Miami—only an expert on
Harpes perradiatus would mention rostral plates in his story,
"Mating Pangea." And Cunning Litmus was Linda Kaufman
from Wyoming State. She was the only paleontologist Harrison
knew who used the phrase "tempo and mode" when joking
about sex.

Discovering paleontological porn three years ago was the beginning of a new and very productive chapter in Harrison's life.
Dr. Borgo made sure it meant something. That it wasn't just another fix. And Harrison was convinced that it was a stepping-
stone to bigger and more interesting things. His writing became
a real facet of his life. He went as far as to envision founding a
new movement of wholly scientific erotica. Forget the ghetto of
paleontological porn, Harrison as Cloverly was headed to the
next level. Scientific pornography that eschewed the dialectic
and went straight for the fantastic. There would be no mention
of taxonomy. No detailed analysis of fossils. Just blue stories as
only a scientist could write them.

Cloverly was famous after all.

The twenty tales that made up the current Cloverly canon
had been reprinted twice. Once by the publishers of *The Maxon
Creek Mixopterygium* in a special double issue called *Cloverly
Phadipose* and once by the editors of *Brutarian* in a book of out-

landish fiction called *Stories for the Geeks: Love, Death and Elementary Particles*. Of the few paleontological porn zines, only the *The Maxon Creek Mixopterygium* reaped the financial rewards. And while it never really took off, it was now, for the first time in its lowly existence, known to more than a dozen people. Copies of the Cloverly issues sold like crack on eBay and countless paleontological porn sites sprouted up overnight.

When Harrison typed the name Cloverly into a search engine it yielded an astounding 11,293 sites. All mentioned or were devoted to the pseudonymous author who had made paleontology naughty.

"I love his use of language, it's so very Gorey-ian," one poster, named Grimly, on the Anti-text Web Journal enthused.

Lost23 posted on MetaFiction: "I've never studied paleontology but reading his stuff makes me want to, even if it is only so I can say things like nuchal gap when I cum."

"He's the next big thing. This goes way beyond the sciences. It'll be an anthem. I was saying that 6 months ago but it's true. I'm going to do my dissertation on this genre," Beetleboy chimed in on Science Porn.

"Cloverly, the paleontological porn artiste, joins the ranks of the movers and shakers in cult culture this week. We're moving him to number 5 on the top fifteen," the Hot Monster Culture Beat site announced.

"I'm sure Cloverly is a kick ass guy. I'm willing to bet he's one of those ultrahot Asian guys with the long bangs tinted red and the black turtlenecks and the green Pumas. I'm sure he's hot and stylish," ReBe gushed on *Meatcab*.

Cloverly was a star, a regular Quentin Tarantino black horse from nowhere sweeping across the edge of culture towards some spectacular end. In fact, after a well-received exposé about the whole paleontological porn genre (and other like-minded literary movements like cryptography porn, organismic porn) was published in *Tasty Callow,* Harrison found Cloverly was evolving toward the mainstream. It was, as Harrison told Amanda on their third date, a calling. She loved the anonymity of it. The mystery. Harrison was a star. And Amanda grew to accept Harrison's porn affliction.

But now, with the *Priconodon* story as proof, the whole thing was falling apart. The art. The science. Everything that Cloverly was famous for was getting lost in the stench of porn. The animal instinct to spray the walls was overriding Harrison's intentions. He was losing his edge. And fuck it all if Hubert wouldn't pick it up and run with it.

Harrison stared out at the snow for a few more minutes as the light dwindled. Then he sat down at his desk and deleted the *Priconodon* story. An hour later he left the office, thirty minutes late to meet Amanda at their favorite bistro in midtown.

"Traffic," he said.

"Maybe you should be a novelist." Amanda's first words of the evening.

"I've thought about it but I don't have the time. My name is not exotic enough. My background pure American Jewish dull. It seems as though all the new authors, the hip ones with the big book deals and best agents, have exotic names and exotic backgrounds. They've got names like Kian Gujarat and were born in Portugal to parents who fled the Kashmir region. They went to boarding school in London, spent ten years in Bali working with the armless refugee children and the long necked ladies who ply their trade on the borderlands.

"Novelists these days are from the remotest lands, isolated mesas in the dense jungles of Papua New Guinea. They've never worn clothing and their heads are tattooed with parrots and jaguars. They're people who grew up in submarines beneath Antarctica and they never wrote a sentence in their life but suddenly they churn out a novel about Victorian England and an affair between an aristocrat and a lion tamer.

"I can't compete with that. I'm Harrison Gelden. Son of Amos Gelden, M.D., and Mrs. Regina Horowitz Gelden. My parents were born here. My grand folks were wealthy immigrants from the Ukraine. I grew up outside Philly and I went to public school. I'm a paleontologist but that's about as boring a job as you can have these days. The bones I study aren't on Cinemax."

Amanda said, "I think paleontologists are sexy. I think you could write a novel and it would be a breakout hit. You can mix in that sardonic humor of yours and maybe talk a little about me too."

"About you?"

"Yeah, I've got an exciting life. Don't I?"

It was a rhetorical question. Harrison was getting better at spotting them. A few months earlier he wouldn't have caught it and would've said something true, something like, "Actually, you've got a very un-novel life." And then he would have been sleeping on the couch and he would have been buying flowers and chocolates and calling his friends to ask her friends what the problem was. He would be on the couch and she'd cry and spit at him and he wouldn't know why. Harrison wanted to stay out of the "woulds." He wised up. He was an expert now.

"Sure, honey. You would make a great addition to my novel. You had an exciting upbringing in Baltimore, the daughter of art historians and collectors. Went to Harvard and studied eco-tourism . . ."

"Ecological management."

"Right and you spent that summer in the wilds of Cedarhurst studying the impact of Orthodox Jewry on the squirrel habitats on the south shore of Long Island. Fascinating research. What was the hypothesis again?"

Amanda laughed. Harrison was past the bad spot. He'd been able to both flatter her and make a jab.

"It was about the foot traffic, to and from synagogue, and whether or not that influenced the squirrels' avoiding certain stretches of sidewalk. In turn, I wondered if maybe the squirrels went a different way and then seeing as they were on an unfa-

miliar street would be more likely to be hit by a car. That was
the hypothesis."

"And the results, my dear?"

"Well, I didn't find any significant correlation between the
two. Squirrels didn't seem to mind waiting a few minutes before they ran across the street."

"Ah, how fascinating."

Amanda kicked him under the table. She had on chunky
blue creepers and it hurt.

"Thanks."

"No problem," she smiled. He could hear her take her shoes
off under the table.

That was her defense—the smile. Harrison always fell for it.
She was so fucking beautiful. He didn't dare say it aloud. No
need to stroke her ego anymore tonight. He did that and he
was bound to wind up cuddling all night talking about why he
loved her. Amanda needed constant reassurance.

She looked exactly like the type of woman Harrison had grown
up wanting. She had an oval face. Large green eyes. Dark hair
that tied up neatly. She was nearly as tall as he was with large hips
and perky breasts. Her skin was smooth. Olive complexion. But
it was her smile. Those pouty lips and luminous teeth that made
him shiver and shake.

Amanda put a foot in Harrison's crotch. She was trying to be
sexy but instead squished his left nut between her toes.

"I've got to go, honey." Harrison groaned pushing her foot
away before the nausea swam up his throat.

Amanda recoiled. Her curled feet went back into her shoes.

"It wasn't like I expected . . ." She didn't need to continue.

There was a moment of silence.

"I've got to go. Meeting the gang."

"Right, your gang," Amanda made it sound as ridiculous as it
was. As sad and tired and childish and ridiculous as it was. "And
what are you and your little creep friends going to do tonight?"

Harrison didn't appreciate the sarcasm.

"For starters we're going to Bossy's."

"Not the fucked up sick crew again?"

"It's the Whole Sick Crew and they are my friends, babe. That's just what we do. We hang out, shoot the shit and have a good time . . ."

"So retarded, Harrison. You guys are just lame. A bunch of late twenty-somethings playing like adolescents and calling it a 'crew.' Wasn't it just like three months ago that Cooper was convinced that there was some conspiracy to poison pensioners in Greenpoint. And the most ridiculous thing was that you all were sucked in by it and by the end of the week it was this 'investigation.' Of course, you didn't find anything. You guys spent like a day at the library looking at microfiche and then it all fizzled out. Whole Sick Crew. Harrison, your friends are just ridiculous talkers. *Whenever there's trouble/we're here on the double/we're the bloodhound gang . . .*'"

Harrison cut Amanda off.

"You don't have to be a cunt about it. Look, we're just having fun. Wolfgang and Rad come up with some wacky ideas. It's all just fun. Just talk. Are you telling me that when you get together with Tiffany, and whatever that other bitch's name is, you guys talk only about politics and the weather and the latest fashions? I've heard you. You guys talk bullshit, too. It's just fun."

Amanda swirled her wine. The red liquid sashayed.

Then she sighed and it came out as *hhrrumpph*. A sound Harrison was sure she'd make frequently as a wife.

"Look, babe, they're my friends. I don't see them that often."

"I just don't get what you see in them. I mean, they're all . . . Well, they're all so jacked up. I mean Wolfgang's got the whole drug monkey. All T ever talks about is his forgotten childhood. Rad's damaged and Cooper . . . Honey, you've spent ten long years with this crew. Maybe it's time to give it a break. Meet some people at the museum. I don't know."

"I'm going."

Harrison waved the waiter over for the check. The rest of the meal was spent in silence. Awkward and at the same time intimately familiar, like a worn shoe. It was, Harrison imagined, the ether that their marriage would drift in. They left the bistro and Amanda caught a cab. Before the car pulled out she waved and smiled. Harrison waved back but really wasn't looking at her. He was looking at the snow falling between his fingertips. The snow was falling in bigger flakes now. Massive protozoan blobs of cold. It looked just like a tide of dead fall.

4

Beth Ann was trying to teach Ethyl Friedman the difference between a Picot stitch and a Crab stitch.

It wasn't going well.

"No, no, no. You don't bring your hand around like that. It's got to be in this direction."

Beth Ann was moving like a contortionist. Her hands wrapping around each other. Snakes caught in a nest of thread.

"I'm not getting it. It's too hard for me."

Ethyl Friedman was a grandmother and a saint. She'd seen the worst the world had to offer. Came to the States as a small child from the ravaged husk of Germany. And here in the bustling breast of New York she set down roots and arranged a small, tidy and simple life. She wanted simplicity.

Ethyl was short, mousy, with a crop of golden curls as delicate as they looked. She had lunch lady eyes, misty but wide, and she walked with a polio limp. And Ethyl didn't have the patience for learning the Picot stitch. Beth Ann didn't have the strength or the motivation to direct Ethyl, to reassure her.

"That's fine. We can work around it," Beth Ann turned to the other women in the room. "Is anyone else having trouble with the Picot stitch? Maybe you can come sit with Ethyl and work on it together."

She spoke loudly to three elderly Jewish women sitting around a big table in a stuffy social room in the Bellaire Assisted Living Apartment Complex overlooking tree-lined Orchard Street on a Monday night. Three elderly women learning to crotchet for their dear husbands. Distant grandchildren. Unappreciative daughters-in-law. Three elderly women with a love of learning. A love of a few rounds of mah jong. A singular taste for herring. This was the Bitch Knit Crocheting senior class, a hopeless case.

What surprised Beth Ann most was that these women hadn't learned to knit earlier. When she asked she learned that they were all special cases. It was that their sister was the knitter in the family. That they were raised by an uncle. That they were trying to assimilate and didn't want to seem too Jewish. And knitting was as Jewish grandma as it got. That made sense. But Beth Ann also enjoyed her role as insurgent. She was there to shake up the ladies of the Bitch Knit Crocheting senior class. She wanted to get the women talking.

Talking about her.

Beth Ann was wearing her Coco Chanel knit sweater, black denim capris and white leather go-go boots. Besides being suitably warm, the Coco sweater was also politically incendiary. It was a pale sand color with the letters C-O-C-O, in red, flush with the surrounding sweater. The Os were swastikas. Beth Ann knit it after reading a short biography of Coco Chanel at the back of a book on 1960s Euro-trash fashion. After learning that Coco spent the war years in a Paris hotel holed up with her lover, a Nazi, she wanted to make a statement about it.

"Chanel. Lagerfeld. They can't just sweep this under the carpet," Beth Ann told her mother on the Tuesday she knit the sweater. "I mean, this is like the Swiss trying to deny they took

Jewish gold and money during the war. This needs to be blown wide open. It'll be scorching."

"But do you really want to walk around the city wearing swastikas? Isn't that a bit over the top?" Luanne Johns had a soft voice. A soothing voice that sounded as if it were assembled, bit-by-bit, from the static that hums incessantly at the back of the telephone. The static that seemed to fill the air of long-distance, late-night calls. It was the atmosphere that early physicists believed held sway over the cosmos. It was the intangible "everything," cold and clear between the words.

"Mom, this is about making a statement . . ."

"But it's anti-Semitic."

"No, that's the point. Coco was an anti-Semite. Here she was, the haute couture maven in the heat of the war, shacking up with a Nazi . . . It's despicable and people are still propping her up like some saint."

"It's her clothes."

"They suck."

"Well, you can't go about wearing a swastika. It's against the rules."

The rules were always Luanne's way out. She abided by them even though they were soft and fast. Runny. Luanne had always made rules for Beth Ann. Rules about rules. Rules within rules. She wrapped herself in a veritable womb of rules and there she was comfortable to gauge her surroundings. To survey a vast safe kingdom of even more rules.

"Mom, nothing's against the rules. You've got to learn that someday. It's just that everything has a punishment. You kill someone and you go to jail. That's not about rules. You don't go to jail because you broke the rule. You go to jail because you killed someone. It's that simple, really. And when it comes to wearing a swastika there aren't any rules. There are emotions. And emotions are what I'm trying to get at."

"Like what? Anger, pain, fear, sorrow . . . That's a sad person to be, Beth Ann, a very sad person to be."

"I'm not trying to upset people. Well, yes, I guess I am. But it's for a good reason. People need to be shaken from their complacency. Coco was a Nazi sympathizer and I think everyone should know it."

That day, the day she knit the sweater, Beth Ann walked out of her apartment with pride. There it was gleaming on her chest, a superman "S" bold and bright. There she was making the statement of all statements. The swastika was loose and she was prepared for the insults. The jeers. The horror. She assumed it would be like when Siouxsie Sioux went onstage in London with a swastika armband in the '70s. As if she had the words "spear chucker" emblazoned on the sweater. But it wasn't. Beth Ann was in New York and nothing was shocking. Nothing happened.

She paraded herself all over Midtown. The Lower East Side. Harlem. Park Slope. Nobody batted an eye. *Maybe they all got the message,* she thought. *Maybe it's all clear.* She put the sweater away. It was a dud. A dummy bullet that looked great leaving the barrel but hit nothing. Went nowhere.

When the old Jewish ladies hired her to teach them the Bitch Knit way, the grasping of feminism by the knitters' thread and needle, she saw a perfect opportunity to bring out the sweater.

I bet these old ladies wear Chanel all the time, Beth Ann thought as she stood in front of the full-length mirror on the back of the bedroom door. *And I'll bet they have no freaking clue that Coco was a Reich bitch.*

It didn't work.

"Why are you wearing a sweater with a swastika? Is that some Indian thing?" Lenore Wolfenberg asked when the women finally noticed her sweater.

"All the kids these days are into that Far Eastern stuff. Drives me nuts," Nellie Gold chimed in from the back.

Beth Ann answered, "It's a political statement."

"About what?" Lenore cocked her blue head.

"Yeah. About what?" Ethyl joined in. Her withered hands cradling a floral patterned teacup.

"About Coco Chanel . . . her Nazi past . . ."

"Oh, that." Ethyl turned.

"Old news, babe," Lenore snorted.

They didn't speak about the sweater again. Not once through the entire lesson. They didn't give half a shit about the sweater. Coco was old news. The swastika was passé. What they were concerned about was the knitting. Ethyl, the saint, had no patience for the Picot stitch. The other women responded in much the same fashion. They griped about it for a few minutes, asked for some help and then promptly turned their attention to something else. And the something else wasn't the Coco sweater. It wasn't Beth Ann's feminism. It was the weather. It was the cost of living in the city. It was the grandchildren. It was the synagogue. It was Beth Ann's love life.

"You need to find yourself a young man, a strong man," Ethyl fired the first shot.

Nods of agreement spread cancerously.

"You've come here for five weeks, Beth Ann. We've heard nothing about a young man in your life. You tell us about this stitch and that stitch, about this technique and that, but you don't tell us a thing about you. You tell us that Coco Chanel was a Nazi—something all of us knew—and you came to prove it with your sweater. But you don't tell us about your family, your mother or your sex life. We're old women, Beth Ann. We want to hear about somebody's sex life." Ethyl smiled.

Beth Ann sat down at the table with the women, her elderly disciples, and decided that she had nothing to lose. The lessons were a flop. Five weeks and the women were crocheting hideous half scarves and atrocious skirts. It was time to talk about something else.

"There isn't much to tell, I'm afraid. But let me start with telling you that I'm going blin . . ."

"Don't start anywhere," Lenore interrupted. "We don't want

you to start. Let us ask the questions. Oh, and if you were going to start off by telling us about your health problems, then let me tell you, we've seen our share. We're all one step closer to the grave and many miles away from you. So, please don't try to match us."

Lenore grinned. Beth Ann let it go. She had wanted the taste of sympathy, the cooing, but she decided it wasn't worth the fuss. For the first time in several years, Beth Ann began talking about herself by mentioning something other than blindness.

"I was dating a man last year. He was older than I was, way older, and he wanted to settle down. He wanted a family and I couldn't give him that. It's because I'm going blind . . ."

There it was. So easy.

Beth Ann realized then that the secret of her existence, every word she spoke, orbited her coming blindness. It was the realization of the hunted animal. The frightened animal that backs itself into corner after corner and takes licking after licking. She was in the corner and The Darkness, the Siamese twin that she couldn't remove, was right there with her, speaking for her. She was a ventriloquist's doll for her own disease.

None of the women batted an eye.

"So sorry to hear that dear," Lenore began. "You know, my sister went blind about your age. She had a hard life. A very bitter woman. But with medicine today you can probably still live a completely normal life. Maybe they can even cure it." She made a slight high-pitched groan like one of those creepy skeletal vulture things in *The Dark Crystal.*

"My husband was blind ten years after we married. I don't think he minded," Ethyl laughed.

"Anyway . . ." Beth Ann wanted to move on. She was embarrassed and read right away that she wasn't going to get sympathy from this crowd. And The Darkness needed sympathy. It lived off of it. Without it, it would be nothing but bad luck. "Anyway, I'm not dating anyone now. But I'm always on the lookout for a good man."

"Well, you will meet someone soon. I'm sure." Ethyl put a soothing hand on Beth Ann's shoulder.

"I don't really mind if I don't. I've got other, more interesting, things going on in my life right now."

Ooos and awws followed.

Beth Ann left the apartment after drawn out hugs and cheek kisses. She stood on the stairs outside watching the snow. It was a beautiful drifting kind of snow. The kind of snow that isn't really falling from the sky but swirling around like in a snow globe. The steps to the Bellaire Assisted Living Complex were stone, marble to be exact, and each one more slippery than the next. It was not at all surprising that Beth Ann fell as soon as she started down them.

She fell on her bony ass and continued to slide until she spilled out onto the sidewalk like a weak trash bag. She lay there for a few moments, her right cheek against the frozen pavement. The snow blowing around her hair. Just lay there. Breathing. Feeling the life slowly pulse back into her legs.

She hadn't fallen because the steps were slippery, though that did contribute to the severity of her fall, she fell because she couldn't see anything.

The world had gone entirely black for a few seconds.

Laying there on the cold pavement, Beth Ann waited until her eyesight returned leisurely. Like a tide slowly filling an empty bay. Thankfully, Beth Ann wasn't cold. The Coco sweater was warm and the '70s yellow and green down ski vest she wore on top of it was insulating. She wasn't embarrassed either.

But she was sad. Deeply, profoundly, sad.

When Beth Ann picked herself up off the pavement a crowd had gathered. No one said a word. They just watched her dust the snow from her pants, then struggle toward the nearest subway station.

5

The Whole Sick Crew huddled around a small table crowded with beer bottles and dusty lines of coke.

Looking for all the world like a half order of the last supper, they moved blithely through conversations about drugs, sex, rock 'n' roll and falafel. Rad Fari, T Radcliff, Wolfgang Brown, Cooper Handsome, Xavier Graff and Harrison and all the spite, irony, bruises and boners that a city like New York inspires. A motley crew, kick-fucking the consumer world with a cynical snarl.

DJ Oppenheimer was at the turntables, spinning a combustible mix of minimal synth and cold wave. The Subterranean Desire night was hot. Thin kids in the know sweating away the evening and spasmodically jerking to heavily accented singers mumbling about nihilism. The place was packed and the Whole Sick Crew was lucky to have gotten one of the tables littering the back of the club.

Rad was going on about pencil boxes.

He was Indian, born Radij in Syracuse, and an ER doc. Rad was a consummate mix maker. His mix tapes were highly prized by collectors and went for hundreds on eBay. He also had a bad habit of cutting himself with razors when he got really stressed out. Hence the irregular scar on his right cheek. A pale, Anglo stripe in his otherwise uniform brown skin. Rad had made the cut several years ago and he thought it looked dignified. Looked like something a villain in a sequel to *Romancing the Stone* would have. Outside of the scar, his face was the same as it had been when he was a child. High cheekbones. Thin, avian nose. Piercing dark eyes bridged by thick eyebrows. His hair, cut short and folded over, was held in place by green goop that he bought at an upscale salon frequented by queens. A good-looking mutherfucker indeed.

Rad worked shifts at King's County Hospital and spent his free time downloading obscure new wave songs. They were at Subterranean Desire for him. Rad's ears seemed decidedly pricked for electropop. He was obsessed with the stuff. Trolled the new wave fan sites, chatting with similarly obsessed wavers and attempting to download every 7-inch and flexi disc of every orphic electronic band from 1982 and 1983. The jaunty, tinny, old synth sound made him feel young again, like he was at Club Navix in Poughkeepsie kissing goth girls. Rad had a special space in his heart for the overweight black lipped girls that crowded the darker corners of Club Navix. Those girls, standing side by side, thick greasepaint and jet-black hair. They wore fishnet stockings, black slips and smoked cloves. They giggled and pointed, made eyes and smirked. They were the sirens of Greek mythology leading the inexplicably skinny industrial and waver boys to their first sexual experience. Something in their smiles, the cherubic cheeks and the flashing teeth. Something naughty. The shadows came alive around them. It caressed their ample curves. White faces that floated along the walls of the club, nodding in time to Front 242's "Headhunter." They were beautiful. Rad remembered that like it was yesterday. Remembered it clearly. He remembered the pencil boxes, too.

"You know, they had Star Wars ones and Star Trek ones and

even some fantasy ones. Maybe a G.I. Joe one, too," Rad
shouted over the din. "Come on. They were awesome. None of
you remember those?"

"I think they were plastic. Maybe aluminum," T said.

T Radcliff was tall, thin, with long, curling sideburns and
slender, pale lips. His eyes were deep set, blue. His black hair
was thinning. He edited a zine called *The Crawling Limpet*. It was
your typical Xeroxed rag with music reviews, essays about art
and graffiti, poems about particle physics and photos of skinny
girls with guns and Bibles. It was very popular in Billburg, sold
well in Toronto and was catching on in Europe. Circulation was
close to 15,000.

T also just happened to be Happy Monster, the widely read
and critically acclaimed blogger at the Happy Monster website.
The site hadn't started as a clearing space for T's ideologies. It
had begun as a cultural review site but people seemed to really
like what T had to say about pop culture. He obsessively covered everything from lo-fi Croatian rock to trading card collecting. The tone was sardonic, fashionable and, most importantly,
abrasive. That was the key with blogging. It had to be abrasive.

T was the one who came up with calling the group of friends
the Whole Sick Crew. He was a keen student of *V.* Said he'd
never read any of Pynchon's other novels, and never felt the
need to. He just liked the idea of the Whole Sick Crew in that
book. Even if they weren't really sick. Just disaffected East Coast
dropouts. Not sick the way his Whole Sick Crew was. Not even
close.

"Right," T continued, lighting up another Gauloise, "I think
you're thinking of those little school supply boxes that you took
to class in first grade, Rad. I think they were plastic."

"No, no, no. They were cardboard. Man, was I the only fucking one?"

"Cooper, don't you still have one? Isn't it your weed box?" T
spoke with his arms, sending hot white sparks flying from his
cigarette to turn dusky red in the dimness.

"That's a lunch pail."

Cooper Handsome was a psychedelic New Romantic. Wore suits and skinny ties and took a lot of hallucinogenics. Brash, his blue eyes sparkled in his rough, unshaven face and his eyebrows were always cocked at some strange angle. He didn't look like or consider himself a hippie. For Cooper, the term had become so burdened with rhetorical baggage that it was almost unwieldy. Hippie was no longer a term of rebellion. In the '00s it meant nothing more than druggie, green and/or liberal. And as Cooper quickly learned, outside of Madison, Boulder and Portland, everyone hates a fucking liberal. No, Cooper was not a hippie. The hippies had gone the way of the dinosaurs. He smoked their ashes.

Cooper was a consciounaut: a consciousness astronaut, exploring the highways and byways of his own reality, looking for the outer reaches of Monad consciousness, to woo and lay the higher light bodies and to hold court with Lord Metatron. And the only effective vehicle for that kind of exploration is hallucinogenics. Mescaline, peyote, shrooms, absinthe, wormwood, acid—all provided, in various ways, the necessary engine to launch a mind into itself. For Cooper the sad fact was humans needed vehicles to reach the inner sanctum. They were no longer capable of doing it themselves. He didn't prefer using drugs. Cooper had tried exercise, eating right, exploring the environment, sex, magick, the world's religions, but none hit that magic button. Just drugs.

"Can we talk about something else?" Harrison spat. He was in a foul mood anyway, something he had Amanda to thank for.

"Sure," Rad smiled. "But I'm going to find one of those fucking little boxes and bring it in here and show you. When you crack the lid on that bad boy and get that whiff of elementary school supplies circa 1981 you're going to be thanking me. Oh, and apologizing profusely."

"Now that I think about it . . ." T clucked.

"Moving on," Wolfgang Brown said, finishing another line of

coke and waving his hand to halt conversation. "Have any of you seen this flick called *Tongue?* It was made in the '70s. A porno blaxploitation flick to cash in on the surge of black culture films that were being made. It's really insane. I can't believe anyone would find it even remotely erotic. You've got this like mute brother with a 9-inch tongue that talks to his pet frog and generally acts all dejected. But when the sistahs on the block find out what he's packing, they come running from miles around to have a night with him. Really insane stuff. First and last blaxploitation porn film."

No one spoke. Wolfgang sighed, frowned.

"I'm sure it's great," Harrison said putting his hand on Wolfgang's shoulder.

Wolfgang coughed. "Fuck off."

Wolfgang Brown was a dead ringer for Christ straight off the cross. He was tall, thin with a close-cropped beard and long, stringy hair. He had a heroin chic that gestated under leather pants and a wifebeater. Scrawny and tattooed, he was all Iggy and walked like he ruled the streets.

During the week he was a high school guidance counselor in Queens, but his real passion was his neo-folk metal band called, naturally, Wolfgang. And he sold coke. Mostly to the teens he counseled. Outside of the counselor gig and the band and the drugs, Wolfgang talked about metal and lusted after black women. The last few months he'd been chatting on-line with some hot 23-year-old with the screen tag Carla45. She said she lived in Queens and wanted to take her time with the whole relationship thing. Said she'd recently been burned. The photo she sent Wolfgang was of a young woman, cocoa skin and a wide smile. She looked fun and happy. Her posts and IMs revealed a wicked sense of humor, a filthy tongue and some very uninteresting ideas about taking it slow. That was the problem. She never did have the time or maybe never wanted to find the time to hook up. Wolfgang was left pulling his willis and dreaming. But the more she denied him physical contact the more he wanted her. And the more he wanted her the more he talked about her. Carla45 had released a monster.

"Doesn't sound very realistic," Rad sneered.

Wolfgang stood up and scratched at his beard with both hands and then threw his right fist out inches from Rad's face, a giant horned silver skull ring on his index finger catching the half-light.

Rad didn't budge. He looked over at Xavier and said, "Will you do something about this shit?"

Wolfgang stood, arm outstretched, ring glaring, oblivious. "We're sixteen days from 2005," Wolfgang said. "More than enough time left for me to kick your ass before New Year's, bitch."

Rad cracked up. So did Harrison.

"The coke's talking. He's just fucking silly," Xavier said and pulled Wolfgang down. The rocker collapsed in his chair with a huff.

Xavier Graff was a local entrepreneur. He ran the Black Light on Metropolitan and the controversial eatery, Trisomy 21, on Berry. At Trisomy 21 all the waiters and waitresses had Down syndrome. The place was raking in big numbers after every news outlet in the nation went after it as cruel and insensitive. But the brouhaha died down quickly after 9-11. Xavier always defended Trisomy 21 saying he was giving people jobs and putting the spotlight on the genetic disorder. He claimed that 15 percent of his profits went to fund Down syndrome research. He spoke at medical conferences. Had a booth at the Special Olympics. He saw himself as a champion of a cause and an entrepreneur. Muscular and lean, Xavier had perfect teeth that he loved to show off. Black hair swirling around his head in an arty perm. He wore a denim jacket and a black turtleneck. Xavier came with T. Always.

Wolfgang made an obnoxious snorting noise. Then he laughed and said, "What the hell do you guys want to talk about? You all are just so racist."

Harrison shook his head, "He's obviously lost it."

"Fuck you," Wolfgang purred, pulling a vial of coke from his coat.

"What do you guys think about that filmmaker that got killed this morning?" Cooper changed gears. The table went quiet, just the chop chopping sound of Wolfgang setting up a line with a credit card.

Cooper leaned in, his eyes on everyone, a clove toothpick stuck in his teeth, "I say something wrong?"

"I thought we weren't going to bring that up again," Harrison said.

"Why not? We haven't been talking about it."

"You haven't, we have," Harrison added. A laser beam, straying from the DJ booth, spun a web across Harrison's brow. Red lines mingled with sweat to produce a liquid rose grid on his skin, flattening his features.

Offended, Cooper asked, "What the fuck? What were you guys saying about it? I was just gonna say it was really fucked up. Nasty. Why on earth would someone kill an indie film director? Was her shit controversial or something?"

"Her name was Veniss," Xavier corrected.

". . . and her sister, that cheese ball pop star Brittany whatever, hung herself afterwards," Cooper continued. "That's just craziness, man. I mean Veniss was a real skanky gal but her sister? I mean that kid pop shit . . . What?"

No one was laughing. Cooper turned to Xavier and asked, "Was Veniss a friend of yours?"

Xavier said, "Yeah of T's and of Rad's."

"Shit, sorry guys."

"She was hacked to death," T spat.

"I know, I read about that," Cooper said.

"Any leads?" Harrison asked.

"No."

Wolfgang said, "Just some random shit, right?"

"No."

"What do you mean 'no,' T?" Harrison caught on.

T said, "I know what's going on. Veniss wasn't the first."

"The first what?" Cooper asked.

"Killing. This wasn't the first," Xavier said, looking over at T as though he needed approval to speak. "T and I have been looking into this. Digging around on the Internet, you know? There are other murders. All in Brooklyn. All hipsters. One of them only two months ago and it was here in Williamsburg."

"What was that?" Cooper motioned for Wolfgang to discreetly slide him a line.

"A record collector was found dead in his apartment . . ."

"Cal Ferrari," T clarified.

"Yeah, yeah. Heard about that. A friend of mine in Queens knew Cal. Did some trades with him. Vinyl rips of obscure '70s funk shit. Crazy. He was shot. But I thought they caught someone on that?" Rad said.

"No. They had someone in custody but they let him go. Alibi. But check this out: The killer didn't take anything from Cal's apartment and it was loaded to the rafters with all sorts of rare and out-of-print records and signed memorabilia. Stuff, honestly, that's worth more than the apartment itself. Killer didn't take anything. In fact, he left something. A copy of Sisters of Mercy's "Doctor Jeep" single. And on the cover of the record he wrote the words *Doctor* and *Jeep* in black Sharpie. I guess the cover doesn't have it written there but on the back. That's like his calling card or something."

"How'd you learn about all that?" Harrison asked.

Rad said, "It's *The* Sisters of Mercy. Can't leave the definite article out. Which release was it, T? There was the 7-inch Merciful release and the 12-inch with an extended mix."

"Does it matter?" T asked stupefied.

Rad shrugged, "Not really."

Harrison smirked, "So, T, how'd you hear about that?"

"A pal with the PD."

"And what makes you think it's connected?" Rad asked.

"Yeah. Did *you* kill that dude?" Cooper said, snorting.

"No. What? Don't be retarded. Listen. Someone killed Veniss. Someone Cal. Both of those were in Williamsburg. But very little to connect them other than the fact that the killer took nothing and both of them were crazy hip. Well, like Xavier said, we found other murders. A performance artist was shot in his car while he was at a light in Greenpoint. Cops assumed it was a failed carjacking. Colin Jaspers. Remember him? He DJ'd the Lo-Fi Europe show on East Village Radio. He was shot in his apartment. Nothing was taken but when Xavier and I got access to the crime scene photos we noticed something that obviously no one else saw. Any guesses?"

"A copy of 'Doctor Jeep'?" Cooper asked.

"Yup. Right there on his coffee table."

"He was a DJ. Why would it be strange for him to have that LP?" Rad asked.

"Just lying out? That's not normal. You look at the crime scene photos, he has a bunch of LPs scattered around his coffee table but it's all stuff like Joost Visser and S/T. Why would a goth rock record be in that pile?"

Harrison responded first. "You're grasping at straws, man."

"Well, there's still another murder. Just last December. It was a librarian over at the Tristram Shandy Metafiction Project. She was shot in a park near her apartment in Greenpoint."

"And what's the connection?" asked Rad.

"Despite the fact that she was a total hipster? Despite the fact that she fucking helped organize a library of books that didn't exist? Well, there was one little thing. A certain something in the crime scene photos."

Harrison said, "Let me guess? Only you saw it?"

"Right."

"Don't tell me there was a Sisters of Mercy LP lying in the grass beside her blood-spattered body?" Cooper chuckled.

"No. But there was a brochure for the new Jeep Liberty found in her purse."

"Oh come off it! Surely, she could have been looking to buy

a new car." Harrison really had to piss but he wasn't leaving. He just hoped the conversation would wrap up soon. That the crew would move off this insanity.

"A Jeep?" Wolfgang asked. Even as coked up as he was he couldn't believe it.

"Alright, let's just say that the killer put it there. Just to humor you. What in the fuck does that prove? Anything? A vast conspiracy involving reclusive goth rock bands and car manufacturers?" said Harrison.

"No. Someone calling himself Doctor Jeep, or wanting to be known as Doctor Jeep, is killing Williamsburg's hipsters."

"You're forgetting Veniss. What Jeep item did she have?" Rad inquired.

"Nothing we know of yet." T's response was blunt. Airtight.

"Yet," Xavier drove the point home.

Bossy's was winding down. The beats had slowed. The lasers sprouting from the DJ booth were off. The only light in the place was the Exit sign. A woman was shouting at the bar and the bartenders were in a huddle, sipping cocktails and laughing.

"And supposing you find something?" Wolfgang asked, his eyes red, coked out saucers.

"Well, that would help solidify our theory. Wouldn't it?" T raised his eyebrows. It was a cheesy move he told Harrison he'd perfected in college, something he called the Andy Sidaris Baddie shift.

"And if not?" Harrison prodded.

"Still doesn't mean anything. Look. I know the deal, you're all being cautious. That's fine. But this isn't a game we're coming up with. I'm totally serious about this. Xavier and I have uncovered a killer at work, someone operating right here, right now. Under the noses of the cops and the public."

"So, let's say you find him. What then, Sherlock?" Rad asked.

"Well, that's the best part. See, we can catch him."

No one responded to that one.

T tried it again and spiffied it up, "We can fucking catch him."

"Besides the fact that that is a very cool but entirely absurd idea. How the fuck would you even think of doing that?" Rad barked. "Are you going to go over to the hardware store and get a serial killer kit? And that's assuming that this is the work of some lone deranged serial killer who's stalking hipsters. Look, I don't know about the rest of you but I'm not exactly your average vigilante. I can hardly lift my own ginormous cock . . ."

Rad paused to let that sink in. He got a groan from Cooper.

". . . all I'm saying is that looking at this crew we don't have anyone I'd call serial killer catching material. I mean look at Wolfgang. The guy looks like Jesus on a bender. Can't believe they let him work with teenaged girls. And then there's Harrison. He's a museum curator, what more can I say. Cooper's always high and when he's not high he's acting like he is. Xavier, I hardly know you, dude, but I know you're not an ex-marine. T, you publish a zine and live in a really fancy modernist house that your parents bought you. And me, well, I can help stitch up your ass when this Doctor Jeep guy hands it back to you."

"I like the idea. I'm in," Cooper grinned. "It's just for fun, right? I mean, we're not really gonna try and catch a killer. This is like when you're in high school and you form a band with your buddies but none of you plays any instruments. You just spend your time making flyers and T-shirts and bumper stickers and thinking of lyrics and constantly change the band's name. I mean, that was fun. I loved that. This is really just the same thing, right?"

"Coop, I think T's serious," said Harrison.

"Really?"

T and Xavier nodded simultaneously.

T spoke, "Look. I had a gang in high school. We called ourselves the Easy Aces. We were like the band that Cooper described but better. We had the bumper stickers. We had the

trench coats. We had the theme songs even. But we also did
shit. Most of it was minor shit—trespassing, graffiti, burglary, a
few assaults—but we were real. It was authentic. Ragged ass
punks, all pent up and spitting Mark E. Smith rage. Some cities
have Crips and Bloods and Vato gangs. Pennington, New Jersey, had the Easy Aces kicking ass from '86 to '89. Once you put
on the uniform, once you commit yourself to the idea of it,
then it's easy as cake. You don't think all those gangbangers
grew up as badazzmofos? They were skinny nerds, too. They
woke up one morning and they was gangbangers. All that takes
is some street smarts and a fucking Glock. Simple stuff, really."

"Sure," Rad said. "But why would you want us to catch this
guy? Why us?"

" 'Cause we're the only ones who can see the pattern. The
cops don't realize that this guy is taking out Brooklyn's finest.
We see it. We can stop it now. Chances are pretty good that this
guy is gonna get away with this. There could be other, even
staler, murders he's committed. We can stop him. And there's
the publicity."

Cooper asked, "Publicity?"

"Yeah, for my zine, for Wolfgang's band, Xavier's street cred,
Harrison's exhibits. Hell, the fucking museum would be super-
psyched if one of their own brought down a serial killer."

"I seriously doubt that," Harrison said. He decided now was
as good a time as any to get up and bleed the lizard.

He took his time in the bathroom.

Urinated slowly. Sighed all the while. He dreaded going back
to the table. Back into the frenzy. The Whole Sick Crew had always been attracted to outlandish ideas. Half the time they got
together one of them would suggest something fucked up. But
Harrison always knew nothing would come of it. It was all talk.
Bravado. T's stripper adoption agency. Wolfgang's cartel
dreams. Cooper's gumball spaceship.

When he returned to the table six minutes later he fully expected that they'd have moved on. Talk about vocoders or *Lon-*

don Fields. But they were still talking serial killer killing. The conversation had moved from mildly outrageous to downright frightening.

Wolfgang was gesticulating wildly ". . . we'll get orange kung fu jumpsuits. You know, put decals on the back. Maybe iron on patches that say, Williamsburg Riffs. And then we'll get some guns, right? We'll need guns, mutherfuckers! It'll be like *The Warriors.*"

Rad stoked the fire. "Warriors, come out and plaaayyy–aaayyy!! Fuck yeah!"

"We know the guy is a hipster," T reasoned. "We know what hipsters like. Where they go. What they do. Fact of the matter is, this guy is probably coming for our asses next. We've probably been in his sights for weeks. Maybe longer. Hell, my zine is pretty well read and the site has been popular for years with the whole Billburg scene. Xavier's bar is always hopping. Wolfgang's band is about to blow up . . ."

"And what about me, T? Anything I do interest Jeep?" Harrison interrupted.

"Well, I don't know, Harrison. Maybe. Is there a reason you think he'd be after you? Anything you do that you haven't told us about?"

Harrison didn't respond.

He knew that T wasn't aware of Cloverly. But it gave Harrison pause. He briefly wondered how easy it would be for someone to connect him with the Cloverly stories. How easy it would be to track it back, through P.O. boxes and cryptic email accounts. And would that qualify as hipster victim material? If Doctor Jeep was slaughtering geeks why wouldn't he be after science porn writers?

Harrison decided it was time to leave. He gestured to the door, "Look gang, I've gotta roll. It's late and I need to be at work early."

No one batted an eye. The fanatical banter continued.

Harrison tried the direct approach. "Been fun. Don't you kids get too out of control here with all this gang talk."

Nothing.

Harrison left and no one at the table noticed.

He caught a cab home and collapsed on his sofa with a groan. Exhausted. Closed his eyes and there behind the lids was Doctor Jeep, a grinning death's head, sitting with a laptop in a café and surfing the net for everything on Cloverly, the paleontological pornographer. Harrison saw T, Xavier, Rad, Cooper and Wolfgang, once the Whole Sick Crew but now the Williamsburg Riffs, in orange jumpsuits doing roundhouses and twirling flying guillotines around their heads. He saw the gangs of *The Warriors* all gathered together at Riverside Drive Park just like in the movie. And the Williamsburg Riffs were there and Cyrus was on the mic but then it wasn't Cyrus it was T, and he was speaking as Cyrus with Cyrus' voice and he was shouting, "Can you dig it? Can you dig it? CAAAANNN YOU-UUU DIG IITTTT!" Harrison slept in his clothes, the hall light on, his apartment door locked, double bolted. And his dreams were blood-soaked.

He awoke around 4 a.m. to the sound of his answering machine whirring into life. Harrison was one of the only people he knew who actually still had a message machine. He thought the whole voice mail system thing was too impersonal. Besides, T had bought it for him. Voice mail didn't lend itself to really long messages. Really long messages like the ones that T left. Tales of T's life, things that never really ended up on his blog but should have. Insights into his existence. Harrison never interrupted the messages. At four or five in the morning, listening to T's ramblings was actually kind of soothing.

"Got another story for you," T's voice echoed in the dark. "I wrote this one a long time ago. Never posted it on the site. Figured it was too fucked up. Anyway, I can't sleep. I figure you can't either. Excitement and all.

"Here it goes," T's reading voice wasn't the same as his speaking voice. It was measured and timed. It was like a performance. It was like he expected that Harrison would save the records for prosperity. As if they would wind up one day on a CD, like T Radcliff's Greatest Hits.

"Sal Solomon. You don't know him but he's a good guy. He's cool, looks like your average faggot with corduroys and slicked back hair. He has a thing for studded boots. He's a karate instructor, or sensei, or whatever. He's like a fucking eighth-level black belt or something. Insane, really. He's also flaming, has guys all over town, and loves that Swedish neo-folk rock that Wolfgang's always dissing.

"So, this one time Sal was giving me a ride on his way back to the city when some fucking SUV dickwad decides to ride his ass. Sal drives some little car and this guy was in this huge white Yukon. This guy is really tailgating hard. Just riding Sal for what seems like hours. Finally, Sal has had enough. He slams on his brakes and the Yukon smashes into his bumper. I was just laughing the whole fucking time 'cause I knew what that poor Yukon bastard had coming to him. I step out and watch the show.

"Sal jumps out of the car. Amazingly there isn't much damage. And as he walks over to the driver's side of this Yukon, a big hulking muscle man steps out of the SUV. This guy's a wrestler, wearing a white T-shirt and backward baseball cap. He's got frat boy and customer service written all over him. He's yelling this and that about how he's gonna kick Sal's ass. But Sal doesn't hear him. He doesn't listen. He just walks up to the mutherfucker and pulls his belt off. I mean, Sal is a fast dude. He's a karate master and when he pulls off this guy's belt it's as though he was able to stop time, pull it off and then restart it. It was as if the belt just vanished and a millisecond later it was dangling from Sal's hand. It was incredible.

"So this Yukon guy's face just barely registers what's happened when his pants drop. He was sagging them, stone washed baggy jeans, and with the belt gone they just tumbled to his sad ankles. The guy's standing there with his fucking pants at his knees. Mind you, it is cold, this only happened about a month ago. This little cock-knocker is standing in the road, fucking thirty degrees out and Sal's got his belt.

"So the guy says something stupid like, "You're going to pay for that." And before he's done with his fucking sentence Sal has whipped off his boxers and has the guy's tiny pecker in his hand.

"I've seen little dicks. Rad showed me a photo lineup of a bunch of the shriveled up little suckers when he was on his urology rotation. We're talking two centimeters, little peckers. Well, this fucking guy had a dick like that. And he shouted and cursed and spat. But Sal just laughs and laughs and walks back to the car. The Yukon guy just stood there in the road as we pulled off, pants around his ankles. Naked, cold, the mutherfucker has been ruined. And you know what I realized after that? I realized that it wasn't that Sal was a black belt or even that he had the monster gonads to do that shit. It was that he knew that it would work. He just knew it.

"Knowing that takes training. It takes discipline. Like a soldier, it's something that you train yourself to do. To be confident that what you are doing, even if it is fucking insane, will work. Even if it doesn't go down the way it was planned. Like if the frat boy had a huge dick or maybe if he had a gun. Something can still be salvaged from that. The operation is always a success when the other side has no idea what you're really . . ."

And the voice was cut. The machine clicked off.

Harrison lay awake in the dark listening for something more. There was surely more. The fact that it stopped prematurely was supremely annoying. Beyond annoying it was aggravating. But not enough to keep Harrison awake.

6

"Dr. Borgo? Sorry to call so late."

Beth Ann pulled an ashtray onto her bedspread and sat back. She lit another cigarette, the third in the past ten minutes, and closed her eyes. She wanted desperately to sleep.

"Beth Ann? What's going on?"

"Sorry. I just . . ."

"No, it's fine. Fine."

Borgo was brusque. Like the biggest Billy Goat Gruff. He was a prototypical psychiatrist. All leather couch and leather elbows on his sports coats. He never smoked a pipe while Beth Ann was in his office but when she pictured him in all his psychiatric glory there was a smoking pipe firmly clinched in his teeth.

"Well, I had a rough morning. I probably should have called you earlier but I waited until tonight because I needed to sort some things out. But now I'm ready. We need to talk about my blindness and my mother. But most of all we need to talk about the meaning of blindness."

"They do seem to go together, Beth Ann. Let's try and tackle one at a time."

She wasn't sure if that was a snide aside or astute clinical judgment.

"Alright, let's talk about the biggie. My going blind."

Beth Ann could hear Dr. Borgo settling in on the other end of the phone. She imagined him getting out of bed, his snoring wife mildly disturbed, and walking down to the kitchen where he would light his pipe and glance at the headlines on a muted television set.

"Let's start."

"I think it's accelerating. I'm really scared that by the end of the week I'm going to be completely blind. Completely."

"As you know, and we have talked about this several times, I'm no expert on macular degeneration. But my understanding is, and this is from Dr. Lombardo whom I believe you have seen recently . . ."

"Yes, I saw him two weeks ago."

"My understanding is that it can happen suddenly, though more commonly it is a slow, painless loss of sight. You've told me that you have spots in your vision. Lines from time to time. Color changes. Have you been using your Amsler's grids? Has any change occurred recently?"

"Yeah, I fell down a fucking flight of stairs today 'cause I couldn't see them."

"Okay, maybe my best advice to you would be to make an appointment with Dr. Lombardo as soon as possible."

"But that's the problem, Dr. Borgo. He can't do anything for me. I'm not taking Thalidomide. This is incurable. It is eventual. There is nothing he can do. That's why I'm calling. I need to talk about the fact that I will go blind regardless of my fear of it."

"You sound as though you don't need to talk to me, Beth Ann. You already know what it is that you need to overcome. You know that you must accept this disease, you must accept your blindness and come to terms with it."

"Any advice on how to do that?"

"Do you have many friends, Beth Ann?"

"No. Not many. But we've talked about this before. Thousands of times."

"Without touching upon your relationship with your mother, do you have family that you can contact and discuss these fears? I know we've surely talked about this before but it is late and I've not got my notes with me."

"An uncle and my cousin. But really no one that I can call up and lay all my shit on. Hence the call."

Dr. Borgo sighed, long and hard. In fact, Beth Ann thought it sounded too long and hard like it was a sigh of annoyance rather than contemplation. A sigh of annoyance would be infuriating and Beth Ann wondered if she should say something. She didn't.

"It's not really my idea originally," Dr. Borgo said, "but I believe most often fear of blindness is closely associated with fear of death. Now, we commonly see this fear of blindness within psychological connotations. You know, people afraid of going blind in place of dying. I'm not sure I'm explaining that clearly. But with you, the blindness is real. And so your fear of death is justified. It all comes down to embracing nothingness. That's the key. Not that I don't worry about death from time to time but what really helped me was the realization that when I die, I will no longer be. There will be nothing to feel. Nothing to fear. Nothing to see. Nothing to know or not know. Life will continue and I will be absent. Nothingness. Learn to embrace the idea of nothing, embrace the void in its antiembrace."

Beth Ann scoffed.

"That really doesn't help me, Dr. Borgo. I'm going blind. Falling down stairs and making an ass of myself. I don't need to embrace the finality of death. I don't give a shit about the end and the grave and the loss of control. I want some help in my journey toward sightlessness. My work. That's all. Just some words."

"Honestly Beth Ann, I can prescribe you some medications

that might help you sleep. Maybe something for anxiety? But you're going to have to face this on your own. I'm sorry. But it's late, I'm tired. You're tired I'm sure. Let's speak again in the morning."

"Okay. Dr. Borgo. You do know you are the shittiest therapist in the city, right?"

Beth Ann slammed the phone down hard on the nightstand. Hard enough that it rocked the ashtray on her bed and spread a fine dust of ash across her pillows. A fine dust of ash that quickly became mud in her tears.

7

The room looked the same.
The same orange rug by the door. The same bed draped
with a blue duvet. The same posters on the wall. The same small
wooden desk and chair. Even the light fixture that flooded the
room with a pale glow was the same. Everything was in place.

The "set-up" had taken seven months to prepare. Paul had
spent his evenings at auctions in the city. Bidding on and winning the pieces that would slowly become the whole. Two weekends ago he got the desk for a bargain price of twelve dollars. It
wasn't the one he had. Not exactly. He brought it home and
using old photos applied the same scratches. The same discol-
orations using erasers, markers, pencils and crayons. And the
figures that lined the floor and dotted the furniture had cost
nearly $760 to acquire again. It took four years to get all the
pieces, all the weapons, all the gear. Long nights spent on eBay
bidding on tiny plastic boots and belts and goggles and helmets
and gas masks and guns. Lots and lots of tiny plastic guns.

It was time for the war to start and it would be better than in

1987. Better by a thousandfold. Paul Achting would call the shots. He would make the first move. It would be so good.

Iceberg, white snowsuit, green goggles and colorless rifle, sat patiently on the L.C.V. (Low Crawl Vehicle) just east of the bookshelf. Beside him, Mainframe, clad in his distinctive gray short-sleeved uniform, manned the battlefield computer. They did not speak to each other. Only waited and watched. High above them on the chair at the desk was Lifeline, his steely gaze trained upon the battlefield and rescue medic kit at his side. He was ready. His time with the Seattle Fire Department had prepared him for anything. He'd seen more in his five years with the S.F.D. than most men see in an entire lifetime.

While Lifeline, Mainframe and Iceberg hung back, Hawk, Leatherneck, Wet Suit and Sci-Fi were on the front lines. They stood in procession, weapons raised, adrenalin pumping feverishly. Anxious for another victory over the dreaded Cobra. Hawk, the original field officer, was now a general. This battle would be the one that defined his military career. The one that would make or break him. Leatherneck, always the traditional soldier, stood just behind Hawk, his gray rifle at his side. Out of his element now for a month Wet Suit was eager to see action. While he would have preferred battle at sea, where his trademark SEAL gear was indispensable, fighting on land was fighting nonetheless. And Wet Suit was always happiest in battle. Sci-Fi's lackadaisical attitude was in check today. The laser trooper in the neon green jumpsuit was leading the charge. Out front, it would be his battle cry that the enemy would hear first.

Behind them Sgt. Slaughter, wearing his distinctive mirrored shades, sat uncomplainingly in the cab of the idling Triple T Tank. He was speaking on a transistor radio to Dial Tone, the communications specialist, back at GI. Joe headquarters. He could smell, almost taste, evil in the air.

Cobra was indeed close.

The Dreadnoks, an elite team of maniacal mercenaries allied with Cobra for this battle, were in the thick of the shag carpet.

The Welshman, Monkeywrench, was lying on his belly. His orange beard blending in perfectly with the orangey-rust of the rug. He had only recently come to Australia. His time in East End, London, being a cavalcade of debauchery and psychedelic music. Beside him sat Zandar, leader of the Dreadnoks and master of disguise though he looked more like a member of Duran Duran circa *Arena* than a crazed killer. To their left was the lovely Zarana, Zartan's sister, sharpening her knife and dreaming of warm flesh. Toward the edge of the carpet, nearest the closet, Zanzibar, the dread pirate who never changed his socks and brushed his teeth with grape soda, was mounted on the Air Skiff, an over water swamp vehicle that functioned surprisingly well on the thick shag rug. Last was Thrasher, the psycho, mounted on the Thunder Machine, a red and black behemoth that was as postapocalyptic as Mad Max himself.

And atop the oak toy chest, high above the swath of carroty shag, sat the core of Cobra Command. The hooded Cobra Commander, looking like a blue klansman, was loading his black laser pistol and making small talk with Destro, the silver headed arms supplier and founder of M.A.R.S. (Military Armaments Research System). Nearby a viper, one of many similarly dressed infantrymen, stood at the ready alongside a ragged copy of *The Haunted Spy,* while a B.A.T. (Cobra android trooper) with a holographic chest paced, anxious for battle, across a derelict copy of *The Silver Chair.*

The air was hot, literally vibrating with tension, and the men on the ground could feel it. They were sweating with apprehension, licking their chops.

And then the fucking doorbell chimed.

Paul waited. The store was closed. It was after fucking midnight. He held his breath. Prayed that a fucking drunk was hitting the bell and would get frustrated and leave. But the doorbell sounded again. And then again. And again.

Fucker! Paul swore under his breath.

The short, muscular red head with a nose ring and a Tiger

tattoo on his neck walked furiously out of the storage room at the back of Wham! Comics and Collectibles.

"What the fuck do you want?" Paul shouted as he violently pulled the front door open.

He expected a scared teen. Maybe a put off geek or a junkie looking for change. But what he found was a thin man with a silver revolver.

The gun was pointed directly in Paul's anger-curdled face.

"I need you to name the six members of *Voltron* in two minutes or less."

"Wha . . ." Paul backed into the store, his hands shot up above his head. "What do you want?"

"I need you to name the six members of *Voltron* in two minutes or less."

The thin guy wasn't kidding. He stepped into the store and ordered Paul down on his belly. Paul's sweaty face stuck to the linoleum floor.

"We're talking about the '80s cartoon show, right?" Paul was shaking. He'd never had a gun pointed at him before. *Not the 'Ayatollah of Comica.'*

"Yes, we're talking about the '80s cartoon about the giant robot."

Paul's mind was spinning. He couldn't believe this was happening to him. Him of all the fucking comic book nerds in Brooklyn. Paul Achting had studied with the best and the brightest. He had toured the country speaking at conventions and on public access television programs like Superhero Xpress. He had hosted the ill-fated comic book segments, taped but never aired, on the defunct Wave Theatre broadcast exclusively on WPIX 11 Alive from 1985-1987. Not that the fucker that held a gun to Paul's head would care. Not that this fucker had even the slightest idea.

Lying there, on the floor of the Williamsburg comic book/ collectibles store he had worked in since 1993 with a maniac pressing a gun to his head, Paul feared his reign might just be over. He began to panic. His heart was exploding. His head swelling. And he worried that the man holding the gun could read his thoughts. It was a ridiculous idea but in his trembling panic he imagined his thoughts were appearing in white comic book bubbles above his head. He tested the theory: *Just shoot me, cocksucker.*

Nothing happened.

Paul thought, *Okay.*

Nothing happened.

Paul spoke. "Okay. You want the names of those little spaceships that flew around and made up the body of *Voltron?* You know, in the early series . . . Or the . . ."

The man with the gun spoke. He sounded really annoyed. "Six members, mutherfucker . . . *Voltron* was two Japanese shows re-edited into a Frankensteinian concoction. The lions were from the show *Golion,* or "Lion Force," and the space ships—the fucking space ships—were from *Dairugger XV,* or "Vehicle Force." When I said I wanted the names of the six, I meant I wanted the names of the lion force pilots."

This guy looked like your average Billburg hipster. Tight white jeans, cowboy boots, a faded Iron Maiden T-shirt, cop shades and shaggy hair. Paul had seen a thousand guys like him and there was nothing different about this one. But this guy did have a gun. A very real gun.

Paul wondered if a sudden surge of adrenalin might give him superpowers. He'd read about that happening countless times. Housewives lifted cars off of their trapped children. Ninety-eight pound weaklings pummeled football stars. Paul thought, *I'll transform into the Hulk in a few seconds. Muscles are tensing. Here I go! No. Nothing. Shit, is he reading this now? I'm about to fucking die and I'm thinking about the Hulk. Pathetic.* Paul needed to focus. He wondered how many seconds he'd just wasted.

". . . the lions."

Paul was no good with '80s anime. He'd watched Japanese

cartoons growing up. He drew pictures of fighting robots in school. Even had a Shogun Warriors sticker on his skateboard. But he wasn't an expert. He could never remember if *G-Force* was the same thing as *Battle of the Planets*. If Tranzor-Z was in any way related to Godzilla. (Or was that Jet Jaguar?) Here he was surrounded by ephemera from the '80s, bits of plastic and stapled paper that meant more to some lonely thirty-year-old computer programmer than a night with Pamela Anderson, and he had to pause to think about which cartoon was *Voltron*. Paul was in the heart of a plastic wonderland and he was struggling.

He sighed. He reached deep inside himself and found a memory there. He shook the dust off it. It was candy striped and electro purple and he saw it was good. But it was hazy. He closed his eyes. Sweat ran in rivulets onto the cold floor.

Paul spoke, "The six members are: Keith . . . Allura . . . Sven . . ."

The thin man said, "Forty-five seconds to go."

Paul wrestled with the names. He knew he had them locked away. He pictured the cartoon faces, those strange Japanese caricatures of Anglo features. Huge eyes, wide solid white grins and the lines, like whiskers, that crossed their oval cheeks. He saw the faces and wanted to laugh.

"Um . . . Hunk . . . Pidge . . ."

Paul was fumbling. The revolver pressed closer.

There was one more lion.

Paul thought, *Who was it? The red lion, it was the red lion . . .*

Paul saw it running, metal legs gleaming, leaping up into the air to join the others. The red lion was the lion of fire. It was the right arm and it held the blazing sword of Voltron, Defender of the Universe.

Let's form Voltron!

"You have twenty seconds."

Fuck, Paul thought.

8

The Slaughtered Lamb was something of a West Village landmark, sandwiched between sex shops and juice bars. It was a pub, hunkered down and British, and the name was from *An American Werewolf in London*. Inside were props from the film. Well, Harrison assumed they were props from the film. That or just crafty geek interpretations.

Taking a seat near the back of the bar, just under the glass case that held a life-sized rubber werewolf tearing off its clothes and howling to the recessed lighting, Harrison ordered fish and chips and a Black and Tan. He was taking an extraordinarily long break from work. Normally he took an hour. But this lunch was approaching its third. No worries, Harrison thought, I'm researching. Researching something or other.

He had taken only a few bites of his fish—he enjoyed it best with a ton of malt vinegar—when a woman walked in and sat at the table adjacent to his.

She was tall, thin and had her head shaved with the front and bangs left long as fringes. He'd seen that before and thought it might be called a Chelsea cut or a feather cut. The only girls he'd ever seen with the hairstyle were punker girls, East Village girls. It was obvious the woman had been crying. Her cheeks were flushed and Harrison noticed that her body would rattle with the after tremors of sobbing every other minute. She was wearing a yellow and green ski vest and Harrison couldn't take his eyes off her.

The woman noticed Harrison staring and smiled when their eyes met.

"Are you okay?" Harrison pushed aside his plate. "Do you need a cigarette?"

"Yes, please," the woman replied. They walked outside together. Both blinking as they emerged into daylight. Harrison pulled a pack of Dunhill's from his leather coat and gave her one. She put it to her lips and he lit it with his trilobite Zippo.

"I'm just having a bad day," she said.

"Why's that?"

"Just shit. Nothing unusual, really."

"Okay."

Harrison let her take a few deep drags before he asked her name.

"Beth Ann Belling. And you are?"

"Harrison Gelden. Doctor Harrison Gelden."

He felt really awkward adding the doctor part. He shook his head and started over.

"It's just Harrison. I don't know why I had to add the doctor part. That was really immature…"

"What kind of doctor are you, Harrison?"

"Ph.D. Paleontology."

"Interesting," Beth Ann shrugged. It really wasn't interesting at all and Harrison noticed that she didn't feign any interest.

"Not, it's really not. It pays the bills and I get to make my own hours."

Beth Ann smiled. The sobbing jags had subsided into jelly quivers every few minutes.

"And what do you do?"

"I knit. Teach knitting."

"Interesting."

"Not really," Beth Ann said.

"You're right, that's not that interesting either. You want to know what I really do? I write truly obscure porn stories."

Harrison was sure that would sink the conversation. Kill it immediately. He cringed for her response.

"Now that's more interesting. Are you some type of pervo?"

"No. Well I don't think so."

"Good. I don't want to talk with some sicko. But if you're not a perv, why do you write porn? I don't suppose you're famous for it?"

"I am."

"Really? Famous for what exactly? Do you write screenplays or something?"

"No. Stories."

"Fetish stuff?"

"I guess, in a way. I really don't want to say what kind of stuff. My pen name has been in the news a lot lately and I want to remain anonymous as long as I can."

"Is that so? A blind girl like me wanders into a bar and sits down with someone who claims to be both a paleontologist and a pornographer and to top it off he's famous for both . . ."

Harrison choked. "Blind?"

Beth Ann nodded. This was her chance to unveil the sickness, to trot out the damage.

"Excuse my saying, but you don't look blind to me."

"Not yet, still going. Macular degeneration. That's the fancy name for it. It began on my sixteenth birthday. I'm in here, crying like a stupid baby, 'cause I blacked out yesterday on some stairs and wound up at the bottom of them."

"I'm sorry to hear that." Harrison had nothing else to say. Nothing he could possibly add but sorry. And sorry again.

Beth Ann must have read the uncertainty in his face, she

switched gears, "Sorry, it's a habit of mine to talk about it. Let's talk a bit more about you and this whole pervo writing thing. Are you like a porn addict?"

"Recovering," Harrison was cool talking about the porn over Beth Ann's impending blindness. It was easier. And he certainly didn't want to mention that the whole porn addiction was starting to overwhelm him. That it was threatening to ruin him. He also realized that talking about any of it was potentially really off-putting, "I can't believe I'm talking to you about this. It's beyond embarrassing now."

"Think of it this way: You're in a therapy session. Besides, I can think of worse things to be addicted to. A lot."

"An addiction is an addiction, at least that's what I've read."

"You don't want to be an addict, I take it?"

"No. No."

"What have you tried?"

"I've met with shrinks. I've tried support groups. Nothing works. It's all a sham and in the end I'm back to where I started. Back to the craving."

"See, that's what has always fascinated me about male sexuality. I don't get it. Women need interaction. Warmth. A look. A smile. Something tangible. Men only need an image, remote and plastic, and they're just fine. That's so fascinating to me. Have you tried approaching it that way? Looking at it from a scientific point of view?"

"If I start seeing these women as they really are, then, well, I might never recover from that."

"You're an idiot," Beth Ann laughed, a snide, coarse laugh.

"Why do you say that?"

"I said you're an idiot 'cause you're obsessed with this whole thing. Look at you, you're practically shaking."

And Harrison was. He was shaking uncontrollably.

"You've got yourself so worked up over this that it's completely dominated your life. Aren't you supposed to work at a museum or something?"

"I am a museum curator. At the American."

"Why aren't you obsessing over that? It's boring, granted, but if you're going to tell a woman that you write porn, and that you're a porn addict, you'd better be comfortable with that. Or at least think it's not such a big deal. Or make it sound like a joke. But you're an obsessed man. You're sick."

"Sick? What about you? You're obsessed with your blindness."

"That's different."

"How?"

"I'm losing my fucking eyesight and that's gonna change my life. You are just playing with yourself and getting all screwed up over it. My blindness is part of me. It's coiled up in my guts and it sings to me every time I speak. It's literally before my eyes when I wake up and when I lie down. I'm trapped. It's physical and I didn't open the door to it."

"You're right. Look, can we talk about something else?"

"Let's go back in."

They stamped the butts of their cigarettes into the pavement and headed back into the dimly lit bar. Then they sat a few moments in silence, just the chiming voices of the other customers at the front of the pub. The rattle of dishes being washed and the distant hum of traffic. "Not Me" by This Mortal Coil was playing on a stereo behind the bar.

"So, what else is there to talk about?" Beth Ann smiled.

"I'm not really like this, honestly."

"I know, I can tell by the pitch of your voice."

"Let me tell you a story."

"Alright."

"It's not going to be a long story. I've got to get back to work. But I think you'll like it. I read this story when I was a kid, maybe in 1982. I was eight or something. I was a precocious child, always reading this or that and particularly attracted to weird tales, strange stories. Normal kids don't grow up to become paleontologists."

"I like weird tales," Beth Ann smirked. "Shoot."

"It was written by a guy named Manly Wade Wellman. Can't remember what the name of the story is. It was about an Indian, a hunter. The story was set in the 1800s when the white people were first branching out into the wilderness but most of it still belonged to the native people. There's this hunter who lives with his tribe at the foot of some jagged mountains. He's the best hunter they have, can take down anything, but even *he* is afraid to go up to the top of the mountain 'cause there's something up there, in a cave, that they call Eagle Eye or Fast Eye. Something like that. No one who's ever gone to the cave of Fast Eye has come back down. In a way, going to see Fast Eye is going off to die—the elders climb the mountain to the jagged peak and meet their fate.

"So, our hunter hero has some accident. Gets something in his eyes or something. Again the details aren't important. What is important is that he goes blind. Not quickly, but slowly like over a period of many years. His eyesight simply begins to drift. Darkness closes in and he can no longer be the magnificent hunter that he once was. Assuming that a blind hunter is useless, he decides to climb the mountain and the jagged rock and meet Fast Eye. Whatever Fast Eye is.

"The ascent is long and treacherous but he finally reaches Fast Eye's cave and without much hesitation he enters. The first thing he notices is that the floor of the cave is littered with bones. The bones, he assumes, of his ancestors. The hunter shouts into the cave, "Come and get me Fast Eye, I'm ready!" But nothing happens. And then a voice appears inside our hunter's head. It's a distant, strange voice and it tells him that he won't die. "Why?" the hunter asks. The answer is simple: Because the hunter cannot see Fast Eye, it cannot kill him.

"Fast Eye, turns out, is some sort of alien. . . ."

Beth Ann giggled.

"Seriously. Come on," Harrison was pissed. "I'm trying to tell you a story. Don't laugh. Fuck, I know it's about aliens and Indians and shit but it's got a moral."

"Okay, okay," Beth Ann stifled her snickering. "Please continue."

"Fine. So Fast Eye is this alien. He crash-landed on Earth millennia ago and lives in the cave because anything that sees him dies. And he feels kind of bad about that. Fast Eye's not evil. Just some poor space chump that has to hide away. He tells the hunter that his face is simply so alien that any Earth thing trying to comprehend him dies. That's kind of cool, right? One look at it kills. Being blind, of course, our hunter is immune. Both he and Fast Eye are relieved. Finally, here is a creature with which Fast Eye can share his knowledge. Fast Eye can see the future. He has longed to communicate with mankind about impending doom but every time a person has come into the cave, whammo!, he's dead. Fast Eye tells the hunter about the coming of the white man. The destruction of the Earth by nuclear weapons. George W. getting elected. Postmodern mayhem. Having told his story, Fast Eye dies. And our hero returns to his tribe a prophet."

Harrison nodded. Sermon over. Score.

Beth Ann squinted, "What's the moral?"

Harrison sighs, "Not that obvious huh? Maybe going blind isn't the loss of something. Maybe it's just a transition. Moving to a new state where you'll gain knowledge that any sighted person couldn't?"

"That sounds an awful lot like fairy tales."

"But it has a nice ring to it doesn't it?"

Beth Ann cleared her throat. A tear rolled down her cheek, leaving a dark trail of mascara. "I don't want to be a prophet. I don't want hidden information. I want to be able to go and see movies and people watch, look out the window of a plane and see the fucking landscape below me. I want to see the transitions of the day to night, of winter to spring. I want to see colors and I want to stare into the sun."

"I'm sorry," Harrison reached out and put a hand on Beth Ann's shoulder.

She wiped her nose and laughed, "I don't know why I'm crying. I'm sitting here under the gaze of a rubber fucking werewolf, talking to a museum curator who writes porn stories and reads weird tales. What the hell am I complaining about?"

Harrison laughed, though he wasn't sure if he'd been insulted or complimented. "The colors and the seasons are really overrated."

"Yeah. People watching isn't though."

"We should do it sometime. I mean people watch together."

"Is that a date?" Beth Ann smiled. "Don't answer that. Let's not start down that road. So, when do you have to be back? Soon, right?"

Harrison looked at his watch, "I'm already running really late."

"Then you need to go."

"Come with me."

"What?" Beth Ann's face registered a joke.

Harrison was serious, "Walk with me over to the museum. It's not far."

"What? 79th Street? That's all the way uptown."

"No, take the B and then walk from 81st with me. I promise I'll behave myself. I'm not like this guy," Harrison pointed his thumb at the werewolf. The werewolf's rubber snarl didn't change.

Ten minutes later they were on the subway, sitting beside each other and giggling like preschoolers. Harrison made a crack about the gutter punk sitting across from them, a wormy guy with a filthy mop and a ratty leather coat with a G.B.H. T-shirt stapled to the back of it.

"Bet he gets a lot of dates."

Beth Ann giggled, "I've got to pee, stop making me laugh."

The gutter punk looked over, the bullring in his nose covered with dry snot. He scowled but it was half-hearted.

"You know that whenever someone tells me that, to stop 'cause they've got to pee, it usually makes me want to tell even more jokes. Makes me want to try and get them laughing even more. It's really not that I want you to pee your pants but it's funny. It's funny that you have to pee." Beth Ann put a bony elbow into Harrison's ribs and he threw back his head in mock agony.

Beth Ann giggled about that, too. But she pulled herself together when a businessman standing across from them threw her a dirty look.

"Harrison, tell me about your life. How did you get here?"

"On this train with you? I woke up feeling . . ."

"No dumbass, tell me about your family. Your home town."

"Nothing too exciting. The usual stuff. I'm Jewish, my dad's a doctor and my mother is a homemaker. I grew up outside Philadelphia. Went to private school. College in upstate New York. Grad school. My grades weren't hot. I got into grad school on a string of good luck and a knack for science."

"A knack?"

"Yeah, I'm a devout rationalist. I worship at the altar of reason. Can't stand superstitious people. Unscientific hokum. I go after ignorance like a fucking pit bull. In elementary school my target was Jim Bercaccio. Jim was a Christian. The type that wore suits and carried a briefcase to fifth grade. Fucking Michael P. Keaton. He assumed that everyone wanted to hear the Word, that the world was built for him to preach in. To pray in. And to eventually flee from with the saved. In sixth grade Jim told me that animals were put on the Earth to eat. And insects—my personal fav—to step on. He said Jesus stepped on bugs. Loved to hear the crunch of their hard shells under his sandals. Jesus loved that.

"I swore for the first time outside of my own imagination that day. Called Jim an asshole. And then the fight was on. It spilled out into the hallway after class. Then it spilled out into the schoolyard. By the end of the day both of us were bruised and bloody. But I won. I beat science into Jim's head using the brick wall by the volleyball court."

"Nice," Beth Ann smiled.

"In high school my science fair entry was a treatise against superstition. It got all the awards but parents were pissed. I was labeled an anti-Christian. That sucked. In college I spent most of my time in the lab. When I wasn't studying in the dark stacks of the library or scanning bones, I was hanging out with my friends, smoking, drinking, dope. College is heaven for science-minded people. People who don't believe that Jesus likes to step on bugs. And the more I hung out with my buddies the less I needed to be in the lab proving shit to myself. There weren't any ignorant asses to hide from. But eventually the hanging out got the better of my grades. I wound up smoking endlessly, flirting constantly and drinking. Casual sex and waking up wearing the same clothes I'd put on two days earlier. I passed out on couches. On loveseats. On divans. On chaise lounges. On park benches. On bus seats. But just as it came, it went. It went quietly one Sunday morning senior year; it went like a fog dissipating, and before I knew it I was back in the labs and applying to grad school and getting in. Anyway, that's just a long way of saying that I'm not into superstitious bullshit . . . How did we get off on this tangent anyway?"

"I asked you about your family and . . ."

"Sorry."

"So, what about the weird tales? I mean they sound pretty irrational to me. Not very scientific."

"No, they're totally rational. It's just exploring the boundaries of science. The story I told you is completely and utterly rational. What the hell is more rational than the thrill of systematic discovery? The lone man who defies the elder's superstition to find out how the world really works? What really happens in that cave high on the mountain? No, it's rational all right. You'd think it was all metaphysical hogwash. That's for idiots who put faith above science. The worst two words in the English language are intelligent and design. That's like weird tales without the big reveal. It's like the hunter goes to the mountain and finds, well, who knows what he finds. That part doesn't matter. Shit drives me crazy. People thinking that evolution is a myth. People thinking that we couldn't have possibly evolved from apes. What the hell's wrong with apes? Is evolution too uncouth for our glorious destinies?"

Harrison was all red. Sweaty. "I sound like a total asshole, don't I? Sorry about my tirade. That was really embarrassing."

He worried he was scaring the shit out of Beth Ann, but she was laughing at him, "At least you care about something passionately. That's totally important. No one seems to care much these days. We need more people like you who get all worked up about stuff. You don't like rednecks. So what? That's no big deal. At least you can get all hot and bothered about something other than a chick with fake tits. I'm not too worried about it. It's really kind of cute."

Harrison said, "You're not gonna start talking to me about changing the world? The bullshit about one man, one vote? How I, me, Harrison Gelden, can start a revolution?"

"No," Beth Ann laughed, "That would be totally retarded right now."

Harrison switched it up, "What about your family? Are they all blind?"

Beth Ann humored his asinine and clunky conversation shift.

"I grew up in Tulsa. Moved here for college. My parents are divorced. That happened when I was two. My dad lives in Wyoming and yes, he's totally blind now. He was an accountant in a prior life. And my mom, Luanne, well, she's a single woman in Tulsa and she works as a stylist. She loves to set boundaries. For herself, me, and just about everyone that she comes in contact with, that's her thing. Setting up barriers. I have no idea why. Anyway, I began knitting when I was twelve.

In college I founded the Bitch Knitters Club, a loose affiliation of knitting chicks with some riot grrrl thrown in for fun. It got big. Made some corporate contacts but decided to pursue other routes to fame and fortune. I wanted to keep it all legit, right? Keep it hip. Stay with the in crowd. I kept knitting in my indie way and I started teaching and lecturing. I suppose it's made me kind of famous around here. At least in the knitting circles."

"Never knew there could be an edgy side to knitting. Like a dirty side to lawn bowling."

"Fuck off. Knitting isn't a sport. It's an existence." Beth Ann looked offended. She was.

"Alright, I got it. Seriously though, I think it's really cool."

"It is. Really. Women knit the fabric of the cosmos, tying the strings of humanity together everyday, all day. We are the builders of reality, from birth to death. Knitting is just our public show, the dance we do. Our display."

"Is that in the Bitch Knit brochure?"

Another elbow to Harrison's ribs.

"So, enough about us. No more stories. I want you to tell me something interesting. Tell me something scientific, Mr. Rational," Beth Ann prodded.

"You trying to turn me on?"

"Sure."

"Alright, since we're on the subject, how about cleavage?"

"On the topic? You've been staring down my shirt?"

"No I haven't. I just meant since we're flirting and all and the whole turn on comment and just . . ." Harrison couldn't believe he suggested that they were flirting.

"We're flirting?"

"Well . . ."

"Get back to what you were going to tell me, the stuff about cleavage."

"Have you ever considered it? I mean, why men are so attracted, so driven, toward cleavage?"

"No. And that doesn't sound like something a paleontologist would know. That's an anthropologist's deal."

"We hang out at the same Star Cons."

Harrison could see Beth Ann liked his talking geeky.

"Truth is, I love geeks," Beth Ann said, "Always have. I went gaga for the nerdy kids who could talk algebra and entomology and linguistics and reason."

"Well, the whole cleavage thing is an evolutionary adaptation. Scientists have always wondered why men would be so attracted to cleavage. They're drawn like magnets . . ."

"I get it, I get it. Move on."

"It's all about the shape. It's the breasts mashed together and the actual crack. The crack is key. You see there's only one other part of the body that looks like that. The ass. Cleavage looks like ass. Why would cleavage look like ass? 'Cause men are nuts for ass. And why would men go nuts for ass? Because it's a bonfire for the vulva. The ass is a roadmap to the sex. The whole thing is a biological sign post. It's like a giant arrow pointing down. Well, what do you think?"

"Sounds like your anthropologist friends have far too much time on their hands."

"Yeah, but it makes sense, right?"

"Sure, if you're a baboon. I can't believe that's the only thing you came up with when I asked you to tell me something scientific. I mean, how about telling me something about trilobites? I don't know anything about them. Or how about something really sophisticated? Like something about cells and genetics or something? That's just fucked up, Harrison. Next time I want to hear something that makes you look really smart."

"I could tell you about trilobites now."

"Lost your chance."

They sat in silence as the train passed through Rockefeller Center.

Then they winked at each other as the train passed Columbus Circle.

They walked from 81st to the museum and in the stairwell to Harrison's office they kissed.

They kissed as though they'd never see each other again.

And when they got into Harrison's office they fucked as though they'd never fucked before. Harrison slammed his office door shut and Beth Ann leapt as gingerly as possible onto his cluttered desk, being sure not to sit on the skulls.

Harrison was less cautious. He threw everything to the floor in a lusty swipe and moved in between Beth Ann's legs and undid his belt buckle as Beth Ann put her tongue in his left ear. He found his way under her dress and felt her nipples stiffen beneath the pads of her bra. Pushing her bra up, Harrison put his face on her chest. Licked the sweat welling up there. Beth Ann groaned and surged. Her hands found his prick and she grabbed it tight, squeezed. He had her panties. Pulled. Stretched. Found a way to get his fingers inside her. Thumb on her clit. And then he was inside her, caught up in the heat. And his skin flushed and the desk groaned from the strain and Beth Ann whimpered.

"I can't see . . . I can't see . . ."

With every thrust Harrison's ass clenched and his legs trembled. Beth Ann closed her eyes, her fingers digging into the wood of Harrison's desk.

"I can't see . . . I can't see . . ."

Harrison worried that he was shaking her retinas loose, speeding up the degeneration. He tried to hold back but Beth Ann pulled him in closer. Wrapped him in a warm blanket of static. The wash of endorphins. And they moved like a locomotive, steam spilling from their mouths.

The desk creaked and as Beth Ann came her nails dug into the soft skin on Harrison's back.

The skulls nodded obscenely, rocking back and forth.

The steam billowed.

Sweat ran.

Harrison groaned.

Beth Ann groaned.

Whimper. Shiver. Shake.

When it was over they were panting on the desk, both covered in that sex sweat and neither touched the other.

"You okay?" Harrison asked.

Beth Ann sighed hard. Pulled her bra back down over her breasts, "Yeah, I'm great," she said.

"I was a little worried there."

"Yeah, about what?"

"Your eyes."

Beth Ann chuckled, a cute nasal rattle. "I've got my cap," she smiled, unstuck her ass from the desk and pulled a red cap out of her oversized purse. "It's my knit cap. It has special powers."

Beth Ann pulled the cap over her head and smiled.

"Like what?" Harrison asked, winded.

"It's the stitch, it's the tightest I've ever gotten it and it makes me focus. Focus my eyes hard. When I do that I put the blindness at bay."

"Sweet," Harrison said distractedly. He was trying to remember if he had put a rubber on. "You know you're really quite talkative postcoitus."

Beth Ann ignored him.

She said, "I've got to get going."

"Oh, you're done, huh? Where to?"

"I've got a class to teach."

"So, you going to call me?"

"Maybe," Beth Ann turned to Harrison and smiled. "You didn't wear a condom did you?"

Harrison blushed, his ass cold on the hardwood. His penis retreating back between his legs. "No."

"I'll be sure and call you for the child payments," she laughed, kissed Harrison and left.

9

The go-go dancer was Russian, her name was Solange Loknar and she was swiveling slowly to Bruce Springsteen's "Streets of Philadelphia" as ten men and one woman watched. There was no alcohol served at Thursday's Strip Emporium so the viewers sipped sodas as quietly as possible.

It was 5 p.m.

Beth Ann sat in the back reading the biography of Darby Crash.

She didn't particularly care for strip clubs. She'd been to many and few of them offered anything more than slight, uncomfortable entertainment. She had no ill will toward the women who flaunted their bodies for the salivating men around them. They were the foot soldiers. For Beth Ann, strip clubs, and dancers like Solange, were part and parcel of an undermining revolution. This place was the last frontier. The Wild West of the gender wars, where skirmishes over flesh were bought and paid for. This is where women made their last stand.

Solange was Beth Ann's former roommate and occasional lover.

She had a nice body, her skin taut and smooth. But she wasn't strip club material. Solange had one of those minor character actress faces. She was that woman in the back of every blockbuster movie. The one crying behind Johnny Depp. The one serving dinner to Sharon Stone. The one driving past Uma Thurman. The one with the beautiful face that was just slightly off. Off enough that it would never land her a career outside of background noise.

Off enough.

But Solange's true attraction was her movement. It was precise. Mechanical. She was less a dancer moving for men's eyes than she was a mathematician plotting out the arc tangent of a falling object. She moved her every part with a deliberation that was calculated and succinct. Watching Solange dance was like watching a professor of quantum mechanics at the chalkboard. Each and every number accounted for and scored. Each and every movement dutifully assigned and expressed. There was a strange, otherworldly, geometry at work in her boogie. And it was more science than sensuality.

Beth Ann thought back to how they had met a year ago at a party in Park Slope.

The party was some big to-do for a movie producer. Beth Ann was invited because she taught the star of the producer's latest indie-epic to knit and she went though she wasn't feeling very social. She'd had a bad day. A sour taste in her mouth and wasn't looking forward to spending her evening on some asshole's leather couch talking to face lifts and rent-a-punks. Solange was serving cocktails at the party and she and Beth Ann got to talking about the minutiae of daily life: shaving, driving, flossing, smelling, reading. It had been a surprisingly robust conversation and Beth Ann found herself dreaming about Solange that very night. Not sexual dreams. Just girly fantasies of hanging out and going record shopping. Maybe there was some hand holding involved. When she learned, indirectly from a client, that Solange was a dancer at Thursday's she decided she had to go and see her.

Beth Ann wasn't embarrassed. The first time she saw Solange half-naked was in many ways like seeing herself half-naked. Solange noticed her, lurking in the darkest recess of the club, sipping a soda and winked. When Solange finished her dance she waltzed over to Beth Ann's table. Gave her a kiss on the cheek. And invited her to visit the changing room.

Beth Ann agreed. There was something about Solange that was simply too intriguing to ignore. Something that sparked a curiosity that dared Beth Ann further. Pressed her deeper. It was like swimming, following a current. The tide.

Stepping beyond the purple velvet curtains that blocked the back from the front of the club was like stepping from sin into church. From decaying London into Willy Wonka's factory. Beth Ann was apprehensive but Solange lead her softly. It felt like a scene from a film. Down a long corridor like in *Last Year at Marienbad.* It was dreamy and gauzy with subtitles.

Beth Ann wasn't expecting to go back to the changing room and have some candle-lit lesbian encounter. She didn't expect a kiss. She only wanted to watch Solange get dressed. To talk to her while she did her hair and look into her eyes and smile. She thought that anything more would ruin the fantasy. This was a romantic friendship, a beguiling first step into something comfortable. And it felt so incredibly good. The scene, a scene from the sleeping mind of a snooping girl, was being replayed in reality.

But when Beth Ann actually stepped into the changing room the fantasy lost its gossamer edges. The changing room was a locker room. No candles. No incense. No lush fabrics or sparkling wines. Clothes were strewn all over the place, lying on chairs and half desks. The room reeked of stale sweat, perfume and booze. Some Euro-slime pop music blared from a deformed boom box in the corner. And they weren't alone in the room either. A chunky girl with large hips was sitting smoking a cigarette and playing with her pubic hair (shaved into the shape of a dolphin) while talking on her cell phone. Illusion smothered, Beth Ann collapsed on a pleather couch. She watched as Solange got dressed.

The chunky girl was talking into her cell, saying, "repossession doesn't always happen that fast." And, "Joe will take care of everything."

"That's Ursula. She's from Prague," Solange smiled.

Beth Ann waved to Ursula. Ursula didn't wave back but she spread her labia and gave Beth Ann a pink smile.

"She's crazy," Solange giggled.

"How long have you worked here?" Beth Ann asked.

"Oh, maybe a year. The owner's a nice guy. He's Russian like me and he doesn't expect . . . Well, you know."

"So, are you leaving now? You want to get a bite to eat?" Beth Ann asked.

Solange dressed casually. A black hooded sweatshirt over a pique short-sleeved polo that read, *I Heart Jean-Hugues Anglade,* brown leather fringed pants and combat boots. She looked entirely natural. Beth Ann found fantasy was creeping back into frame.

"Where do you want to go?" Beth Ann asked.

"Wherever," Solange's accent was strong. Playful. She made her way over sultrily, like Cat Woman licking her lips, and sat on Beth Ann's lap. She sat hard. Grinding her hips into Beth Ann's thighs. Pressing the muscles against bone. It hurt. Beth Ann ground her teeth. She wasn't aroused.

"You hungry?" Solange asked.

Beth Ann gave Solange a half smile. It was a return smile like a kung fu move. Maybe some form of drunken mantis fu. The dreaded eagle claw. It was a way of simultaneously disarming an opponent and enticing them. It worked.

Solange backed off, stood up and stretched.

She wasn't wearing a bra and Beth Ann could read the fine bumps on her areola like a cartographer.

"So, are we going to lunch or what?"

Beth Ann preferred Indian food.

They sat across from each other at Royal Delhi on 17th. Beth Ann ordered tikka masala and Solange a curry. They didn't speak until the naan came and when it did, Beth Ann asked Solange about her childhood.

"I was a child genius. I have no problem saying that or maybe admitting that. I never wanted to grow up and be a dancer. I never really wanted to grow up and do anything. I'm here 'cause this is where life took me. I was in college at NYU. Math. But that's not in my future."

"Mathematics?"

"Yeah, I'm a math prodigy." Solange shrugged.

"I was never good at math. In fact, I fucking sucked at it. Made me crazy, really. What the hell does "a bit" of a math prodigy mean anyway?"

"It means that I'm a chick who rubs her boobs on your head and at the same time factorizes RSA-200."

"200?"

"A number with 200 digits."

"Of course."

"Anyway, it's not important. My childhood was nothing but butterflies and throwing stones . . . That's really true. I spent my childhood catching butterflies and throwing rocks into the bay. And then came school. Other people. Boys. Girls. And books. Studying and studying. College and then here I am. Simple."

"I've noticed your dancing. It's very precise."

"Yeah, I like to enact theorems. I like to solve complex equations in my dance routines. I didn't realize it was that obvious."

The main course arrived along with Solange's mango lasse. She stopped speaking, put a straw in the lasse and sipped it with her eyelids fluttering. She was either really enjoying the drink or she was having a slight, butterfly kiss orgasm.

"So, stripping? Is there an agenda?"

"Oh, I get that all the time. You're really asking, 'What's a smart girl like you doing working in a strip club?' I get that question more than I get asked out. The truth is rather lame: I started dancing 'cause I had nothing better to do. I'm a lot like you, Beth Ann. A lot more like you than you realize. I am looking for power too. But I'm not the philosopher or the worker bee that you are. I looked at myself and said, 'Let's make some money.' And it works. I'm in control up there. I'm reducing men to squirming eels and at the same time I'm reducing equations. Calculating percentages. Playing with the numbers that make up the world. It makes me happy to dance. You burn off your energies on knitting. I dance. Both are physical feminist actions. I'm not deluded, I know I'll only be able to do this for a few more years but in the end I got what I was—what we all are—looking for."

Solange leaned across the table, put her hands on Beth Ann's and smiled. All her teeth—even the crooked ones on the periphery of her lips—were immaculate.

"What's that? What are we all looking for?" Beth Ann asked.

"The meaning of life."

"What?"

"I discovered it. It's my little secret."

Beth Ann sat back, her eyes settled on Solange's.

"What is it?" She cracked a smile.

"A secret."

"Oh, come on now, you calculated it and you're not going to tell anyone?"

"Oh, I've told people. And they were all quite pleased with the results. They found, in fact, that it changed their lives."

"Why won't you tell me?"

"You're not ready to hear it."

Solange put her fork down and then stood up.

"I've got to go. You want to meet me at my place?"

That first night was a long journey. A rolling down a verdant hill into the arms of a mirror body and when Beth Ann awoke next to Solange the morning after, breathing softly under Solange's duvet, her arms entwined with the mathematician dancer's, she wasn't exactly sure what it all meant. Solange was looking for a roommate. They moved in together. Not as lovers but as friends. As soldiers in the same platoon. Bunk mates. Solange helped Beth Ann hone her sexuality, showing her that subtlety was always the best defense, and Beth Ann taught Solange the trooper's history she never had. Taught her the meaning behind the movement. Solange's message was toned. Her method perfected. Beth Ann's resolve was strengthened. Her femininity recharged.

A month after living together, a month after sharing a bed, Solange told Beth Ann her secret. The meaning of life.

It was a cool morning in April. The sky was clear of clouds. The sun cold but brilliant. Beth Ann was reading Reed's *Mumbo Jumbo* for the tenth time when Solange curled up on the ratty sofa beside her, a steaming cup of tea in her hands.

"I think it's time I told you my secret," Solange cooed.

Beth Ann looked up and took a depth breath. She put the book away and nodded her readiness.

"The meaning of life is being watched. That's what it's all about. That simple, really."

Beth Ann was instantly annoyed, "First off, that's not math. I thought you were going to give me some formula, maybe even a single number. And second, why on earth would you think I wasn't ready to hear that?"

"Yeah, it's not math. I did come up with a number once, 7609. But that's not it, that's just an illusion of meaning. No, the meaning of life I learned while stripping, it was the movement of my body while my mind was out calculating. And that's when I realized it. It's so simple you just don't see it . . ."

"Yeah, right."

"No, seriously, it's beautifully straightforward. All life wants is to be seen. Everything exists to be noticed. And we're no different than the smallest microbes or the largest whales. Our lives—every action that we instigate, every breath—are geared toward someone else noticing us. In a vacuum, without eyes or ears or a nose or fingertips, we don't exist. And that's hell, Beth Ann. That's the absence of life. The meaning of life, the purpose of our existence, is to see and be seen."

Solange beamed as though what she'd shared would change Beth Ann's life immediately. As though Beth Ann would pop and scream to the sky that, Finally she understood. *Finally!* But Beth Ann didn't. She sat stunned, eyes wide.

She began to cry and said, "Fuck you, Solange. If you hadn't noticed, I'm losing my fucking eyesight."

And The Darkness bit hard after that. Beth Ann moved out and spent her time working feverishly, desperately. The Darkness raged like an angry, insolent child in the midst of Beth Ann's renewed vigor. Solange tried frequently to patch things up. But she had nothing in her acrobatic bag of calculus tricks that could make Beth Ann see again. Beth Ann ignored her calls. They saw each other only at random parties. Strangers until a chance encounter, a line of coke and a good cry, and then they held hands again while they watched *Antonia's Line*. That was a week ago. Now, Beth Ann was back, watching Solange dance and hoping to talk to her about love.

When Solange finished her dance, she threw on a robe and plopped down next to Beth Ann.

"What's up girl?"

"I think I'm in love."

Solange screwed up her face. "What?"

"Seriously."

"Who?"

"A guy I met at a bar today . . . We talked forever and then . . . He's just incredible. And I really feel alive right now."

Solange's screwed up face, all twisted lip pout and squinting eyes, relaxed and smoothed out. Her nose whistled. She laughed. "That's fantastic sweetie."

"Thanks."

"What's his deal?"

"He's a paleontologist and a pornographer. Tall, dark. A bit of a paunch."

"Awesome. So what's he got that I don't?"

"About seven inches."

"You're dirty, Beth Ann. Look, babe, I'm really sorry . . ."

"Forget it," Beth Ann kissed Solange on the cheek. "You were right after all. I guess those of us going blind just want it more than anyone else."

"It?"

"To be seen."

10

Wolfgang Brown sat at his dining room table in front of his laptop.

The glow of the screen created a blue chiaroscuro pattern on the wall behind him. He was plugged into his iPod, checking out a few Vacant Grave tracks and ashing into a bowl of cold spaghetti. Between the sickly white strands of congealed flour and water were thirty cigarette butts. Beside the bowl of spaghetti and butts, three empty Miller High Lifes and a half-finished Schlitz.

Wolfgang was checking his email. Most of it was for Wolfgang, the band, and consisted of the usual fan mail and assorted detritus that a local band gets. The majority of the emails went something like:

"Yo, the Aston show ROCKED!!!! You guys really kick azz!
Keep up the excellent work and let me know when I can come
down and help you out. I'm here for you guys!"

Wolfgang had a bad habit of automatically deleting them.

It was a snide commentary on his assumed fame. Rock stars

don't respond to email. That's at least what he told himself. And in Wolfgang's world he was indeed a rock star. Maybe he didn't have the big record deal. Maybe he didn't have the legion of roadies and hustlers but he was on his way up. That enough gave him license to delete the fan mail. It would make him more glamorously remote, untouchable. For better or for worse.

An instant message popped up.

> Carla45: hey sugar

Wolfgang took a last sip of Schlitz and poured the dregs out into the bowl of spaghetti. He lit another cigarette to cool the rush of emotion he got at the very sight of Carla45's IM tag. He typed slow, punching out letters with his index finger.

> Wolfchant: whats news babe?
> Carla45: usual. b.s. at work and then come home to find natasha left the oven on.
> Carla45: thank god the place didn't burn down. you heard that happening right? whole apartment complex just 2 blocks away burned down.
> Wolfchant: sux
> Carla45: all brothers thought crooklyn was burning again.
> Wolfchant: again? wtf
> Carla45: don't you remember that it was last fall
> Wolfchant: lets talk about us
> Wolfchant: romantik
> Carla45: like what sugar?
> Wolfchant: just type something sweet i had a long day
> Carla45: jus want to imagine ur sweet cock
> Wolfchant: sweet enough

Two months of this chat. Carla45's picture, a jpeg posted to the Hot Monster dating site, was the background on Wolfgang's laptop. She was laughing, thick lips and straightened hair, sitting in a leather chair, a lava lamp behind her right ear and curtains to the left. Carla45 had a rounded face, a flat nose as smooth as marble and widely set. Light hazel eyes. Her skin was mocha blended with a dark chocolate. He could hear her laugh or at least imagined he could. She said the photo was taken a year ago, at a friend's party. She was drunk in the picture. Having a great time. Laughing uncontrollably. She was beautiful. Carla45 also had a way with words. A certain pornographic language that a white woman could never wield. It was raw. It was fast and furious. Carla45 came on like a tortured teen. Her heart racked with lust.

> Wolfchant: you get the photo?
> Wolfchant: that was the shw at the Aston
> Carla45: you look hot but its a dark photo.
> Carla45: nice leather.
> Wolfchant: that's snakeskin.
> Carla45: yummy when are we going to finally meet up
> Carla45: and i can taste what your wasting?
> Wolfchant: my unloading? nice
> Carla45: ur kisses those sweet lips. these pink and choc late lips
> Wolfchant: like what?
> Carla45: don't know. i think maybe if you came by my place
> Carla45: see the real world for once in your pamper life
> Wolfchant: huh?
> Carla45: white boy guidance counselor at a suburban school come on.

Carla45: your pampered. whole band thing must be your bid to look rough and tumble.

Wolfchant: not true don't where you get

Carla45: so cute

Wolfchant: first of all, I wasn't pampered. dad left when I was 4 mom was a drunk. is still a drunk.

Wolfchant: we haven't talked for 10 yrs put myself through college and grad school.

Carla45: boo hoo

Wolfchant: raked up a shit load debt too and I don't have a fucking trust fund

Carla45: band gets the

Wolfchant: the band is my release. my expression.

Carla45: cute again and the drugs?

Wolfchant: what did I tell you

Carla45: left that out now right boy

Wolfchant: what?

Carla45: 2 mnths ago you were talking a lotta shit about bein a drug dealer. mister counselor?

Wolfchant: me being silly. nothing. what about you?

Wolfchant: 2 months ago you were a jive talking ass flapping hoochie momma.

Wolfchant: now yur some academic holed up at a community college teaching finance

Carla45: econ

Wolfchant: that ain't too street, babe.

Carla45: shit. im blacker than you could ever imagine. inside

Carla45: an out

Wolfchant: nice

Carla45: when am i going to touch u

Wolfchant: I don't know as soon as possible.

Carla45: watch the stars. say you need to be here this weekend.

Wolfchant: anytime.

Wolfchant: just tell me when youre ready.
Carla45: soon baby. very soon. xxx. im hot already
Wolfchant: spirit on you
Carla45: mmmm
Wolfchant: much love.

Two months and Wolfgang was smitten with this enigma. After their first few email chats Wolfgang printed the photo of Carla45 and stuck it on his desk at school. He turned the cheap frame out slightly so students sitting in his office would be able to catch just a glimpse of it. Then he waited. And sure enough the very first kid that came in his office commented.

"Who's the picture of, Mr. Brown?" Tobe Larkson asked. Tobe was one of the brighter kids. One of the kids with a future. If it hadn't been for his face full of whiteheads he may have even gotten laid his senior year.

"That's my girlfriend." Wolfgang smiled.

Two months of lust and love.

And now, tonight, two moons later, what was there? More cryptic emails. More chat room banter. Wolfgang sighed heavily, smashed out his cigarette, shut down his computer and took a much needed nap at his kitchen table. Thoughts of black sugarplums in his head. He reminisced about high school but then his dreams were twisted into nightmares. Nightmares of drug hungry teens. Imaginary loves. A serial killer whose face was the grill of a Jeep.

11

Harrison stayed late at work.

He had no plans. After Beth Ann had left and the haze of passion had finally cleared from Harrison's cranium, he decided to hunker down to try and get some writing done.

But he couldn't.

It was impossible. He simply couldn't think of anything other than Beth Ann. Her failing eyes. Her peach and bleach scent. If anyone were to have called him in those postcoital, sex savaged hours and asked him about his fiancée he would have looked up with a blank stare. *Who?* It was a bit scary when he realized that he wasn't thinking of Amanda at all. That he hadn't thought about her in what felt like days. That he wasn't thinking of her beauty or the two thousand dollar rock he'd popped on her finger. That he wasn't thinking all these things made him panic. And the panic birthed a big ass headache. A throbbing thud-thudding blood-pulse behind his eyes that made everything go dark. For a second he wondered if it was what Beth Ann felt and he liked the thought of that. To know her pain. Even if it was just a taste. But this was too perfect. This insta-headache was all mental games.

Harrison had this same self-induced icepick behind the eyes twinge attack before. It came on when he was in trouble. Usually when he was caught red-handed. Or felt that he should be. He got the behind-the-eyes brain fucker the worst the first and last time he shoplifted. He was eight years old and full of bile. All mop of wretched hair and filthy socks. Harrison was with his mischievous friend Billy, the punk who was known around Miller Elementary as the kid with no dad. Billy had goaded Harrison into stealing something from the corner store near Harrison's house. Billy said Harrison could steal anything, so long as it was more than candy. Harrison walked around the shop. His sweaty hands in his green cords. Eyeing everything and blinking constantly. The neon orange rabbit foot key chains were twenty five cents. Harrison palmed one, went out of the shop whistling and when he showed it to Billy, Billy whooped and hollered. According to Billy they were now badass crooks. When Harrison got home with his purloined rabbit paw he locked himself in his bedroom and cried for three hours straight. It wasn't the pain of guilt but the skull crushing headache. Harrison's body was punishing him. Crippling him. Harrison went back to the corner shop after dinner. He made some excuse about needing another pencil and as soon as the rabbit foot was dropped back into the bucket from which it had been pinched, the headache stopped. Just like magic. Just like a remorse on-off switch.

Harrison hoped there was an equally simple solution to his new love problem. He figured the solution probably involved telling Amanda that he had just fucked another woman. Probably involved his admitting that he was a filthy cheater. He thought about that for a while and the pain bit at his optic nerves.

He decided a walk would help. He bundled up, wrapped his swelling head in a scarf and marched out into the freeze of the city. The cold air was good. But with each hard step from curb to curb, the pain fluttered. His brain wanted out.

Stopping at 72nd, Harrison lit a cigarette and envisioned himself sitting across from Amanda and admitting his sins to her. Her crying and spitting into her pasta. Mascara running like spider legs into the corners of her mouth. Him shaking uncontrollably. His heart palpitating. Sweat boiling up. As he smoked and thought, each plume of breath removed a morsel of pain and Harrison began to calm down. The twinge of the headache compared to the scene Amanda would create was minuscule. In comparison, the headache actually didn't seem so bad. *Screw telling Amanda,* Harrison thought, *I can live with a headache for a while.* And that thought made him even sicker.

He decided to call Rad.

It was an unspoken rule that when Harrison had women problems he called Radij. The rest of the Whole Sick Crew didn't get women. They were all too white. Too apathetic. Understanding women required something macho. Something studied and earned. Rad was a ladies' man. He was debonair, wealthy, experienced. He knew the ropes just fine.

"Hello?"

"Hey, Rad, I have a question for you."

"Women?"

"Yeah. But first, let's not talk about the serial killer thing. I don't want to hear any reference to The Sisters of Mercy or anything remotely related to conspiracy. Let's just talk like normal people with normal problems."

"Okay. So, tell me about her."

"Beautiful. Fucked up. And she's smart."

"This isn't Amanda."

"Nope."

"What's the deal? You cheating?"

"I am . . . I guess, yeah."

"When did this happen?"

"Today."

"Seriously?"

"Yeah."

"So, you're in serious trouble."

"I'm in deep shit. I've never felt like this. It's insane how I feel. I understand that it's all chemicals and hormones and brain mapping but somehow just the very smell of her hot breath makes me crazy."

"What about porn? You been thinking about porn since you saw her?"

"No. Not at all."

And that made Harrison pause, made him swallow hard.

"Surprised. Yeah, I'll bet you never stopped jerking off while you were in love with Amanda. You see that's something there."

"Yeah, something."

"You gotta go with what your gut tells you, man. You can't just assume this or that based on whatever empirical evidence you've collected in your overly rational mind. You need to just go with the gut. The feeling that is sick is either excitement or pain. That's all."

"I get bad with trembles just thinking about her. But I don't even know her. I just spent the afternoon with her. Maybe like three hours."

"You'll have your whole life to know her. You know what you need to do though. You need to tell Amanda. The engagement. I'm betting that's off."

"Kill it?"

"In some words, yeah. You need to be happy. It's unfair to Amanda to marry her when you're pining over this other chick. Or the next chick that walks into your boring life. Do it dude. Pull the trigger. Kill it."

"Any other words of wisdom, master?"

"Yeah. Hotch-Potch, Hugger-Mugger, Bow-Wow, Hara-Kiri, Hoo-Poo, Huz-Za, Hicc-Up, Hum-Drum, Hexa-Pod, Hell-Cat, Helter-Skelter, Hop-Scotch."

Harrison replied, "And that's supposed to mean what, Rad?"

"Nothing really, it's from Kleenex's 'Split' but I've always wanted to get that into a conversation somewhere. Look, bro, you need to dump Amanda. Curb her. It's over. You're effectively dis-engaged. Sorry."

And that made Harrison feel even worse. He stood on the corner, steam pluming from his chapped lips. His hands growing numb. He wanted to get on the train and head back to his place, maybe shower and have a drink, but he couldn't bring himself to move. He couldn't will his legs toward that familiar space that smelled and looked and felt like Amanda.

Harrison stood watching the traffic. Breathing. In and out. The headache was gone now.

He decided to call T. Talk about something else.

"You get my message?" T asked.

"Yeah. What was the deal? It like cut off half way through," Harrison asked.

"Nothing in particular. I had a call on my other line, clicked over and lost the connection," T sounded distracted.

"You got a call at four in the morning?"

"Sure. Why not?"

Harrison let it drop, "So, anyone getting together tonight?"

"Yeah. But, um, well . . . I mean two nights in a row . . ."

"What are you trying to say?"

"Well, it's just that Amanda doesn't usually . . ."

"Fuck Amanda. I want to go out again."

"We're meeting up at Arcadia. The Crew. To talk about Doctor Jeep. We've got a swell plan, Harrison. You sure you want to be there? It's going to be lots of paranoid discussion. It'll be planning and plotting and, well, I'd lie if I were to say there wouldn't be coke."

"I'm game," Harrison said, "Even though the thought of listening to more of that Doctor Jeep bullshit makes me sick. A glutton for punishment, I guess."

"Good. Around nine."

"Fine, I'll see you all there."

Harrison went back to his office. He jerked off hard and then sat in his sweat. Masturbation as a teenager, when he was just an awkward kid pulling on himself, was always indescribably incidental, almost, accidental. Harrison didn't know his body. Didn't know his limits. Rather than feeling like a jungle explorer, or Indiana Jones, he felt like a klutz that had stumbled upon something good but couldn't find it again.

He almost longed for those days, that innocence. He was a hardened masturbator now. The act was entirely routine. Wholly functional. Masturbation involved no pleasure. It made Harrison sick to realize that. The true adventure, the real fix, came with the finding of porn. He'd been all over the Internet. From every ingloriously lowbrow girl-next-door site to every expensive manicured model high-class site. He'd seen it all from girl-on-girl, black-on-white, fat-on-thin, fake-on-flabby. Every seething and cum spattered inch of the net had been pried into. And after the first ten sites, the repetition had set in. Seeing the same act a million times, whether it was a woman giving a blowjob or raking the lawn, slowly hollowed out a space within Harrison's soul. A place where only longing went. A place without satisfaction. It was a hideous existence. Harrison felt like a pariah in his own life.

He prayed to rational gods that Beth Ann might be able to free him from his compulsion. He knew Amanda couldn't. Harrison fell asleep at his desk, the skulls and flat trilobite fossils his only companions, and awoke around 8:45 p.m. He was stiff, his spine wedged oddly into the back of his chair, mouth dry and his eyes encrusted. He felt filthy, smudged.

12

"What're they called again?"

"The Suburban Reptiles."

"Right, right."

"Freaking incredible. Like a Kiwi version of the Sex Pistols."

"No."

"Crazy shit, man. They did the soundtrack to this wacked out movie called *Angel Mine*. It's about this couple who get all caught up in their own wish fulfillment games. They have these doppelgangers that are like uninhibited versions of themselves, all in black leather. The crazy thing is the movie is interrupted by fake commercials for this libido drug called, of course, 'angel mine' . . ."

"That'd never be a movie here. That's for fucking sure."

"No, actually, I heard rumors that Ron Howard was gonna remake it."

"Fucking Hollywood."

"Indeed."

"Rod," Swank took a long, hard drag of his Lucky Strike and blew smoke into the phone, "Tell me more about his other one you were talking about the other day. Something about Santa Claus?"

"Death May Be Your Santa Claus?"

"Yeah, tell me more about it. Slowly, I want to see it."

Swank closed his eyes and turned up the volume on his stereo system, Ladytron's "Blue Jeans" flooded his studio. The bass throbbed in the air and Swank could feel the small hairs on his cheeks stand up while the cigarette burned, sending smoke serpents into the humid night.

And Swank drifted, he spun behind his eyelids. He wasn't sure if it was the glass of absinthe he had downed twenty minutes earlier or just the faint stirrings of a headache, but something was different. *A bad buzz? Nasty.*

". . . where Mott the Hoople got the song title. About this black power militant brother out to stomp . . ."

Drifting, woozy.

". . . of course it was banned. And now it's completely and utterly lost . . ."

Spin dry.

Swank opened his eyes and looked down at his hand. The cigarette had gone out. No burns this time. He let the room slowly ooze back into focus, the furniture settle again on the floor, the paintings flap on bat wing shadows back to the wall.

Rod was yelling something. "Swank? Hey, fucker, did I put you to sleep or something? You there?"

"Yeah," Swank stretched his eyes wide, "I've got to get back to work here, man." He blinked five times, tossed the cigarette butt to the hardwood floor and rubbed his cheeks. Then he slapped himself red. Five times. That was his deal. His OCD. Swank didn't treat it, not with what Dr. Borgo prescribed, because he figured he'd lose his artistic spark. That or he'd go limp in the sack. Heard that happened all the time. Doing everything in fives was a hell of a lot better than having a floppy.

"Swank?"

"Hey, Rod. Sorry, I'm just kind of . . ."

"Absinthe?"

"Yeah."

"You gotta stop swilling that shit, man. You've got a show next week. You need to have that series done, bro. Get it going. Besides, it's still fucking morning."

"You don't need to tell me, Rod."

Fucking Rod, Swank stood up and stretched. *Fucking guy.*

"Alright, bro . . . Hang on just a sec . . ."

Swank tossed the phone on the paint speckled leather chair he'd been lazing in for the past hour and stood up and jumped up and down in place five times.

Fucking Rod.

Swank knew that when The Tibbles' *Ghosts and Nominal Beings* album hit the charts, became the "must have" album for every college nerd, his life would change dramatically. He'd painted the cover for that little lo fi trashsterpiece in a matter of days. And now everyone wanted a painting. After The Tibbles he did Cosmoster and the Le Tigre LP and then it wasn't album covers at all but gallery work. And it was postcards. Ashtrays. Bomber jackets. Bowling pins. Lithographs. Suddenly, Swank's bachelor pad meets The Munsters style was everywhere. Now, even in the pages of *Juxtapose,* there were copycats. Copycats like the "Bachelor Illusionist" series by that fucker Rod Tibble, the fucking lead singer of the band that put Swank on the map. Now even *that* bastard was an artist. Even signed his name with a red crayon like Swank had always done.

It didn't make it any better that they were friends.

"That's always been my style," Rod countered when Swank attacked him after reading a favorable review of "Bachelor Illusionist" in the L.A. Freepress. A review that went so far as to say, "Tibble's work trumps Swank's."

Trumps? Swank thought at the time, *Who the fuck says trumps, anyway?*

"You never painted. Since when did you start painting?"

"I've been taking lessons," Rod said.

Swank didn't speak to Rod for a month after that. But then he got word that the Lizard Gallery in Seattle would love to do a retrospective of his work and host the debut of his new series. He let the grudge go. So long as he was on top, one step ahead of the poseurs, he was comfortable. He could breathe.

Swank picked up the phone again.

"You still there?"

"Yeah, what the fuck?"

"I had to stretch a little . . ."

"So, what's the new work like? I can't believe you've kept it secret this long. That's rare today, rare for someone as popular as you've become."

Like you'd know, Swank thought. *As if you'd know.*

"It's still a secret, Rod."

Swank knew that this series, the one he'd slaved over for ten months, would be his return to the top dog spot. *This series would change lives. It was art, not just wall hangings.*

"Is it sick?" Rod's favorite word.

"Of course, the world is sick, Rod. This is going to be as sick as it gets."

"Can't wait to see it."

Swank paced and stopped before the latest painting he'd completed for the series. A spiraling panorama of the Beats in Hell titled "The Ninth Circle." And he knew it was good.

There was a click on the phone.

A click normally associated with someone else picking up and listening in. Swank knew the sound well. It had been etched into his memory as a paranoid child convinced that his parents were listening in on his conversations with his girlfriends. Years later he came to find out that they had been. Paranoia is always real. It's just the degree that matters. Swank listened intently, hearing past Rod.

". . . and that's the newest, best shit, man. That's the cutting . . ."

There was someone there.

"Hello?" Swank whispered into the phone, holding it away from his head and eyeing it as though he were looking into a seashell.

"Yeah, dude, I'm talking," Rod's reply muffled another voice. A smaller, quieter voice.

"Shut the fuck up, Rod. Don't speak."

And then Swank tried again, "Hello?"

Rod babbled to someone in the background, *"I don't know who he's talking to. The guy's losing it over there. Hon, I told you he was going to crack . . ."*

Hon, Swank knew, was Gloria. Rod's overweight and over-indulgent wife.

". . . he started drinking that stuff trying to be poetic . . ."

The other voice came out over the shadows, hulking and brutal.

"Swank, I'm going to make you famous."

"Who the fuck is that?" Rod barked. Then aside, *"No, hon, there really is someone on the other line!* Who the fuck is that Swank? Is that at your house?"

Swank remained silent. He turned slowly on his heels, scanning the room.

It was empty but the front door was ajar.

"I'm here, Swank. Right now. Behind you. On the other telephone."

Swank turned like a ballerina, smooth as silk. It was a move he'd perfected in high school, he dubbed it "the slow turn," and he always thought it would impress girls who loved *Moonwalker.*

"Hon, shut it, I'm trying to listen here . . ."

But Swank didn't know if "the slow turn" would impress the man standing on Swank's porch. The man with Knight Rider sunglasses. A thin handlebar moustache. A Roxy Music T-shirt.

". . . I'm going to make you famous, artwork . . ." The man said into the phone.

"Swank, dude, is this a joke? Swank?"

The man walked slowly forward into the light. Swank stumbled backwards. Falling over paintings and knocking into a bookshelf before crashing to the floor beside a stack of LPs.

The phone clattered from his hand.

Rod was shouting all the way, "Swank! Swank! What the fuck is going on? Who is that guy? Swank! *God dammit, hon, get your cell phone . . .*"

The man in the Roxy Music tee pulled a knife from his snakeskin cowboy boots.

It flashed like a fish. Silver arcing in the halogen light.

". . . artwork."

13

Arcadia was a noisy joint with a tiny dance floor and loads of classic arcade games lining the walls.

Frogger. Zaxxon. Centipede. Ms. Pacman.

Harrison didn't really like the place. It was too self-consciously geeky for his tastes. The games were rarely, if ever, actually played. Most of the cool kids that hung out at Arcadia were too young to know what arcade games were. They stood around, eyes half closed, and laughed about the games. They joked about the graphics. "So fucking retarded, seriously." And they laughed about the joysticks, "Were people in the '80s handicapped or something?"

This was theme night. It was the same across the city. Tonight was Retro Chango at Arcadia. Over at Bossy's it was Gnosis Thrombosis. At Lush on 15th it was Deep Sleep. At Dionysius it was Hotel Ozone. Arcadia's resident DJ, Electra Glide, was playing power pop and punk. Ramones, Angelic Upstarts, Midget Submarines, Orange Juice, the usual suspects. The kids mocking the video games ate it up.

Rad and Wolfgang were sitting at the bar downing PBRs

when Harrison walked in. Rad was overanimated. His hands flickering like spastic bats above his head. Harrison was sure he was also spraying enthusiastic spittle all over the bar. Rad was giving another sterling rendition of one of his ER stories. Harrison pulled up a stool next to Wolfgang and Wolfgang gave him an immensely cheesy high-five.

Rad's demonstration stopped.

Something on Zaxxon squealed like a stuck hard-drive and a kid in sweats cursed.

"Sorry to interrupt," Harrison smiled. There was an uncomfortable silence. Harrison spent the few seconds looking around the room, wondering why no one was playing Frogger.

Rad sighed and said, "No problem." But he didn't start his story over.

He paused and then continued, "So, he's got pain in his groin. I take a look and all I can find is this red mark, a big bruise, obviously some internal hemorrhaging but nothing external. I ask him what it is and he says he was shot. I take another look at the guy and there is no wound. None. Just this red spot that's getting bigger and really starting to look nasty. But it's under the skin.

"I tell the guy he couldn't have been shot. There's no entrance wound. And if you're shot there is always an entrance wound. Anyway, I take him into surgery and can you guess what they pull out of that nasty red bruise? A bullet. A fucking bullet. I'm beginning to lose my shit. I go into the guy and tell him we found a bullet in him and he just nods and yeses up and down the room.

"I ask the guy what he was doing when he got shot. He tells me he was running from someone and he jumped over a fence the moment the gun went off. He felt some heat on his back and then the pain in his groin. So, I decide to take another long look at him.

"I ask him to roll over and then take a look at his ass. Nothing on the cheeks, no blood. Nothing. I spread 'em and then I see it. His asshole. The sphincter is burned around the edges and raw, bloody. The fucking guy went over the fence and at the very moment that his ass was in the air. Sticking up like a target. That bullet snuck right into his asshole. Maybe he'd relaxed his sphincter to fart. Maybe it was just karma. But that bullet went right up his asshole and landed in his groin. Fucking crazy shit."

Rad laughed and held his sides as if his ribs were bruised. Every time Rad finished a story he laughed as though he was on a line of nitrous. And every time he held his ribs as though he were worried his fragile Eastern frame was going to buckle under the strain of these earth-shattering chortles.

Ms. Pacman burped.

Harrison was already bored. He yawned and shrugged and wanted to say something like, "Yeah, that's a great one, Rad, but I've got a more interesting story for you two." But he didn't. He didn't because T, Xavier and Cooper walked into the club wearing orange jumpsuits. Across the front of them, in bold white letters, was stitched, "Williamsburg Riffs." They looked like self-conscious kids pretending to be subway maintenance workers. Those rat exterminator teams.

T was carrying a terrorist-sized duffel bag.

The orange threesome plopped down at a free table. Wolfgang, Rad and Harrison moved over to the table slowly, cautiously. Harrison wound up sitting right next to the neglected Frogger box. It chimed as though it were happy to have some company.

"Holy shit!" Wolfgang exclaimed, eyeing T's jumpsuit.

"You're kidding, right?" Harrison asked.

"And me?" Cooper smiled. His eyes were bloodshot. He was completely and utterly obliterated. T's eyes were the same way. Xavier looked half-asleep, irises peeking out from his heavy eyelids.

"We're a full-fledged gang now, boys." T pulled three more orange embroidered jumpsuits from his duffel bag and handed them out. There was a poppy bleeping over at the Pac-Man.

Harrison held the jumpsuit up in the half-light and gri-
maced.

"A joke, right?"

"No joke. I'm not laughing," Cooper said.

"We're gonna make this happen," T smiled. The smile, lopsided to the right and wet, meant that he'd inhaled a line and
now, giddy as a true cockhorse, he was trying to keep his
synapses from firing all at once. Putting off some death knell
brain-gasm.

The bleep-bleep of Frogger became deafening.

"Are we going hunting?" Harrison asked. And he realized
that he was the only one at the table asking. The only one at the
table not enthralled by the orange jumpsuits. The only one at
the table not salivating over the thought of hunting down a serial killer dressed in *Clockwork Orange* gear.

T said, "He whacked Swank. And yesterday he shot Paul
Achting on the floor of his comic book shop like a fucking
pig."

"Fuck. Paul?" Wolfgang was shocked.

"Yeah, you friends with him too?" Xavier asked.

Wolfgang nodded.

"Didn't know you dug comics," Cooper scoffed.

"Fuck you," Wolfgang said. "You read Grant Morrison, Frank
Miller. You read *Shaolin Cowboy. Rocket Raccoon.* That shit'll
change your life."

Xavier said, "Damn skippy. Not for kids anymore."

T and Xavier high-fived.

Harrison couldn't take anymore, "Who else? Did you say
Swank?"

Cooper clarified, "Yeah, dude that did that tattoo art. The
new Daniel Higgs. He was gutted a few hours ago. I guess he
was drinking some absinthe, having a time of it, when a dude
walked in and sliced and diced him. Poor mutherfucker was totally cut to shreds . . ."

Rad nodded.

"Yeah, I heard about it earlier this evening. Swank was butchered," Rad's voice quivered in anticipation. It was show time. Doc time. "He had his throat slashed, a long lateral cut through the trachea. Almost decapitated, bled out in a matter of seconds. Probably didn't even know what hit him . . ."

"Like a ritual butcher. You know, kosher style," Wolfgang said. His off-the-cuff statements always being entirely perverse.

Harrison looked at T.

He nodded.

"And what's the evidence this time, T?"

Spotlight on T. "Harrison, you've doubted this shit since the get-go . . ."

"No, just doubted that we should have anything to do with it," Harrison felt it important to clarify that immediately.

". . . right, anyway, when they found Swank they found a scrap of a painting of a white lion with eighteen eyes standing guard over an ornate swimming pool. Written in black ink in the center of the swimming pool were the words: *Meanwhile in the Sheraton/ Doctor Jeep plays on and on and on* . . . What, my friends, do you make of that?"

"Fuck," Rad grunted.

"Fuck," Cooper agreed.

Harrison wanted to smack both of them.

"Five murders, all of raging hipsters, many directly mentioning Doctor Jeep. This last one seals the deal," T beamed. His shit had hit.

"So, what's the deal?" Wolfgang asked.

"This guy's driven. He's like a rock star," Xavier said.

"T, where will this go?" Harrison felt the need to interject.

"Like I said, we're gonna catch him. We'll be the ones to bring him in. We know the score here; we see the pattern."

"So, how?" Rad asked.

"That's the best fucking part. He's coming after me next."

14

The table was silent, just the pulse of bass vibrating the air like a hornet's wings.

T lit a smoke and settled in.

A short guy at an adjoining table said, "You can't smoke in here, bro."

T glared back at the guy and flicked him off. He said, "Stop me, pussy."

T turned back to the table. Harrison, Wolfgang, Xavier, Rad, Cooper, all of their mouths open waiting for the other shoe to drop. T took another drag, said nothing. He had it timed perfectly. Just enough to get the anxiety rolling. Make the whole thing seem bigger and badder.

Then he said, "Yeah, he's coming after me next. I got the post on my blog last night."

"Don't you get crank shit all the time, T?" Rad inquired.

T had been getting oddball emails ever since he started blogging. Most of what T got was the usual government conspiracy and right-wing bullshit. The quacks who thought T was in on some big secret. Knew about some alien base on a Navajo reservation. An AIDS vaccine. And the church quacks who thought T was dragging the rest of the world down into a moral morass with his cheap shit Xerox zine.

"So, what did this comment say?" Harrison asked.

"It said, Love the site, super 'swank'y. It was signed, Humming AOR—Williamsburg."

"I don't get it. What's that mean?" Wolfgang asked.

"That's one of the lyrics from a Sisters of Mercy song," Rad said.

"What song?" Cooper was really in top form.

"The fucking 'Doctor Jeep' song. And the 'swank' bit, that's fucking obvious," T said.

Cooper cringed. Settled his nose back over a line.

"You're kidding, right?" Harrison's eyes were rolling wildly. "Just 'cause some dude signs his simple post Humming AOR you assume it's Jeep? And 'swank'? I mean that's actually a word, shit heads. That's not just a name. And are you assuming that there's just one person in Williamsburg who's a fan of Sisters of Mercy?"

"*The . . .*" Rad corrected.

"Fuck off, Rad!" Xavier spat.

"Look, man. This guy isn't just some schmo from Billburg who's got a hard on for my site. You still don't get how this cat operates. He's subtle. But if you can read the fucking signs he can be as obvious as the Brooklyn Bridge. This is a goddamned message to me. It's a bold fucking hint. Maybe Paul got the same thing but he didn't listen. Didn't read the writing on the wall. Same with Swank . . ."

"Alright," Harrison interrupted. "So, if this is the same guy and he's got his eyes on you, then how are you going to trap him? I mean how would you possibly know when he's going to strike next?"

"I don't," T shrugged.

"Great."

"But I know how to bring him to us."

"Okay, let's hear it," Harrison said.

"We're having a party on Friday night. Just the Whole Sick Crew. I've invited him. He'll show and we'll blast him."

"With what?" Wolfgang asked.

"With some Crips," Rad said. He turned to T. "You've been planning this shit out since I told you about that, huh?"

T nodded.

"Gangbangers?" Cooper was jarred to life.

"Yeah," Rad said. "Lil' Chris is one. I met him at the hospital a few weeks ago while treating one of his homies for a gunshot wound. This fat gangbanger called Balls, shot in the balls. He wasn't going to make it. His wounds were actually serious. I couldn't do anything about it. Lil' Chris was fucking pissed, called me all sorts of names. Two hours later Balls was dead. I didn't bother explaining it all to Lil' Chris but the guy didn't care. He was just like, whatever, nigga had it coming. The guy's tough as nails. He's a street killer."

"Yeah, I like it," Wolfgang snarled. "We'll hire that gangster dude to fucking blast Jeep."

"You guys are killing me here," Harrison scoffed. "You're going to hire a gangster to kill a serial killer. Ridiculous. And how the hell is this party thing going to work anyway? You're just going to invite this Humming AOR dude and assume that if he shows, he's Jeep? That's totally fucking retarded. What if it's just some fucking dumb-shit from down the hall that hears a party and decides to stop by?"

"Harrison, I've got it under control. This is the guy and he'll come. He's itching to get me. He's taunting me. I'll play dumb. Assume that I don't know the gig. He'll just trot into it and fall. Sure, maybe he won't show but if any strangers do appear, well, we'll know it's not him. And if he doesn't show we'll just have a good time."

"And if he does show, we'll be ready. Right? I mean, Rad's gangbanger is legit, right?" Cooper asked.

"Sure, right," T answered. "Rad says he's the real deal. He's definitely a bad man. Oh, and let's have it at Wolfgang's pad. Easy to get to and nothing expensive to break."

"Fuck you," Wolfgang said.

T said, "What's the problem? We can't have it at my place. Too far away. And besides, there's always gunfire and break-ins on your block. There's a crack house across the street. I always see gangbangers hanging around. Come on man."

Wolfgang tentatively agreed.

T shot him a big grin. Xavier clapped.

Frogger belched.

"So what's next?" Cooper asked.

T replied, "We cough up some dough and make Lil' Chris an offer."

"How much?" Cooper wiped white from his nose.

"Whatever we can afford. I'll throw in $25,000. That's what I've got," T proffered.

"Fucking rich asshole," Wolfgang capped a grin.

"That'll do, I'm sure," Rad said.

Harrison looked at his friends, all smiles and bright eyes in the smoke. He realized that he couldn't stop this. This was out of his control. It was happening whether or not he agreed with it. Whether or not he was down. He wondered what it would be like, killing someone. Standing there while someone was gunned down. Standing silently. Spattered in blood, most likely. Spattered in brains. But he didn't wonder long, because Beth Ann walked in the bar that very moment.

She was wearing a black T-shirt that read *WWJJD (What Would Joan Jett Do?)* and incredibly tight jeans. Her eyes raccoon-like, buried beneath dark makeup. Her lips ruby red. Cheeks pink. Harrison thought she looked incredible. The jeans hugged every inch of her legs and he couldn't help but stare at her ass. She really didn't have one but those jeans wove some spell— the illusion of a magnificent, swelling ass. A sharp heat spread across Harrison's lap.

He got up and walked over to Beth Ann. Put a hand around her waist. She turned around and smiled. He said, "Hi there."

"Hi," Beth Ann squeezed her smile for all it was worth.

"So, what brings you here?"

"The usual, out with a few friends."

Beth Ann nodded to three elderly women at a table near the bar. They looked very out of place. Two of them were knitting.

"Who are they?"

"Some of the ladies from my knitting class. Thought I'd bring them out," Beth Ann shrugged.

"You think they're having a good time?" Harrison asked, a bit worried.

"Sure," Beth Ann waved to one of the women. The woman waved back. "That's Ethyl. The one with the hat is Nellie and the other is Lenore."

"This like female empowerment? Like taking back the night or something?"

Beth Ann smiled, "Maybe a little bit. More it's just that I didn't have anyone else to go out with tonight and I kinda was hoping I'd run into you. They're psyched to be here, I think."

Ethyl was sipping a beer and eyeing the crowd, Nellie and Lenore were knitting and Lenore was nodding in time with Let's Active's "Waters Part." She genuinely seemed to enjoy the music.

"Who are you with?" Beth Ann asked.

Harrison pointed out the Riffs crew.

Beth Ann cracked a smile, "What's with the get ups?"

"They're jumpsuits."

"Right."

"It's stupid . . ." Harrison said shaking his head.

"Anyone I might know?"

"Nah, bunch of psychos."

"Introduce me?" Beth Ann asked.

Harrison led her back into the bowels of the club. The boys

at the table were oblivious to Beth Ann standing there until he cleared his throat.

"Guys, this is my friend Beth Ann."

A round of breathy introductions followed.

Harrison told Beth Ann, "They're trying to catch a serial killer."

"Nothing wrong with that," Beth Ann elbowed.

"No. Really. They want to catch a serial killer who's killing hipsters around town."

"Right . . ."

"No. Seriously, they do."

Harrison shot T a glance that said, Check this, mutherfucker.

T's smile turned upside down.

"She gonna help us, Harrison? You know, every gang needs a moll," Cooper said.

Beth Ann sat down in Harrison's chair next to Rad, "You guys are starting a gang, huh? And catching a serial killer?"

"No, it's not really . . ." Wolfgang played interference.

T cut him off, "No, it is a gang. It's totally a gang and we are, like Harrison said, hunting a serial killer."

Beth Ann looked over her shoulder at Harrison. He shrugged.

"I want in then." Beth Ann lit a clove.

She was totally serious.

"You're kidding?" Harrison caught an eyeful of smoke.

"No, I'm totally serious. I've always been one to run with the boys. If you have something cool going on then I want in on it."

"Beth Ann, they're full of shit."

T shook his head. He was on his fifth beer and his eyelids were drooping.

"Who's the serial killer?" Beth Ann leaned in.

"Tell her, T," Cooper said.

Harrison skipped the retelling. He played a few rounds of Frogger. The goddamned otters always got him. When he returned to the table Beth Ann nodded to him and said, "T's serious."

"I told you."

"So, Beth Ann, you game?" Cooper asked.

Wolfgang and Rad raised their beer bottles in toast.

"Sure," Beth Ann got up and kissed Harrison on the forehead. "Give me a call when you guys meet. I'm down for anything."

"Friday night," Xavier slurred. "We're having a little get-together."

Beth Ann sauntered off back to Ethyl, Nellie and Lenore.

"Man, your new girl is awesome," Wolfgang grooved.

Harrison blushed and downed the rest of his beer.

"She thinks you're all crazy. She thinks it's for shit."

"No, she knows it's real," T said.

T nudged Wolfgang and Wolfgang, like some automaton, produced a small bag of coke that was promptly placed on the table. Unwrapped and divided into four fine lines with a Metrocard. It had been years since Harrison had snorted. Last time he could remember doing a line was at a party in the late '90s celebrating the completion of his thesis. He'd really enjoyed the high. It made him feel cherished. It made him shudder. Harrison did one line and decided he should leave.

"Oh no, no, no. Not yet, Mr. Bones," Xavier put his hands on Harrison's shoulders and pushed him down into his seat.

Harrison laughed cautiously, "Why's that, Xav?"

"Well, we've got plans tonight."

"Stop being so fucking mysterious."

"We're going to meet Lil' Chris," T clarified.

Rad said, "What?"

Harrison laughed, "You're fucking kidding me." He added a very melodramatic yawn.

"Yeah," T said, "I figured why wait. I looked up Lil' Chris, talked to him a few nights ago. He remembered Rad from the

ER. Said he was cool with everything. If this shit is going down at the end of this week then we have to meet tonight. Lil' Chris needs a little time to plan."

"Seriously?" Rad asked.

T said, "Seriously."

Harrison stood up again, "I can't guys. I'm already sick of playing gangster."

"You're coming with us. You've got to," T said.

Cooper said, "You've got to."

Rad said, "I'm going."

"What else are you going to do?" Xavier said. "Go visit your fiancée? Oh, wait, that's right . . ."

"If you're a real Riff, you'll be there," Cooper drooled.

"Fuck all of you." Harrison sat back down and took a good look at his friends. This sick crew. He was feeling the coke.

"What do you have to lose?" Rad asked.

Wolfgang said, "Bring it on."

They met up with Lil' Chris at a club in Bed-Sty.

"I hate bar hopping," Cooper said as they walked into Club Zebra. It was clogged with smoke and populated almost exclusively by heavily built and heavily armed men. There were a few tables scattered around but only one was occupied. Harrison guessed right that Lil' Chris was the cat with cornrows and an eye patch sitting at the table. He looked just like Bushwick Bill, if Bushwick weren't a midget. All sour mug and dour eyes. Lil' Chris waved the gang over. Rad got some beers at the bar.

Lil' Chris started off as soon as the Riffs' asses hit the seats, "So, what exactly do you mutherfuckers have in mind?"

"We're talking about a hit," T said.

Lil' Chris laughed, "Do I look like a wop to you? I don't do *hits.*"

"We're looking for a killer," Cooper said.

And that was good.

Lil' Chris nodded, "You came to the right nigga."

"Who have you killed?" Xavier asked.

Cooper looked at Xavier funny.

So did Lil' Chris. "What do you need to know, muther-fucker?"

"Do you want his resume?" Harrison added.

"No, I just figure we need to know. I think that's totally rea-sonable. I mean if we're going to be paying a shit load of money we better make sure we know what we're getting."

"I ain't a used mutherfucking car," Lil' Chris spat.

"I think it's good to shop around. Make good investments. It is my money after all," T replied.

The conversation stopped and everyone looked uncomfort-able. It was as if the entire club stopped bumping and attention had turned to the wiseass white guys. Harrison sensed it imme-diately. He took a gulp of his beer, tried to relax. The music swam back in. The bass rattled the floor tiles.

"So, who did you kill?" Xavier asked.

"I was in a few drive bys, knifed a mutherfucker who owed me some cash. The regular shit."

"You're a Crip, right?" Cooper asked.

"Yeah, 88th street."

"So, you've got some good firepower?" T asked.

"Wait a sec. Wait a sec. Who the fuck am I supposed to be killing here? You mutherfuckers ain't given me anything yet. I wanna know what this is going to be about."

"We want you to kill a serial killer," Wolfgang said through a veil of smoke, his hairy skull face luminescent.

Lil' Chris busted a nut over that. He almost rolled off his seat.

"What the fuck? Like Bundy an' shit? Some fucking subur-ban white fucker who's cutting up hookers? Are you fucking crazy, boy?"

"No, we're serious," Rad said. "He's a serial killer in Brook-lyn. He's killing people like . . . Like us. And the cops aren't doing . . ."

"Fuck, you don't even need to tell me 'bout the cops not

doing shit. Look at me, I've been punked by the fuckin' cops my whole life. An' the one thing I know is that they don't ever know shit 'bout what's really going on in this city."

There was a pause.

"So," Lil' Chris continued, "You boys need me and one of my associates to assist you to do this job 'cause you can't do it yourselves?"

"We wouldn't know where to start," Cooper said.

"And you guys know who this serial killer bitch is?"

"More or less," T smiled, shrugged. "We'll get him to you. We know that. We're going to throw a party and he'll be showing up at a certain time. You guys just need to be there and do what you do."

"How 'bout weapons?" Lil' Chris asked.

"We've got nothing," Xavier said.

" 'aight. Don't matter, I've got enough. I could see myself doing this. I'll ask my homeboy, Tank, to see if he's down."

Lil' Chris called Tank on his cell, said a few words. Then he nodded.

"Tank's down."

"Tank, huh?" Wolfgang grinned.

"Yeah," said Lil' Chris, "Tank the Niggatron."

An uncomfortable silence followed, no one wanted to make the obvious jokes.

No one even giggled.

"Look," Lil' Chris leaned forward, his lone eye studying the faces of the drunken white men around him, "I'm just gonna lay this shit straight for you. I know what you muthafuckers is up to. You think I'm some black asswards nigga that you can run up against your demons and do all your killing and none of you muthafuckers is gonna get as much as a scratch on your perfectly styled hairdos. Well, it is true that I'm a killer. And it's true that you're not. I'm sure your mamas told you all not to fuck with killers. It's like kicking a hornet's nest. It's just shit that you don't do. But you seem overeager to fuck with a killer—despite all your money and all your brains—and if you're going to do something that fucking stupid you'd better have someone like me backing you up.

"But what all this shit boils down to is money—pure and simple. I know you Williamsburg muthafuckers have this idealized vision of the muthafucking world. You think that you shine brighter than every other cracker in this world and you've got enough pity for the black man to steal his hip. You catch my drift, right? I'm not interested in breaking down your fantasy world of cooler than this, cooler than that, but I will tell you all I don't believe in any of it. You can eat all the brown fucking rice you want and wear the fucking faggot ass girl's jeans, but you haven't convinced anyone but yourselves that you're important. This is economics, fools, nothing more."

Lil' Chris leaned back, "So, I'm gonna do this shit for you. You muthafuckers are gonna give me a load of cash and I'll help you out. But understand one thing, this is all business. I have no love for you or your kind. As far as I'm concerned, if this serial killer mutherfucker hired me to kill you fools I'd do it in a heartbeat. Clear? I'm gonna check up on some shit I got goin' on."

Lil' Chris stood up, "You mutherfuckers have a good time here, hang out. I'll see you fools in two days."

15

"It's not pronounced. It's just a symbol. Yeah. A symbol."

"Like Prince, when he did that masculine-feminine symbol deal?"

"Exactly."

"But then who's Freur?"

"Then record execs, radio DJs, somebody, decided that it simply wasn't reasonable for a band not to have a name. Remember, this was the early '80s and everything was market-driven. Bands had to have images. Videos. Names. You couldn't not have a fucking name."

"So what's Freur mean?"

"Nothing, that's just how you pronounce the symbol."

"So they kept the symbol then?"

"Yeah but now they had a pronunciation for it."

"Sounds like art-school fag shit to me. So, what'd you do last night?"

"Hung out at Arcadia with the crew."

"Fun?"

"Always."

"What're you guys talking about now? I read some of T's stuff recently and it was kind of blah. He got something else going on that he's obsessing about?"

"Nothing he's shared with me. Look, I've got to go, Bill."

"Later, Rad."

Rad hung up and threw his cell phone on the passenger seat. Thursdays at the ER sucked. Just always did. That's when all the gunshots came in. When the abused kids turned up. The junkies who shoved pencils in their tracks. The psychos with broken lightbulbs in their assholes. And that was when Bill Conte always called. 6 p.m. on a Thursday evening. Every. Single. Fucking. Thursday.

Rad had met Bill in residency and immediately disliked him.

He was a high pitched and sullen prick with an over-the-top theatrical edge that made every molehill into the fucking Swiss Alps. But he had fantastic taste in music. Not as deep and rich as Rad's but unexpectedly broad. Bill knew the Factory back catalog as though it were tattooed on the back of his hand. He had amassed, with the help of a sizeable trust fund, a record collection that rivaled most critics'. But he was ignorant when it came to electropop, the early stirrings of the now ubiquitous electronic music. Rad had no idea how a man like Bill could listen to Depeche Mode and mew at the most recent Underworld album, and not have the faintest knowledge of Freur, the great unsung—and unnamed—Welsh art-school electropop band that, in fact, became Underworld a decade later.

Rad had a procedure at ten, which left only four hours to grab some Cuban food and meet up with Cooper. And maybe smoke a bowl in the Lexus. If he planned it right, and Rad was a master at scheduling, he could eat, meet Cooper, smoke a bowl and still have time to stop by Earwig for the LP he'd ordered, Plastic People of the Universe's agitpunk pop, *Egon Bondy's Happy Hearts Club Banned*. The LP was nearly impossible to come by and when the guys at Earwig told him that they had heard someone in California was selling a decent copy, he moved in quick. It would be a perfect addition to his latest mix. Volume VI in the greatest mix CD series ever made.

Like any child of the '80s, Rad had grown up swapping mix tapes with his friends. Most of those early abominations were cheaply recorded, little planned and poorly executed. The songs would run from genre to genre, theme to theme with little or no semblance of an overarching agenda. Sure, Rad had made a few love tapes for girlfriends. Those had a theme and it usually involved trying to get laid. He had enjoyed staying up late and picking the songs. Listening to each one at least three times to catch all the lyrics. There couldn't be anything like "I love you" or "you're the only one for me" in the songs. That would both scare a teenage girl off and embarrass the tape maker.

No, every song had to fit perfectly and as Rad grew older he honed his skills. By college he'd made some of the finest mix tapes to ever grace a co-ed party. He quickly became snobbish. Branding his tapes and making sure the little tab on the top of the cassette was plucked out so the tape couldn't be copied. Throughout med school he made tapes. In residency it was minidiscs. Rad's mixes were sent around the world. Played at the biggest parties in New York and London. And Rad quickly acquired a sweet tooth for the fame. He wrote for *Rolling Stone* and *Spin*. His columns on tape making were fixtures in over twelve zines. Then came work at King's County and his interest faded, the greatest mix CD series ever sat gathering electric dust on his hard drive. Volumes I—IV were complete. Fantastic even. V was a bit shoddy. Rad figured he'd just redo it later. VI was never ending. These days, only every now and then he'd stumble across a song he'd absolutely need to include. The fireworks would go off again. He'd suddenly get that surge of adrenalin associated with collecting. But it wore off sooner than it used to. These days, Rad just didn't get enough from the record fix. These days, it just wasn't the same.

Rad arrived at Little Cuba later than he had hoped. The place was packed and he knew that getting shrimp paella to go would be an effort in futility. He decided on empanadas. He called Cooper on his cell while he waited.

"Cooper, what's the deal? You gonna meet me?"

"Nah."

"What the fuck?"

"I just embarked on a hero trip."

"A what?"

"I just ingested 50 grams of wet shrooms. Not that dried shit."

"So, you're spending the night tripping?"

"Yeah."

"Fucker."

It took ten minutes to get the empanadas and with over three hours to kill, Rad went straight to Earwig.

Earwig was one of those organic record shops that grow on side streets. It was a pulsing cultural nerve center in Williamsburg. A ganglion through which passed the chi of youth. Despite its having stood at the same graffiti ridden corner for nearly two decades, the store was always vibrant. As Rad pulled up he noticed a tight knot of Latino kids with pompadours and leather coats. They were smoking cigarettes and as Rad walked into the store he overheard one of them breaking into a hideous rendition of Morrissey's "First in the Gang to Die." Rad laughed, *At least they have Morrissey to keep them warm.*

The lanky guy at the register was Jeff Bashlow. He started working the counter of Earwig three years ago, before that he'd been at another shop called Cherry Red Records. Before that he was at Lay Low. Before that Revival and Vinyl Destiny and Def Con 3. Rad had heard Jeff's stories about each and every one of those shops. The time he was working in Lay Low in the early '90s and talked politics with Monks frontman Gary Burger. Or how he met Tuli Kupferberg at Def Con 3 in 1986. Most of the stories were riffs on the tired music-was-so-much-better-back-when-I-was-a-kid rant that Jeff had perfected. For Rad, it was all too incredibly irritating for words.

"You here for the *Happy Hearts Club Banned*?"

"Yeah, is it in?" Rad asked standing at the counter and thumbing through an old copy of *Classic Record Collector.*

"Sure," Jeff said as he pulled the LP out from a stack on the back wall. "How do I know you deserve this though?"

"What?" Rad asked. "I thought this was a clean copy."

"No, the record's in great condition." Jeff slipped the record from its sleeve and looked at it, tilting it in the light. Then he carefully slipped it back into its sleeve. "Yeah, great condition. It's just that I don't sell these to just anyone."

"How's that, Jeff?" Rad was annoyed. Anyone worth his salt in the record collecting scene knew that Plastic People of the Universe's *Egon Bondy's Happy Hearts Club Banned* was a underground classic. It was canon. An example of rock 'n' roll at its most challenged and challenging.

"Thing is," Jeff placed the LP on the counter and leaned in, eyes locked on Rad's. "This album is super rare. I could get you a quality copy of *Leading Horses* for $150, easy. But this, this is something that only comes along every now and then. I mean this is the original Invisible label release, bro . . ."

"You're saying that I won't appreciate it, right?"

Jeff nodded. If anything, he wasn't shy.

Pissed off, Rad said "Jeff, just give me the goddamned record. I'm paying you a shitload for it, shouldn't matter if I know the fucking band or not."

He grabbed the record, threw down his credit card and stared back hard at Jeff.

"Look, man," Jeff backpedaled, "I just really respect this music. It goes beyond worship in my book and I just need to make sure that when a record like this—practically a relic— leaves the shop it's going to good hands. I've seen you around here enough to know you appreciate good music but I just need to be sure. You know? You get it, right?"

Rad signed the receipt and mumbled, "I know the fucking band, Jeff. This is an investment."

"I'm just saying," Jeff sighed. "If you want I can at least fill you in on the back story behind this release. It's not like everyone knows that this album is really just a bunch of demos people snuck out of the country and printed without the band being in on the . . ."

"I don't need your burnout back story, Jeff. I got the memo. I'm not one of those kids just walking in off the street and picking up random vinyl 'cause it'll look good framed on my bedroom wall."

Jeff put his hands up in surrender. "Alright. Alright. I'm glad you care, man. Enjoy."

Rad started for the door but then turned back around and said, "You don't even know who I am, Jeff. I've been shopping here for years and you don't even know my name. But let me tell you something, after this weekend this album isn't going to mean anything compared to the shit that's about to go down. I'm about to be immortalized, Jeff. And you know what? You're going to be adding a new story to your dusty repertoire of rocker tales. You're going to be telling everyone who comes in here that you sold records to the guy who took down Doctor Jeep."

Jeff looked confused. "I don't know what you're talking about," he shouted as Rad stormed out to his car, got in and slammed the door. Rad drove around the block to McCarren Park, stopping across from the empty tennis courts. He grabbed a scalpel from his leather briefcase and began to cut a long, thin line across his forearm. The pain was exquisite.

And as he cut and as the blood ran in thin rivulets down his arm and into the palm of his hand, Rad thought about Doctor Jeep. About Paul Achting. About Veniss. Swank. Lil' Chris. He thought about the blood that would be spraying walls in just one day. He cut deeper and the deeper he cut the less he felt.

Only we can do this, Rad thought.

Only we can stop him.

16

Thursday was bad for Harrison too.

He decided to break off his engagement with Amanda that night. He called in sick to work and slept most of the day but awoke at two in the afternoon and couldn't get back to sleep. He was too anxious. His heart pounding.

They met up at Tomfoolery's, a dinky place renowned for its great corndogs just a few blocks from Amanda's apartment.

Amanda was actually excited to see him.

"Feels like we haven't seen each other in weeks. I don't think we've gone days without talking to each other in months. How weird."

Harrison apologized.

"Stop apologizing. I was busy, too."

Harrison smiled.

"So, I'm glad you called me. Have you seen this yet?" Amanda handed Harrison a folded sheet of newsprint. It was *The Times* "Arts and Culture" section.

"Look toward the bottom of the page."

Harrison did and saw something he hadn't hoped to see for

a very long time. Something he'd hoped he wouldn't see until he was old and better established and more comfortable in his own skin. It was a brief paragraph, lengthened on page 12, detailing the expanding cult of Cloverly. Written by *Times* lit critic Craig Leftbetter, it expounded on the "joyous delirium and intellectual super-specialization" of Cloverly's "enigmatic tales of lust."

"You're really famous, baby!"

Amanda grabbed Harrison's hand and squeezed.

"We're not going to get married, Amanda."

It just came out like that. Across the table, over a half-eaten plate of cheese fries and corndogs, through a cheap shimmering candle and into Amanda's reddening ears. And when Harrison realized what he had said, when the depth of it jumped a synapse and slammed like a falling mammoth carcass into his cramped brain, he knew that a whole world of hurt was about to follow.

But first came, "Ha, ha." Which quickly turned to, "Did you just say that?"

Amanda retracted her hand.

"I can't."

"What?"

"I can't marry you. I'm in love."

"What?"

"I'm in love with another woman."

"What?"

"I can't marry you."

Amanda's face drooped as though she'd had a sudden stroke. An emotional stroke that went physical and dropped her flesh.

"What? What the fuck?"

"I can't, Amanda. I don't know how to say it."

"You are joking."

"No."

"You are."

"No."

"Then you're dead. My brother's gonna kill you, you fucking twerp."

Amanda's claws came out.

"Sorry."

"You're so dead."

"I didn't know how to tell you this, it was sudden. I met her at a . . ."

"I'm not going to listen to this."

Amanda's tears began and the room spun around.

"Please, Amanda. You have to understand, I didn't mean for this to happen."

"And?"

"And it was a strange accident. I just met her and it was right. It's love."

"I suppose you want me to be happy for you." Her eyeballs bugged in fury. "How can you do this to me?"

"I didn't mean to."

"Of course you didn't mean to. Who does? Who means to break someone's heart and tear their life apart? Now I see why you wouldn't settle on a wedding date. You never really intended to marry me, did you?"

"I did, I did. This was a fluke."

"So you're going to leave me for a fluke? Some bitch?"

Amanda's voice rose. It rose like a thunderstorm coming over a mountain and drowned out the clangs and clinks in the kitchen.

"I'm so sorry."

"You're so dead. Dead." Amanda stood up and stormed out.

Harrison put his head on the table, his fingers in ketchup.

"I'm dead."

It took Harrison an hour to get home. Normally it took twenty minutes but he purposely missed the F train and sighed all the way back to his apartment. He felt sick. But at the same time he was enormously relieved. He did it. It was over. Harrison threw his arms into the air and shouted like he'd never done before in his entire life. There had never been a need to shout at the top of his lungs. And the city responded with a hail of car horns and cat screeches, rumbles and belches.

17

Jakus Balk stepped out of the back entrance to the El Torreon Ballroom and lit a cigarette.

The alleyway was dark. Lined by garbage cans and illuminated by the pale phosphorescence of a single street lamp. Jakus let out a plume of smoke with a sigh. It was cold out. Cold enough that the smoke hung in the air like a despondent ghost before dissipating.

There was someone standing beside him.

He was sure the alleyway had been empty when he stepped out of the sweltering shriek of the ballroom. Rampant Mismanagement, a digital-rawk band from Detroit, was on stage taking chainsaws to shopping carts. The noise was stupendous. But there was someone in the alleyway now. A younger man, maybe mid-thirties, wearing a sweatshirt and a baseball cap emblazoned with the words, Border Blaster.

"Look buddy," Jakus preempted any conversation, "I'm tired. I've already gotten four blow jobs tonight. One from a guy. I'm just too tired to even think about another one. We'll be playing here again tomorrow night, come on by then and maybe I'll sign something for you."

The man stood there. Silent. Hovering.

"Buddy," Jakus was getting annoyed. "Just go, man."

"I'm not here to suck your dick, Jakus," the man in the baseball cap said quietly.

"Then what do you want?"

"To talk."

"Look man . . ."

And that was it. Everything went white and then black. Jakus could feel his toes curling. Burning. Stretching out into infinity.

He awoke with a start. Sweat running into his eyes.

Jakus found himself bound to a chair in a nice hotel room, the kind that businessmen reserve. Two queen-sized beds. Each with pale duvets. A small teak desk with a leather chair. An entertainment cabinet. Some decidedly muted abstract paintings hanging above each bed. The room was somber to a fault. Clean and crisp, it reminded Jakus more of a mortuary waiting room than a place to crash for the night. This was the lair of a late night commuter. The den of the salesman.

The man from the alleyway behind the ballroom was sitting on the bed nearest Jakus. He didn't have his ball cap on but he was wearing huge, square-framed sunglasses and a five o'clock shadow that softened his high cheekbones. He was ordinary, an everyman. He offered a Camel.

Jakus nodded. The man put the cigarette to Jakus' lips. Lit it. And as Jakus took a drag the man leaned back on the bed and smiled.

"I told you I just wanted to talk. Sorry about the taser."

Jakus was groggy. His body was sore. He felt as though he'd been run over.

"You can call me Doctor Jeep," the man said calmly, toying with the taser. "Don't make me use this again. I just want to talk. It'll be a real simple, civilized conversation and then, if the stars are aligned, I'll let you leave. Alive."

Jakus nodded. The gag came off. Sweat and the taste of room freshener.

"You, Jakus Balk, are not only the lead singer of the popular electroclash/folk band, The Corporation, but are also considered one of the premier new wave trivia enthusiasts alive today. You've won, I'm guessing, at least six national new wave trivia events . . ."

"Seven," Jakus didn't like to fuck around when it came to his awards. Even if he was tied to a chair in a hotel room with a maniac. He just didn't.

"My mistake, seven, new wave trivia events. That's quite a store of information you've assembled. So many wasted brain cells."

Jakus said nothing. This was the same talk he'd been given a thousand times from his parents. He said nothing to them when they asked how it was that he could fail general physics and yet have every Smiths' lyric memorized. It was a matter of principle. Of priorities.

"I'd like to test your knowledge," Doctor Jeep said leaning forward on the bed and scratching at his stubble. Jakus could see himself reflected in Doctor Jeep's sunglasses. Tied to a chair, sweating like a fat girl at prom and wishing this had been about a blow job. Jakus saw himself crack a smile.

"Are you a trivia fan, Doc?"

"Yes, you could say that. I've got a good feeling that I know more about new wave music than you do. That's why I want to challenge you. It's a duel."

"And if I win you'll let me go."

Doctor Jeep nodded.

"And if I lose?"

Doctor Jeep drew his index finger across his throat and made the universal throat slitting sound, a distinctive *sssssssssss-llllleeeeeecccchhhhhhhh.*

"What if I don't want to play?"

Doctor Jeep shook his head.

"So no choice."

"No choice."

"Can I at least get a drink? Maybe another cigarette?"

Doctor Jeep complied. He got up and broke open the wet bar. He made a screwdriver and helped Jakus sip it. Then he lit another cigarette and held it to Jakus' lips. There was an eerie silence. Two actors playing out a domestic scene on a stage. When the drink was gone and the cigarette butt ground into an ashtray, both men sighed, smiled at each other and then nodded. The game, so to speak, was on.

"I'll begin with easy questions, like any trivia game, and then get to the harder ones. Most of the stuff you seem to know is about postpunk. So, I'll focus on that. My first question is a simple one. Who, or what, is Echo of Echo and the Bunnymen?"

"The drum machine."

"Good. Easy one. Alright, what was the name of Ian Curtis' first band with Peter Hook and Bernard Albrecht?"

"Joy Division. . . . No . . ."

"It's a tricky question."

". . . Stiff Cats?"

"Close, Stiff Kittens. I won't take any *points* off for that."

Jakus closed his eyes and wished himself away. He was clawing at the inside of his brain. Scratching away the velvet lining on his skull. He was as uncomfortable as he'd ever been. The trivia contests were difficult but he enjoyed the competition. It wasn't rote. There was some strategy. No strategy here. Just survival. Reliance on brain cells and God above.

"Alright, what's the B side for Ultravox's 'One Small Day'?"

"'Easterly.'"

"What label was Tubeway Army's debut album on?"

"Beggars Banquet."

"Tears for Fear's debut album, *The Hurting*, was inspired by what psychologist?"

"Janov."

"Who is Jed Holie?"

"Howard Jones' mime."

"Stephen Duffy left what band to join who?"

"Duran Duran to join Lilac Time."

"First name for Frankie Goes to Hollywood?"

"Hollycaust."

"Propaganda's first single?"

Jakus paused. He asked for another drag of the cigarette. Doctor Jeep complied. There was a moment of silence as Jakus took a long, graceful drag and then released a long column of smoke.

"'Dr. Mabuse,'" Jakus said.

"Good. Yello's Dieter Meier was a member of what sports team?"

"The Swiss golf team."

"Martyn Ware and Ian Marsh were . . ."

"Human League."

"No, before that?"

"Dead Daughters."

"Frankie Nardiello was in Special Affect with whom?"

"Al Jourgensen."

"Who gave Altered Images their start?"

"Siouxsie Sioux."

"1978, the Misfits, became what band?"

"The Go-Go's."

"Bernard Sumner's last names?"

"Albrecht."

"And?"

"Dicken."

And then the game stopped. Doctor Jeep got up off the bed and stood by the window staring out of the thin curtains to the parking lot down below. He sighed. "You won, Jakus. You're good. Really good."

"So, you can untie me now?"

"No. Now you need to stump me."

Jakus closed his eyes. Hung his head to his chest. He would

ask one question. That was all he could stand. There would either be an answer and then maybe a knife slowly cutting through the stubble on his Adam's apple or he would feel his bounds being undone, the taser put away. At least he hoped those were the only two options.

Jakus had to come up with something that only he knew. Something personal.

It came immediately.

"On whose album did Simple Minds sing backup in 1979?"

Doctor Jeep thought a moment.

"David Bowie."

Jakus laughed.

"Close. Very close, Doctor. He was in fact producing in the studio next to Simple Minds in 1979 when they were hard at work on *Real to Real Cacophony.*"

"Yes, so?"

"But it was actually Iggy Pop's album. Bowie was there with Iggy. Simple Minds sang backup on "Play it Safe," among other songs. You lost, you sick fucker. Now let me go."

And Doctor Jeep obliged.

He untied the ropes. He opened the door to the hotel room and let Jakus walk out.

And as soon as Jakus' feet left the hotel room carpet and the door closed softly behind him, Jakus ran. He ran like he was trying for first place at track and field day. He was a marathon man and his guts, his lungs, were sore to bursting as he ran out onto the open roadway just beyond the lights of the hotel.

Jakus realized quickly that he was outside of Queens, but just outside. Somewhere in Long Island. Free. Jakus prayed for the first time in twenty years. He offered thanks to God for the first time since he was 13, when he had merely asked for a stereo system. This time it was unadulterated praise. This time it was loud. Shouted out in hoarse breath over the freezing wastelands.

Jakus didn't have a watch on. He had no idea what time it

was but he was sure that if he just ran along the street he would find a car. A car like the car that slowly came up behind him. A car that offered salvation. A car that would take him home to his friends and family. To his life of music. His newfound faith in humanity and goodwill and Christian divinity. A car like that would carry him, a changed man, to the promise of another morning alive. A car like the one getting closer and closer.

Jakus stopped. Waved his arms.

Almost there, Jakus beamed. Almost there.

The car was close. So close now that Jakus could see that it was a black truck, or a Jeep, or an SUV.

So close now that Jakus could see that it wasn't slowing down but speeding up. Squealing tires and steam in the moonlight.

And Jakus could see that he needed to run. That there would be no salvation tonight. That despite his winning the game, he'd lost the war. And Jakus realized that the moment he'd been picked up, the moment he looked into Doctor Jeep's eyes, he would never see another tomorrow.

But Jakus couldn't run. His legs wouldn't move.

There was a rush and a push and the speakers in the Jeep twanged with something heavy. Jakus heard guitars crunch and thought it might be Metallica. Thought he might actually know the song.

Jakus wanted to scream but he couldn't.

The Doctor's black Jeep ran him over too quick for that.

18

"You hear about Jakus Balk?"

It was 8 a.m. and Beth Ann was half awake, eating Cracker Jacks and watching a kung fu movie on Channel 19. She didn't catch the title but it had something to do with dynamite and cranes.

"What about him?" Beth Ann asked.

"He's dead," Solange said.

"What?" Beth Ann turned the TV off.

"Someone killed him."

"Seriously."

"Yeah."

"I bet I know who it was."

"What?"

"Yeah, don't worry . . . I'll get it all sorted out. We're going to take him . . ."

Beth Ann paused and wiped the encroaching crust from the corners of her eyes. She was starting to get anxious—the gears were turning—and with the bruised sunrise glazing the horizon, she worried about the night to come. She wondered if everything would go down as smoothly as T predicted. He seemed to think that this whole thing was like a game. Just a matter of snakes and ladders. Avoiding the bullets and having a good time. For some reason, only a day earlier it hadn't bothered her a bit. It was nothing. Just a bit of violence to set the world right. It was a stitch in time. But that changed as the day blossomed and the fear of the unknown began creeping into her soul.

The one thing she wasn't worried about, the one thing she had totally distanced herself from, was the fact that they were going to kill someone. Blood would be spilled. Yet Beth Ann was sure it would all seem cinematic. Fake like ketchup blood. Not really killing. Maybe it was that this guy was a cold blooded maniac, undeserving of life. Maybe it was that Beth Ann wouldn't be doing the actual killing. This was going to be like a military operation. Dropping a bomb from afar. Leave it to the gang bangers.

"What?" Solange asked. "I didn't get what you were saying."

"Nothing. Just babbling."

"So, what are you up to tonight?" Solange clearly wanted to meet up. "You know, we could get a drink. Talk about this new guy you met."

"Sorry, I've got plans."

"Oh yeah?"

"A party. I'd love to bring you but it's just a small get-together at this one guy's place and it's going to be really mellow . . ."

"You just don't want a stripper there, right?"

Beth Ann laughed. "Solange, that's not what I'm saying."

"No, it's cool. Look, give me a call later and we'll find a time to hook up. I don't mean that sexually or anything. Just to talk."

There was a long pause. Beth Ann didn't have a response. She was far too wired to think of something clever. She asked something obvious instead, "What are you doing up so early?"

"I've got to dance in an hour."

"Seriously?"

"Yeah."

"There are guys looking for tits this early? I thought most everyone would want coffee and a newspaper, not G-strings and nipples. Morning woods or something?"

"This is it, babe. My life. Appealing right?"

"Yeah, definitely."

"Give me a call later and do let me know how your mellow party goes."

"Sure."

Beth Ann hung up and ate a few more handfuls of Cracker Jacks. She chewed slowly, letting the flavor baste her tongue. Then she called Dr. Borgo. Got his voice mail.

"Hey, Doc, it's Beth Ann. Just thought you should know I'm going to be killing someone tonight. It's cool. He's a serial killer so no loss there, right? I'm hoping that maybe the adrenaline will kick my eyes in high gear. Maybe like a preventive move. Like with the knit cap. I'll let you know if it works."

19

Beth Ann met Harrison at the museum. He was staring into the eyes of his recently acquired skull and she joked he looked like Hamlet.

"I never read the play," Harrison said. "That's embarrassing isn't it? I only took one English lit class in college and it was postmodernism. We read Camus and Dave Sim's *Cerebus.*"

"Yeah, I didn't take many lit classes either but I did read *Hamlet.*"

"What's the name of the skull again?"

"I think it was Yorick."

"That sounds right."

"Well, I named this one Leftwich."

"Why's that?"

"Well . . . It just seemed to make sense. Come here, let me show you something on the computer." Harrison stepped aside and let Beth Ann have a seat at his laptop. He opened up a file and let her read it.

She looked at it, then said, "I can't really read well on computer screens. Why don't you read it out loud to me?"

Beth Ann jumped up on his desk and crossed her legs.
She nodded her readiness.

"Okay," Harrison said sitting back down. "It's not really a full story. Just a piece of something. I've never read you any of my porn stuff but this is a bit different. Let's just say it's more literary, even though neither of us would really know what that meant."

"I'm ready."

"So, here it is," Harrison took a deep breath and began: "Leftwich stepped out of the sweatbox of the roaring jungle, the pads of his feet raw with blisters. He'd walked for nearly two days to arrive at the edge of the green hellhole and the abutment of the vast savannah. The journey had been grueling, the parasites that slowly nibbled away at Leftwich's malodorous brain were doing double-time in the haze and buzz of the jungle. Leftwich would never know the reason for the humming in his head, sometimes he looked to the sky and the eye that sat brilliantly burning down on his pate and offered up a curse that was too young for language and too foul for depiction.

"But he would never know that it was the larvae of some prehistoric worm gnawing endlessly that created the noise that kept him awake at night; the noise that drove him on past the ferns and spiraling foliage and into the great floodplain.

"And all the way he sang:

Ain't nothing gonna break my stride
Nobody gonna slow me down, oh, no
I've got to keep on moving

Ain't nothing gonna break my stride
I'm running and I won't touch ground, oh, no
I've got to keep on moving

"And the whole time his penis throbbed, throbbed like a beacon hanging between his hair shanks: calling, a lighthouse to lust. Forecast a humping, a plowing. Moving to the savannah, away from the dark, moist interior of the forest and into the light where slouched females, their breasts dangling, rose nipples, and pudenda screaming pink would howl in lust at the edge of the world."

Harrison ended and leaned back in his chair, gave Beth Ann a half-smile.

"What do you think?" Harrison asked when Beth Ann didn't respond immediately.

"I don't know . . ." She started.

"Fuck, I knew it. It sucks," he interrupted.

"No, Harrison, it's really good. I like the writing but it's just . . . You know, honestly, I've been thinking about tonight and I think it's just really fucking crazy that we're sitting here, right now, talking about your stories and looking at a skull. Tonight we're going to be killing someone. Doesn't that seem fucked up to you?"

Harrison chewed his lower lip. "No," he said. "This whole thing is totally fucked up. I mean it's way beyond just normal fucked up. We're going to a party where my friends are going to be in orange jumpsuits, they've formed a gang, and we've hired some gangbangers to kill a serial killer for us. I mean, the whole thing couldn't get any more surreal. I'm just trying not to think about it really."

"I can't stop thinking about it."

"Yeah, well, give me another few hours and I'm sure I'll be there too."

Beth Ann got off the desk and sat in Harrison's lap. She kissed him.

"The story is very interesting," Beth Ann cooed. "I think you're a brilliant writer and I love that you threw that song in it."

Harrison kissed her back. Cupped his hand over her left breast. Squeezed.

"Let's go back to my place," he suggested.

And they did and they had sex, in fits and starts, until close to 9 o'clock.

"We've got to go," Harrison said pulling the sweaty sheets from the small of his back. Beth Ann was sleeping on his chest, her hair in his face. Harrison nudged her awake.

"Alright, alright," she grumbled.

"Wake up, time to die," Harrison laughed.

"Not funny," she said.

20

Cooper Handsome hated riding the subway. Simply fucking hated it. But it was too cold to walk and he was already too fucked up.

While the mescaline did nothing for his gait, it took the edge off the train ride. Added a bit of Stan Brakhage solarization, the kind you see in '70s drive-in movie trailers. It made the concrete columns that drifted past the train pink and purple. And puffy. Other than the color changes, Cooper's hatred of riding was unchanged.

It wasn't that Cooper was afraid. He actually thought traveling under the city, speeding through the subterranean night, was really freaking cool. He supposed it was comparable to his own soul searching. The problem was that it also made Cooper sick. He was okay with motion. What made Cooper sick was the stench of American culture. Not the stench of unwashed bodies, though he'd encountered that many times before, it was the stench of a Western society, of greedy, opportunistic capitalism. It was being trapped in a can with a bunch of imperialist pigs with no exit between stops. Cooper shrank from flying too.

Just like he shrank from a trip to the mall. Or a suburban outlet store. Or, God forbid, a McDonalds. The smell was just too strong.

The stench of an American adult was one of murder. A murderer always smells. Once you've got blood on your hands, human blood, and it's sunk down in deep, into the folds and creases, you can never get it out. And then it begins to rot. Tiny molecules of another life rotting in your skin. And all the Scrubbing Bubbles in the world can't remove them. They don't become a part of your being. You don't absorb them. They just coexist with your own molecules and cause a stink. A wretched smell that only those with psychically attuned wills can sense. *Dogs, too,* Cooper thought, *dogs can smell a killer from a mile away.* Americans murder small third world children, old folks and cripples with astounding regularity. It's all in the way big business is done. Americans want cheap clothing. So kids in sweat shops die making it. American adults want lower taxes. So the homeless die freezing in the streets. American adults want their children to be ignorant of any science. So third world children die of curable diseases and have babies when they're ten. For Cooper the pain of being surrounded by death and disease was tight. It was raw. But it wasn't as sharp as the pain of living "undercover."

Cooper considered himself to be a "plant," an undercover operative for the larger world. The spiritual world. The hidden world. The world of higher light forms and Lord Metatron. He was undercover in America to observe and report on the goings on, the changes and the interminable destruction. It was a difficult assignment and he'd only become aware of it two years ago.

Cooper realized that his life was a facade after a particularly compelling dream. He knew that he had been flying in the dream. Soaring over a primordial landscape led by a throbbing pink light and a feeling of duty. A feeling that Cooper knew every soldier must have when the flag is raised and the trumpet blown. Cooper awoke from that dream and went to take a shit.

That was the hilarious subtlety of it.

Everyone had to shit at one time or another. Some women

went three days between dumps. Some guys went three times a day. But it was natural. Needed. And it offered Cooper the perfect excuse for alone time. Time to offer up a message to the ineffable geniuses obviously represented by the pink light. Cooper was Horselover Fat come real and the pink light, be it by any name, was calling him to task.

Cooper knew two things from the dream. First, that he had to communicate, psychically, with the higher elemental forces most likely represented by the pink light. And second, that he had to do it as he dropped a log. He had to psychically blog to the pink light. The Lord Metatron. Valis. It didn't matter the name. Straining on the toilet, separated from the world, provided him with the inner peace, the focus, to communicate outside his body.

Cooper found it worked brilliantly.

In the men's room at the library. At Rad's apartment. In his own home. When Cooper sat on the porcelain he could instantly connect via some sort of cosmic wi-fi hookup. He didn't report every time he took a dump. Only when the signs were there or he had some important information to relate. The method was quite simple. Cooper would sit down and as he shat he would stare at the floor. It didn't take long, especially if the floor was tiled, or patterned in some manner, and images would begin to crop up. Maps. Faces. Figures. Numbers. These formed in the spaces between the tiles or in the patterns of the bath mat or cracks in the linoleum flooring. Once the picture came Cooper knew he was in. Then he began his psychic transmission.

It usually went something like this:

Hey guys. Just reporting in, know it's been a little while. I was out on a reconnaissance mission earlier and it's taken me awhile to find a suitable communication hub. (Cooper liked to make the higher light forms think that he was always out doing something on their behalf.) *But I'm here now and I've got some exciting news to report.* (Cooper always tried to have exciting news to report.) *I've just been over to blank and I noticed that the Americans have begun a new campaign of blank. I will watch the progress closely as I think it may have something to do with blank, as we discussed in great detail last time I radioed.* (Cooper often called it "radioing in.") *I will try and radio in soon, I'll let you know what my latest intel is within the next week. I should go now; I think they might be suspicious.* (Cooper always ended his transmissions with a line like this. It was intended to leave the higher life forms on edge, maybe a little concerned for his safety. If they were concerned then they'd assume that the work he was doing was generating good leads. Heck, maybe he'd even be promoted off the planet soon.)

Staring into his reflection in the subway car window, Cooper couldn't wait to get to the party. He couldn't wait for the fireworks. He'd have so much to tell the pink light afterwards.

Cooper thought he was sitting alone. But when he turned away from the window, he saw that a man was sitting next him. The guy was a big, fat geek. Maybe 350 pounds and struggling to breathe. He was also sweating like a stuck pig. The guy was wearing jeans, stone washed and far too tight. White sneakers (the biggest insult to any eye). And an enormous gray sweatshirt that read Cal State in faded blue letters. Geek had jowls, an unshaven neck and glasses. Not to mention a hideously cut mop. His smile was a bit off. A little toothy. The fat guy was reading a ragged copy of Leonard Cohen's *Beautiful Losers.* Though he wasn't really. Hidden inside the book was a magazine, an academic journal called *The Serpukhovian Age.* Cooper felt sorry for the poor fucker.

Cooper turned back to the window and flowed.

The dark monotony only inches away from his face faded quickly as pink clouds rolled in. Pink cumulous clouds billowing over the graffiti. The clouds followed the train, calling Cooper with a voice that sounded like wind chimes. And there was a light, a bright pink strobe light . . .

"Excuse me, what'd you say?"

Cooper's eyes snapped open. He'd been asleep.

"What?"

He turned to see the geek staring at him. Asking him the same question, "What?"

"I didn't say anything," Cooper replied rubbing the sleep from his eyes.

The geek said, "No, you were talking about a pink light."

"A pink light? What did I say?"

"Something about your mission."

"Nothing else?"

"No."

"Thanks," Cooper turned back to look out the window. Nothing but darkness beyond.

"You read Philip K. Dick by any chance?" the geek asked.

"No, not recently. What? The pink light I was talking about was his pink light?"

"Maybe. Maybe not. You talked about pink light. And your eyes were closed but my guess is that you weren't asleep."

Cooper thought the conversation had just made a very awkward turn.

"Who are you? What do you know about me?"

The geek was taken aback, a slight ripple of trepidation washed over his eyes, "I'm just a fellow traveler. I don't know anything about you."

"If I mumbled something about a pink light then that's what I did. That doesn't mean anything. Not to you."

"It might," the geek repositioned himself and put his book down.

"And?"

"Well, I've been in contact with a pink light too. It happened a few months ago. I had never dreamt of a pink light before. At least one that talks. But suddenly there it was. I read Philip K. Dick's *Valis*. I just assumed it was a psychotic break that he had. He just put his experience into words and made it fiction but I never doubted that it was just one of his episodes. But then the pink light spoke to me. It called me across an abyssal plane. It told me things that I never knew were possible. And you know what, it was right. Everything it told me was true. It told me the future. You want to know the future?"

Cooper nodded.

The geek said, "Then you need these."

He handed Cooper a small envelope.

"What is this?"

"Acid. Three tabs. Use it wisely, my friend. Take two and you'll see the pink light at a distance. Take all three and you'll speak with the light and you will hear the answers to all of your questions."

The rest of the train ride was uneventful. The geek read his book quietly and Cooper looked at him closely. Studied the shallow rise and fall of his chest. Looked closely at his fatty neck. And oddly, the more he looked at it the more it looked like rubber. Like the guy was actually wearing a fat suit with a big fat rubber neck. Cooper was spooked so he turned back to watching his reflection. His attention was so rapt he failed to notice the geek disembark.

In the men's room at a cafe, Cooper paused to make contact. It took him a while to find a clean stall. One had a blizzard of shit swirled around its edges. Another simply stank too much of stale piss. The last stall on the left was clean enough. Cooper settled in there. His hands on his chin, he gazed patiently at the tiles on the floor in the space between his shoes until they began to spin and shapes appeared. He began transmission.

Hello gang. Cooper radioing in,

I got the message you sent on the train. The guy next to me, the fat guy, he knew everything about the pink light, about Valis. *About me. Surely, you sent him as an emissary. I know he was really there 'cause I got the tabs from him.*

I wanted to let you know that I've been thinking recently about my life and I've come to the conclusion that it's better if I completely let go of the material world that's holding me back. But the tabs, I suppose they are the key. Alright, talk to you later.

Thanks for being there for me.

A block from Wolfgang's apartment he popped all three tabs of acid.

21

When Harrison and Beth Ann got to Wolfgang's they saw Lil' Chris and Tank were waiting in the stairwell. They didn't go in the building but smoked a few cigarettes outside. Harrison gave Lil' Chris a weak what's-up-yo nod. Lil' Chris acknowledged him with a slight tilt of his head and a flash of gold teeth.

Tank the Niggatron was a dead ringer for Tupac. With gold teeth and flared nostrils. The two of them together looked a little too gangsta. Like they'd wandered off a music video set. And despite Harrison's being pumped up, he couldn't help but worry. He could tell Beth Ann was concerned too.

"So, those are the guys," Harrison said sneaking another look at Tank.

Beth Ann smiled and said, "I'm sure we have nothing to worry about."

Cooper rounded the corner with Rad.

"Look who I found on my way over," Rad said, patting Cooper on the head like a lost puppy. "He's pretty fucked up."

"Acid," Cooper smiled. He pointed at Lil' Chris and Tank, "These two dudes are gonna be killing Jeep?"

"Fuck yeah," Rad said.

The foursome entered the building and Lil' Chris introduced Tank the Niggatron.

"I hear you're some sort of robot?" Cooper asked, snickering.

"I'm the Niggatron, mutherfucker," Tank said.

"And what is that?" Cooper giggled.

"A killing machine."

They made their way to the lobby and T and Xavier were there lounging on the prewar furniture. They both had their jumpsuits on. Both had the deadened coke glare.

"You'll all have to suit up upstairs," T said.

"What the fuck you fools wearing?" Tank asked.

"Jumpsuits. We're the Williamsburg Riffs, mutherfucker," T replied cocky.

They all went upstairs to Wolfgang's apartment and Wolfgang, always the perfect host, brought out warm drinks and cool lines of coke. T passed the jumpsuits around and everyone changed leisurely.

Wolfgang's place was just three rooms. A bedroom big enough for a futon. Kitchen with all the appliances mashed together. And a main room with a television, two bookshelves, a black leather chair, a couch and three hanging plants. The small bathroom was in one corner of the bedroom. The place was dark. Wolfgang had hung opaque curtains on the few windows and it made the place womblike. The revelers hovered around the kitchen, sipping drinks beneath a poster of *Mean Streets* at a thrift store folding table with skateboard stickers plastered all over it.

Around 10:30 the anxiety in the air was nearly tangible. Wolfgang and Rad tried to diffuse the tension with jokes. Everyone else settled for more liquor. More drugs. A round of shots. A line. A bong assembled from an antique vacuum cleaner. Everyone but the Crips. Lil' Chris and Tank didn't partake. They sat at the table and cleaned their guns, examined their ammo and generally seemed removed from the nervous banter and worried laughter. Harrison and Beth Ann sat quietly on Wolfgang's couch talking. Mostly, it was Harrison distracting Beth Ann from his friends' drunken shenanigans. Wolfgang singing along to Eddie Murphy's "Yeah" with a bra on his head. Cooper snorting A-1 steak sauce. Xavier popping some of Cooper's backup mescaline.

At 10:45 Cooper shouted, "Let's do this!" And for a moment everyone froze, not sure how to respond. There was an uncomfortable silence afterwards and a line formed at Wolfgang's small bathroom.

At 10:49 it was decided by hand vote that Lil' Chris and Tank would open the front door when the knock came. Lil' Chris and Tank nodded in unison.

Beth Ann and Harrison moved from the couch to the kitchen table. Harrison wanted to be near the large window that led to the fire escape. Harrison's mom had always made sure to point out exits to Harrison when he was growing up. She'd point them as soon as they'd enter a movie theatre. Or when they boarded a plane, or entered a crowded restaurant, or took a train. Despite his being royally fucked up, Harrison had enough wits about him to ensure that he and Beth Ann were nearest an exit.

At 11:12 the knock came.

The room went quiet and Lil' Chris and Tank stood stiff. Assumed business fronts. At that moment Harrison suddenly realized the absurdity of what they were doing and he told Beth Ann. "This is fucking insane," he said.

She shushed him.

He said, "Seriously, this is totally retarded."

The knock was like a stick of ammonia clearing a concussion fog. Suddenly everything was in sharp relief. Harrison looked at T and Cooper and Wolfgang and then he looked over at Lil'

Chris and Tank. He started to laugh under his breath. The Riffs jumpsuits. The fact that two hardened gangbangers were going to take on what everyone assumed was a brilliant and calculating serial killer. Wolfgang's cheap apartment. Cooper's fried brain. It all added up to a major joke. Harrison laughed because he knew that this would most likely be the last night of his life.

Beth Ann saw the look in his eyes, read it efficiently, "Harrison, Lil' Chris and Tank, they're killers. Jeep is only one man."

Harrison saw Beth Ann was scared. Fear quivering like jelly in her. And he knew she wanted desperately to believe that Jeep was just one man and that one man could be easily overcome and killed. Destroyed. She wanted to believe that, just as surely as she believed that knitting a cap could cure her. But there was doubt. And from the doubt welled fear. And the fear was obvious enough that Harrison grabbed her and held her tight.

"I'm afraid we're going to die," Beth Ann whispered.

They cringed as Lil' Chris opened the door.

The man they assumed was Doctor Jeep looked taller than any of them had expected. He was tall and rail thin, a prototypical denizen of Williamsburg. His hair was dirty blonde, cut shaggy with a few stray locks curling down into his eyes and over his ears. Unshaven. Fashionable stubble. The man wore tight jeans and cowboy boots. He had a coat on. It was an olive green army jacket with a fur-lined hood.

The man was holding a box. It was gift-wrapped, white with a silver bow.

And he had some sort of brown haired animal on a chain pacing back and forth in the hallway. Harrison wasn't sure if it was a mangy pit bull, he hadn't seen a long haired variety before, or a hyena. He'd seen the latter at the Bronx Zoo and on PBS as a kid. They were nasty fuckers. In a zoology class he read that female hyenas have elongated clitorises and that they tend to act more like males. He found himself really hoping it was a shaggy male pit bull. But he couldn't really get a good look at it.

"Evening," the man said.

No one moved.

The animal paced and made a snarling sound.

The man may have thought he'd wandered into a break dancing convention, what with all the orange jumpsuits and gangbangers. Afrika Bombaataa's "Wild Style" was humping out across the room, moving the dust in the corners. The whole scene must have looked like a Far Side cartoon with a caption like, "And then the serial killer paused, worried that he'd interrupted the wrong party." But the man in the doorway didn't appear confused.

"So, is this the party?" he asked.

Beth Ann whispered, "What is that animal?"

Harrison shook his head.

Lil' Chris and Tank stood on either side of the door frame, their hands deep in their pockets, fingering their guns.

"What do you think this is, fool?" Lil' Chris stepped up.

The man smiled.

"It looks to me like this is a party. I was invited after all."

Up until that moment Harrison had been cradling a fragile hope at the back of his mind that this wasn't really Doctor Jeep. That this was just some dumb fuck that'd happened to knock on the wrong door. Some guy in the wrong place at the fucking wrong time. *Happens all the time,* Harrison figured. In the movies there's always that one accidental guy. He's a red herring. He's the cat that jumps out and scares the big-titted heroine as she searches for the killer in the basement. He's the crow that screeches from the undergrowth as the lynch mob makes its way through the graveyard for Dracula's tomb. The skittish nerd hiding under his desk that everyone thinks is the Hatchet Killer of West Bedford, IL, but is in fact his twin brother. But this wasn't the wrong guy.

The wrong guy was never invited.

Lil' Chris moved forward. He was stealthy. Cautious. His right hand in his sweatshirt. The gun pointed right at Jeep. The animal stuck a snout into the room, flashed its teeth.

Cooper said, "Is that a monkey?"

Rad told him to shut the fuck up.

That's when Doctor Jeep stepped into the room, drew a gun and shot Tank the Niggatron square in the forehead. It was so sudden and brutal that Harrison stopped breathing. Tank fell to the floor, eyes black lakes, and the back of his skull slid down the wall behind him.

Lil' Chris let out a noise that was either a wheeze or a gasp and then he pulled his gun from his sweatshirt and pointed it at Jeep's chest. The thing that Cooper called a monkey shrieked and came barreling into the room. Doctor Jeep knocked the gun from Lil' Chris' hand and threw two slugs in his chest. The stocky gangbanger folded in a wet clump. Dead.

Both of the hired assassins were dead.

Jeep walked into the room, gun raised.

He looked at T and Xavier and scowled, "You've decided to fuck me over, huh? Well, you've just fucked with the wrong guy and I'm about to go Cobra Kai on all of your little *Death Wish* asses. Go, Faggot!"

The animal skittered across the room like a spark and leapt onto Xavier.

It howled and bit deep into his neck and that's when Harrison realized it was a baboon. A big fucking male baboon with a bloated red ass. A big red assed baboon named Faggot.

Jeep wheeled in and grabbed Rad in a chokehold. The kind older brothers use when they want submission from weak siblings. He didn't appear to be particularly strong but he was fast and he was agile. He was a well-oiled machine. A killing machine. What Tank was supposed to be.

Faggot had Xavier pinned to the floor. There was a lot of blood and loose fur.

Jeep called over to T, "What's the story?"

T said nothing.

Faggot was a having a field day on Xavier's face.

Jeep put the gun to Rad's head and Rad closed his eyes. When Jeep cocked the gun Rad turned white. Harrison thought back over the past few nights and wondered just what exactly he'd been thinking, what exactly had they all been thinking. He wondered how he could have possibly convinced himself that this was a good idea. And he hated T and Xavier and Cooper and Wolfgang at that moment. He hated them. But not Rad, Rad was screwed. He couldn't hate Rad.

"What have they been telling you?" Jeep turned to Cooper. Rad followed. Head in a makeshift Jeep neck brace and an animal look in his eyes. Cooper spoke casually, "They've been telling us about you. About your deal."

Jeep laughed.

"My deal. What's my deal?"

Faggot snarled and sat on Xavier's bloody chest licking his paws. Harrison couldn't tell if Xavier was still alive.

"You're killing hipsters."

Jeep reached back and pointed his gun at the lumps that had been Lil' Chris and Tank, "Looks like I'm killing more than just hipsters now."

Faggot was panting.

Beth Ann whimpering.

Harrison had forgotten she was even there. She had just become a soft extension of his body as the bullets flew. He prayed that she didn't feel safe there. That she wasn't going to get crazy just because she had his weak-ass arms around her.

"Who are you?" Cooper asked Jeep.

"And what is that?" He pointed over at Faggot.

"That's a baboon. I named him Faggot after the poodle in that Clint Eastwood mountaineering movie. I saw it as a kid and thought it was funny. Who did T and Xavier tell you I am?"

Faggot leapt off Xavier and padded over to Jeep, chain dragging at his side. The baboon's flanks were red with gore. Jeep patted its head.

"A sicko," Cooper said.

Jeep smiled.

"T, you're getting awfully imaginative."

"Fuck you, Alistair," T stepped forward. He had something in his hand, something silver. It was a gun. A really little gun.

"Nice pussy gun," Jeep snickered.

And Harrison laughed. He couldn't help it. It welled up with the panic that was bubbling at the back of his throat. T's gun was really, really small and it looked so ridiculous. Jeep had a bazooka of a gun and a trained killer ape and T was threatening him with something that women put in their stockings in the Wild West.

Rad's eyes widened in Jeep's armpits and he shook his head slightly, cautiously.

Jeep smiled his off-kilter grin.

Cooper said, "I can't believe the dude's name is Alistair. That's so Gorey."

Then his eyes suddenly widened.

"You," Cooper said. "You're the fat ass on the train that gave me the acid. I can tell by your smile."

"Enjoying the trip?" Jeep asked.

"Fuck! This went really bad . . ." T said looking down at Xavier's mangled face.

Beth Ann suddenly came alive in Harrison's arms. She ripped around, wearing him like a coat, and glared at T. "What the fuck do you mean, T? What the fuck have you gotten us into?"

Beth Ann squeezed Harrison's hands like a wife squeezes her husband when she wants him to back her up. Harrison thought it was the squeeze a husband gets when they're meeting with the principal, trying to explain why Jimmy really is a good boy and why he shouldn't be kicked out of school for trying to poison his Spanish teacher. The squeeze when the principal says,

Give me one reason why I shouldn't boot your child. And the wife squeezes. *Your turn,* the squeeze says.

Back me up here, it says.

Cooper shouted, "You're the fucking guy!"

T looked mad. He had a huge vein pulsing in his neck.

"T, why don't you tell them what exactly is going on here," Jeep said flippantly.

"You're the fucking guy!" Cooper shouted again.

And then, just as Cat Power came on the stereo, T and Jeep started shooting at each other. Jeep let go of Rad and Rad fell to the floor with his arms over his head. Beth Ann and Harrison ducked under the table. During the firefight that followed, Faggot squealed like a rusty storm and Harrison prayed the baboon would catch a bullet. Jeep was one thing but at least he was human. The fucking screaming baboon was scaring the hell out of him.

The gun blasts sang out like Wagner.

Harrison, curled up under the table, hoped the shooting would be a stop and start thing. Shoot and then duck behind furniture. Wait for the other guy to shoot and then stick your gun over the top and shoot again. Like in a Western. But it wasn't like that at all. T and Jeep just went nuts with their guns. Shaking like Parkinson's patients and sending bullets ricocheting off every surface. They took out the television. The potted plants. The fridge. The bottles of booze lined up on the kitchen counters. The stereo system. Framed photos on the mantelpiece. Everything was shattered. There were fragments of it all scattered across the floor.

And then, the fire fight just stopped. The apartment was silent save for Faggot's panting. Harrison guessed that Jeep and T were out of ammo. In the midst of the mayhem, as bits of plaster and plate fell to the floor in snowy tinkles, Cooper was still standing. Exactly where he'd been when the shooting started. He was smiling.

Cooper walked in between T and Doctor Jeep, his hands

raised like white flags. Like time-outs. And he opened his mouth to say something but his head exploded. Cooper's head had been there, all bright teeth and receding hair, and then a nanosecond later—just a jump cut—it was a million bits of corpus colossum and eyeball juice. It was like his smile got so wide and bright that it evaporated the face around it. Poof!

T stood, his gun outstretched and smoking.

Jeep said, "T, I really had some respect for you. You always were at the top of the game. Honestly, Mother and Father were really, really proud of your zine. But you're obsolete now my friend."

That's when Harrison noticed that Rad wasn't lying at Jeep's feet anymore. He'd somehow stealthily made his way behind the leather chair near Tank's splattered body. And he made a very noticeable move for Tank's gun. Harrison saw it. T saw it. But Jeep was the one who put a bullet in Rad's cutting hand. It didn't go in clean. Left a ragged seared hole that smoked like a Halloween gag. And Rad screamed bloody murder.

Harrison didn't dare move.

Beth Ann didn't breathe.

Everything was still again.

Hiding, huddled on the floor under the table, seemed plain silly. Something overcame Harrison. Something stupid and fuzzy. It was like curiosity and suicide at the same time. He was tired of crouching. His legs were aching and Beth Ann had such a grip on his arm. He needed his blood to move. He needed desperately to stand and stretch. Even though he knew it was the stupidest thing he could possibly do at that moment, he stood up anyways.

"Hey, Doc," Harrison said as he emerged. He thought maybe if he was cool and casual about it Jeep might cut him some slack. Maybe he'd be in a better place to bargain for some lives. And for the first time that night he wished he had a gun.

Faggot, crouched at Jeep's side, made one of those dog yawns. Followed by an eager squeal.

"Harrison. I love your Cloverly stuff, bro. You're going to want to get out of the way . . ."

And then the lights went out.

Harrison didn't have time to think.

He just crouched in place, his hands on the floor. The fact that Jeep knew his pen name didn't register at the time. Harrison was merely acting on instinct. Running on baser victuals. A cool combination of adrenalin, love and lack of sleep.

He assumed that Wolfgang had shut the lights. Or hit the fuse box. The apartment was pitch black. The only light a few glowing star stickers that Wolfgang had stuck on his ceiling above the couch. The fact that Wolfgang had hung such thick drapes made the place a thousand times darker than it normally would have been. A thousand times darker than an apartment in the city should have been. As his eyes adjusted to the dimness, Harrison made out rough shapes. He saw jagged edges of furniture and bold paler splashes that he assumed were the walls.

T spoke up from somewhere near the couch, "Listen, Alistair, this went down all wrong."

"Hostile takeovers are a bitch aren't they?" Jeep said from somewhere in the center of the room.

"This is our scene, Alistair. Xavier's and mine."

"Your scene? Look, T, this is capitalism. Survival of the fittest. You didn't listen well enough to Father. He made that clear."

Harrison could hear Beth Ann breathing to his right, still under the table. Shallow. Thin. It was like she was on the top of a mountain. Her lungs struggling.

"Are you alright?" Harrison whispered to her.

"Just scared," she said. "Where's that sick fucking monkey?"

Harrison hadn't thought about Faggot for a minute. The baboon could have been anywhere. Black lips peeled back over Dracula fangs. Sniffing them each out one at a time.

"What the fuck is going on, T?" Rad shouted. He was somewhere near the bathroom, in the back of the apartment.

"Nothing, Rad. Nothing at all," T said.

Then T fired two shots toward the bathroom. The flashes from the muzzle lit the room like a strobe light and a distorted image of the furniture, of Jeep smiling, gun raised, was etched into the shadows. There was a second shot, from Jeep's direction, and again the flash of light. Jeep's bullet hit one of the heavy curtains with a low thud and then the glass behind it shattered.

"Alistair, you don't know who you're fucking with here!" T shouted. "We're not just gonna ignore your trespass."

"Who's we, T? Xavier's dust. Are you going to come after me alone?" Jeep fired again at the leather couch.

The flash revealed that T was no longer behind it.

"Just let us go," Wolfgang asked from somewhere near the front door. "Just let us out of this, T. Please. We'll just walk out of here and you guys can continue with your beef."

"Sorry, Wolfgang," T said. He was in the kitchen now. "I can't let any of you leave here. Sorry that everything went so wrong. Rad, those Crips sucked, man."

"Amateurs," Jeep laughed. His disembodied voice rumbled through the room.

Harrison thought that maybe he could get out. He grabbed Beth Ann tight and told her to lie flat and move over to the window. They rolled under the table to one of the drapes, ducked under it and emerged into a surreal blue moonlight. Beth Ann's eyes were wide. Eyebrows quivering.

Harrison held a finger to his mouth. Made the universal sign for *Quiet down or we're gonna get fucked.* Then he reached up and unlocked the window. Bent down. And slowly, painfully slow, began lifting the window up. He stopped when T shouted from the kitchen. "Alistair, when did Mother tell you?"

"I've always known, T," Jeep sounded further away. He sounded distracted.

Harrison looked at Beth Ann. She was holding her breath. Her eyes were closed tight. And she was beautiful. Her skin smooth in the blue light. Her eyelashes sparkling. Harrison looked out the window, out beyond his reflection, and saw that the blue light wasn't the moon as he'd assumed. It was a neon Michelob sign on the corner below Wolfgang's apartment building.

His hands on the window, Harrison began to slowly pull it up again. It creaked once. He stopped.

T shouted, "Alistair, you realize that you're not getting out of here the way you came in! I'm bypassing Mother and Father on this one . . ."

"Like all the other ones?" Jeep said.

And T answered, "No. No, Mother and Father knew about those. But I've been surveying the playing field and I'm not convinced they're being aggressive enough."

"So, you're just removing all the obstacles, huh? Clearing a path to what, T?" Jeep said.

Harrison could hear that Jeep was on the move, stealthily inching toward the kitchen. He stood up again, bathed in the light of the Michelob sign, and worked on the window. Beth Ann tried to smile as she rubbed Harrison's back but her eyes kept darting to the room beyond the curtain.

T was speaking, "I'm looking at new markets, Alistair. Expanding my portfolio, so to speak. There's been a lot of movement recently in the world of Nambian pop. And I've been hearing great things about that spaghetti western director . . ."

"Miles Deem?" Jeep asked.

"Yeah, but we're gonna sell him under his real name. I've always focused on the long term, Alistair. You know that. By the by, what's in the box?"

Jeep answered, "Oh, the present? Well, you'll never find out now."

"Please don't tell me it was Pink Floyd's *Household Objects?*" T barked.

"You're good," Jeep said.

T answered with a groan, "Fuck, I really, really want to hear that."

Harrison had the window open enough for Beth Ann to wiggle through. Then things went nuts again. Bullets flew. Harrison grabbed Beth Ann and pulled her down. The bullets punched through the curtain, perforating the space where Harrison and Beth Ann had just been standing. They lay on the floor. Breathing hard. Holding hands and staring at each other. Teeth clenched as splinters of glass fell around them.

It seemed to rain glass forever.

Harrison's head was spinning. He closed his eyes and waited until the silence was overwhelming. When he opened them, he saw Beth Ann had lifted the drapes and was looking out into the apartment. The lights were on.

Jeep was gone. T was gone.

Beth Ann dropped the drapes.

Harrison whispered, "What do you think?"

Beth Ann whispered back, her lips pursed, "I don't know. I think they're gone. I saw that the front door is open."

"Think it's a trap?" Harrison asked.

"No."

"What do you think happened?"

"Maybe they killed each other."

"Where the fuck is that baboon? I think we need to wait longer."

Harrison counted to sixty.

"Now?" Beth Ann looked eager to move.

Harrison could hear his heartbeat in his ears like he was deep underwater. He waited for the scrabbling of Faggot's claws against the hardwood floor but the sound never came. Beth Ann smiled and lifted the drapes again.

The apartment was still empty.

Beth Ann stood up, walked out.

Harrison stood and stretched. Glass crunched.

Beth Ann peeked into the kitchen. Empty. Harrison motioned for the door and Beth Ann nodded. They walked out past Cooper's headless body and that's when Harrison saw Rad, lying behind the bullet-riddled couch. He was bleeding badly from his blasted hand.

He crouched down, "You all right?"

Rad groaned, "I need to get to the ER pretty bad. Probably gonna have to amputate."

"What the fuck do you think happened?" Beth Ann asked looking around.

Sirens began to fill the streets outside. Harrison wondered if they had been blaring the whole time but he just hadn't heard them.

"The cops are coming," Wolfgang said stepping out from the bathroom. Harrison was relieved to see that Wolfgang was still intact.

"Where's that baboon?" Harrison asked.

Rad said, "How long have the sirens been going?"

"What the fuck do you think happened?" Beth Ann asked again.

Harrison told Wolfgang and Beth Ann that they needed to leave. Now.

Beth Ann said, "I'm not going to jail."

"Neither am I," added Wolfgang.

"So let's get the hell out of here," Harrison said.

Beth Ann grabbed Lil' Chris' gun.

22

Harrison, Beth Ann, Wolfgang and Rad stumbled out onto North 6th Street and walked to the intersection with Berry where the traffic was light.

They needed a car. Wolfgang took the gun from Beth Ann and carjacked an elderly lady in a green Honda. Harrison watched as the old woman was ushered from her car with all the subtlety of a bum rush. She rolled out onto the asphalt and into the slush.

"Are you guys coming or what?" Wolfgang shouted from the driver's seat.

They all piled in. Harrison in the front with Wolfgang. Beth Ann and Rad squeezed into the backseat with the old lady's laundry. As they sped off, tires squealing, Harrison looked back to see if the geezer they'd just royally damaged was all right. She was still lying in the gutter and a guy from the grocery store on the corner had come out to help her up. Harrison felt sick to his stomach. Beth Ann was shaking.

Wolfgang took a hard right at North 7th Street and nearly plowed into Doctor Jeep. The killer was standing in the middle of the street shooting. A bullet hit the Honda's radiator and steam billowed onto the windshield. Wolfgang, ducking to avoiding being shot, plowed the Honda into a parked car.

When Rad opened his door to get out, Faggot leapt in.

Doctor Jeep appeared at the driver's side window. He was grinning like a drunken prom queen, "Good to see you all again."

Harrison reached over and pushed the stick into reverse and slammed his left foot on the gas. Jeep's face vanished. Wolfgang took the wheel again and slammed it in drive.

"Where's the fucking gun?!" Harrison shouted.

Beth Ann was screaming and Rad cursing beneath a flurry of red and brown. There were masticating sounds, as if Faggot were actually eating. Chewing.

"Where the fuck's the gun!?" Harrison screamed.

Wolfgang veered onto Driggs Avenue and handed Harrison Lil' Chris' cannon.

Harrison spun around to a chaotic scene. It looked less like Rad and Beth Ann struggling with a rabid animal than some disgusting German performance art involving gallons of blood and reams of matted fur.

Harrison knew he couldn't pick a spot and fire it into. It was cramped enough in the backseat of that Honda that if he were to have fired he'd have hit all three of them. The key was getting Faggot out the window.

"Roll down the windows!" Harrison shouted to Wolfgang.

Wolfgang was too busy weaving in and out of traffic on Metropolitan. The car didn't have automatic windows. Harrison had to reach back and roll down the window on Rad's side himself. In the process he got a few good nicks from what he assumed were Faggot's long nails.

"Throw it out!" Harrison yelled.

Faggot was screeching.

Beth Ann screaming.

Harrison looked back and saw a shark attack in a bottle. Rad was trying valiantly to toss the enraged animal out of the car but Faggot had his claws deep in Rad's arms and every attempted push only got them in deeper.

Harrison told Wolfgang to speed up. Wolfgang did.

And when the car hit around 35 mph Harrison told everyone to brace themselves and pulled up the emergency brake. Rad crashed into the back of Harrison's seat. Faggot was thrown loose and slammed into the dashboard in a wet hard smack. The car rocked to a standstill. Wolfgang said he was fine. So did Beth Ann. Rad groaned. Harrison reached down and grabbed Faggot and put a thumb in the twitching baboon's left eye just for good measure.

The eye fought back, the slick surface surprisingly more resilient than Harrison imagined it would be. Eventually, using the nail to dig in, the eye gave and Harrison's thumb sunk deep into the orbit. He crammed it in as far as it would go. Faggot wasn't moving. Harrison threw the hairy body out of the car then looked back to see Rad and Beth Ann.

Beth Ann was shaken. Had a few cuts on her face and hands, but nothing like Rad. Rad was bleeding bad. It was enough that his hand was shot through but now he had deep angry gashes on his arms and face. The entire backseat was dripping. Rad weakly asked Wolfgang to drive him over to Greenpoint Hospital. He said it was desperate.

Traffic was relatively light and the Honda actually had some pep so they got there quickly. Harrison knew that in movies they dump someone out of a moving car in front of an emergency room when shit was bad. That happens, he was sure, but they didn't want to do that to Rad. That was just cruel. They stopped the car and Beth Ann and Harrison helped Rad over to the front doors.

"I'll be fine," Rad said as they laid him in front of the sliding glass door. "I know a few of the docs here. They'll take good care of me and I'll tell them I got into it with a pit bull or something."

Harrison pointed out the bullet hole in Rad's right hand, "And that?"

"I'll make something up. You guys should get going."

Beth Ann kissed Rad's forehead. Wolfgang honked the car horn with a fist.

"Go," Rad said, "You've got to bail. Get out of the city. You need to call the cops or something, with both of them out there. I'll be safe in here."

They didn't bail. They pulled over onto a side street just around the corner from the hospital and sat in the car and talked. The windows were rolled down and every one took deep gulps of fresh air. It was snowing, little flakes so thin that they melted before they even hit the car. Wolfgang lit smokes and handed them around.

"What the fuck happened?" Wolfgang was the first to ask.

"I'm not sure," Harrison said.

Beth Ann added, "That was a setup."

"For who?" Wolfgang asked.

Beth Ann said, "For us. For Jeep."

"For Jeep," Harrison agreed.

"What were they talking about? I thought I knew T really well. And fuck, man, Cooper's dead. Cooper's dead. And those gangsters and Xavier. What the fuck happened?"

"They were talking about business," Beth Ann said. "They obviously knew each other well, like they were in on the same scheme. Like they worked together."

"Fucking killers. Cooper's dead," Wolfgang said again.

"Yeah, they'd have killed us too. That's a given," Beth Ann cracked her knuckles.

"What are we going to do?" Harrison asked. "As far as I see it we only have a few options. We cut and run. Maybe head somewhere innocuous, like Dover. We could contact the cops but that just brings up all sorts of hell. I mean, we talk to the cops and we'll for sure be in jail. And I'm not ready to serve time.

The only other option is really fucked up. We got ourselves psyched up to kill a killer. Why not finish the job? Get them before they get us."

"That's a retarded idea, Harrison. You're tired. You're talking stupid," Beth Ann shook her head.

"What do you suggest?" Harrison fired back.

She said, "I think we need to bail."

"Nah," Wolfgang said. "We run and this shit won't get resolved. I say we stay here. Chances are they aren't even looking for us. Honestly. Besides blasting Cooper they were after each other. They'll probably kill each other and that will wrap it up. They won't be looking for us."

They sat in silence as they finished their cigarettes.

Harrison's thoughts turned to the backseat. It wasn't their car but he really felt like they needed to clean it up. Beth Ann didn't seem to notice the blood. She didn't say anything about it. Harrison knew if it had been him back there, he'd be complaining about how his ass was wet with gore. But Beth Ann was too hyped up. Too jazzed on adrenaline. Harrison figured she'd start complaining when the buzz died.

Beth Ann asked, "What if they do come after us?"

"Wolfgang, you knew T better than I did, what did he really do?" Harrison tossed his cigarette butt out the window and his eyes traced its faint red arc as it fell sizzling. "It's a stupid question, I know, but I really don't think I knew him . . . Well, I certainly don't now."

"He published the zine and had the blog. He always said he was dirty with money."

Beth Ann asked, "What is his real name?"

"T. Radcliff," Wolfgang said.

"But what's the T for?"

Wolfgang replied, "Travis. I think."

"How about people he hung out with?" Harrison asked. "I mean, I only ever saw him with us."

"I did meet a friend of his that I'd never seen before, or since. T was wasted, it was at a gig at Giger's and he was there with this dude called Fluke. He was real edgy. Real nervy. He really didn't like that T introduced me to him. He's like a DJ, runs a pirate radio station, horror rap . . ."

"Fluke?" Beth Ann interrupted. She said she had heard the name before but wasn't sure where or why.

"Yeah, like the parasite," Wolfgang smiled.

"And where does this dude hang out?" Harrison asked.

"I heard a rumor that he hangs out in the fucking sewers."

"What?" Beth Ann asked.

"The sewers. Weird shit, huh?" Wolfgang stopped when his cell phone beeped. "It alerts me when I've got email."

Harrison turned to Beth Ann, "Carla45."

Wolfgang nodded. A bit self-conscious.

"Maybe she knows who T really is?" Harrison joked.

Wolfgang gave him the finger.

Harrison tried to get some focus back, "Look, I need to get some sleep. We all need to rest a little. We can't go back to Wolfgang's place. And I'm sure the cops are gunning for several freaks in orange jumpsuits right now."

"At least that fucking monkey's road kill. Let's go to my place," Beth Ann said.

They went to Beth Ann's pad and Harrison took a shower while Beth Ann showed Wolfgang some of her knitting. Beth Ann's apartment was suitably girly. It was clean but it wasn't floral. She had nice furniture. The design would be best described as midcentury. Harrison found it odd that the very first time he was at her place, he was there with Wolfgang. That just seemed perverse. Then again, the night had already been nearly apocalyptic.

The shower felt good. Harrison used all of Beth Ann's body wash scrubbing the blood and sweat from his body. When he came out Beth Ann was demonstrating the mattress stitch and Wolfgang was surprisingly attentive. The scene was almost domestic. If it hadn't been for their blood-spattered jumpsuits and wild eyes, it would have appeared downright Rockwellian.

It was good to focus on something as innocuous as knitting for a while. Harrison figured Beth Ann would find it really fucking annoying that he referred to knitting as innocuous.

After a few minutes, Beth Ann gave Wolfgang the reins. Let him go nuts with the knitting while she inspected Lil' Chris's gun.

Harrison told her to be careful with it. She told him to fuck off.

Wolfgang was moving quickly, finishing his first row, when Harrison decided to go home. He couldn't sleep. Despite being completely and utterly spent. Despite feeling every cell in his body withering to nothing. He couldn't close his eyes. He just wanted to stop by his place and pick up a book. He wanted to change into something clean.

"What are you talking about?" Beth Ann snarled. "We're wanted. There's a killer running loose out there. You just blasted his doggie, he's looking for us. You can't go home. I've got clothes here, I'm sure something that'd fit . . ."

"I just wanted to pick some stuff up," Harrison said. He didn't care if he wasn't thinking clearly. He didn't care if he was shell-shocked. Or if he had a bullet in his cranium wedged somewhere on a precipice of paralysis.

"You're insane, man," Wolfgang looked up from his knitting. "What the fuck, dude?"

"I'll be quick. I'll take a train, just get my stuff and head back."

"Can you explain why?" Beth Ann demanded.

Harrison shrugged, "I just need to get out."

"So fucking retarded," Wolfgang mumbled.

Beth Ann shook her head. She mumbled something incredibly crude. When Harrison went for the door they shouted and screamed obscenities. But they didn't physically try to stop him. And Beth Ann didn't cry.

Harrison told them he'd be back soon.

He added, irreverently, "I am being completely honest."

They told him it was fun knowing him. Beth Ann said she'd visit his grave. Harrison thought there was something sweet to that.

23

It felt great getting out and hearing the life of the city again. Being among people who weren't in shootouts. People who hadn't spent that evening brawling for their lives with a monkey. Just the sweet citizens of New York. Happily wrapped up in their own private endeavors. Their quests for love. Food. Cheap housing.

Seeing his apartment building was like seeing his mother.

It was like coming up from underwater and seeing his mother's face in the sun above him. He walked into the foyer sighing, coming out of a nightmare, and ran head long into Justin, his ex-fiancée's gorilla-like brother.

"I've been waiting for you," Justin said with a fist.

Harrison fell back on the marble floor. Swallowed a tooth. Gums raw and stringy like spaghetti squash. Justin was on him in a moment and with the second punch Harrison felt something in his nose crack. He knew there were no bones there, in the tip of the nose. Just cartilage. But the sound was such that if he had heard it in a hospital he would have assumed it was the sound of a sternum being cracked open.

And then came a pummeling. A crush.

That was the best Harrison could think of to describe it. He'd been swimming once on Fire Island and was caught up in an undertow and dragged against the rocks. He was eight or nine at the time and the sensation of being slammed, endlessly, against those black rocks was the most painful and desperate thing he had ever felt. His lungs were ready to burst. Combusting. Until his father dragged him from the water. He sat coughing and vomiting on the beach for half an hour after that. Coughing and vomiting and looking out at the ocean, a dark green heaving mass that flung itself tirelessly toward him, seeking to reclaim its lost booty. There was no dad to save Harrison this time.

He just backed into himself, folded in, and waited for the pummeling to stop. Deep down he knew he deserved every minute of it. He'd broken a heart. It took only thirty seconds to ruin Amanda's evening. Her month. Her life. He could handle two minutes of ass kicking. Especially after the evening he'd had. This was just an encore.

As Justin's left hook landed on his cheekbone, Harrison recalled the decline of the trilobite. How the most successful creature on the face of the Earth vanished into oblivion in a matter of a few million years. A nothing. A blip in terms of Earth time. Here one day. Gone the next. If anything, thinking about the trilobite cemented his near pathological insistence that Beth Ann was indeed the one. There wasn't time to go off and marry the wrong woman. Harrison had to be right. His time on this planet was nothing but a millisecond in the life of the universe.

Toward the end of the beating he started seeing his life flash in front of him. But it was like the projector showing his movie was broken. It was fucked. Images came in stops and starts. Fits and coughs. The first were from his youth.

He saw himself in the Batman cape, the one he got at Kmart in Saratoga Springs on vacation. The one he bought with his allowance. There he was at the beach on Siesta Key, the white sand sparkling between his toes. Whites blossomed and exploded as the film caught in the projector and the images crusted with black. A jump cut and the next images were high school. It was fast and furious. Waves. Making out with Jessica Steward behind the curtains on stage. A disco ball. Running from the football team after the horseshoe crab incident. His locker. The bumper stickers on his best friend Todd Lark's Beetle. A beaten up cassette tape of Suicide. Walking in the park with his mother. Turtles. Eating an apple by a fence. His junior year chemistry exam. A skull. Going under the table for his pencil and catching a glimpse of Lisa Brock's pink panties. A beer with dad. Playing the drums after school in a moldy basement. EMF. The first time he kissed a girl. And then nothing.

And then another fist jarred the frames free.

He relived meeting his freshman year roommate, Bill, for the first time. The awkward handshake, the uncomfortable silence that followed. Flash forward to sophomore French. *Toujours pour la premier fois.* The recitation slowed to a crawl. He watched a beetle make its way slowly across the windowpane. Outside rain, the campus lush and the University closing for summer. Black. Junior year and he feels up Christy Tanner as they smoke joints and watch *Rock & Rule.* Junior year ends snorting a line of coke off of Christy's left breast. *A Cold Night's Death* and eating éclairs and it is senior year. A block party and long discussions about reality. Denim jackets and long hair. Everyone is so thin. He graduates and mom cries. And Harrison thinks that these aren't his memories.

Black again and it's peaceful but Justin's not done.

Round three.

Grad school and rain. Driving across town to his new apartment in a rental car. Amanda and cigarettes. Amanda changing the towels in the bathroom and joking about how Harrison's always late to dinner. Porn time and for a few microseconds he sees the faces of every woman he ever rubbed his rod for. They all have names but he can't remember any of them. Then it's Beth Ann and her eyes closing as she sighs on the train. Then it's Jeep's snarl and the sound of breaking glass.

And then it was over.

Justin backed off. His face a tangled black melanoma of fury. "That's what you get, dickface."

Harrison curled up fetal. The marble floor was cold but the blood-saliva mixture that oozed from his broken lips was warm.

He just lay there. Numb. Blissfully beaten.

A year passed. Maybe ten.

24

Beth Ann found Harrison on the marble floor of his apartment building. He was curled into a ball on a mattress of saliva and blood.

"Harrison. Harrison."

"Yes," he said through cracked teeth. Broken lips.

He didn't move. Curled like a pill bug.

She lay down beside him. Spooned him.

"Harrison, I'm here," she whispered.

"Yes."

"Glad you went home now?" Beth Ann asked but didn't let the sarcasm poison the poignancy of the moment. Her cradling Harrison. Her loving him.

Harrison uncoiled. Pushed his legs and arms out and he moved from fetal to ready for birth. Then to stand and walk. It took a few minutes but after a slippery period of fumbling, Beth Ann had him propped up. A few minutes later, she had him standing. Leaning against a wall.

"Does it look bad?" Harrison cackled like a crab's claw.

"No."

"Yeah, right."

Beth Ann guided him to the elevator. She imagined that his every step was a jarring thrill ride of nerve raging pain. A roller coaster across the plains of hell.

"Yeah," he said, "It hurts like fuck."

The elevator was a brief respite from the agony. But then they were on the fourth floor and walking down the hall taking baby steps to Harrison's apartment. And the whole while he tried not to speak.

"I don't want my few remaining teeth to spill out," he said.

Once inside Harrison's dark apartment, and after a few panicked moments stumbling about for the light switch, Beth Ann helped him onto a green crushed velvet recliner. He promptly passed out.

She caressed him as he slept and she studied his face carefully. The freckles on the bridge of his nose. The grey hairs sprouting up in his beard. The seashell curve of his ear. She cried and thought about the sick hipster cap. She thought about how it was such a blessing that her eyesight hadn't failed her recently. The party. The battle in the backseat. The miracle of the knit cap. Beth Ann thought about Wolfgang back at her place knitting. She smiled at the thought of having a protégé. And wondered if that was the correct word.

While Harrison slept, Beth Ann studied herself in his bathroom mirror. Studied the scrapes. The cuts. The bruises. They added something battle weary. Something Joan of Arc-ish to her already chiseled features. She thumbed through a stack of CDs she found beside Harrison's bed. Put on Os Mutantes and it seemed to rouse Harrison.

She sat back down next to him. Ran her fingers through his hair.

"Are you okay enough to go to the ER?" she asked.

"Isn't that the point of an ER?" he replied. "Aren't you supposed to go there when you're not okay? I doubt anyone has ever been not okay enough to go to the ER."

"Alright, smartass. What do you want to do? I'm happy taking you over there."

"No. I hate hospitals. Especially the ER part. Rad says that if you go in there and you don't leave within five hours then you're stuck. And very few people who get stuck in the ER ever come out. The place is a death trap."

Harrison spat a thick mixture of saliva and thick, knotted blood clots. The spit didn't go far. His lips couldn't get into alignment to make the spray fly further than his chest. The blob of bloody goop landed on his shirt. Just below his chin. Beth Ann wiped it away with her hand.

"Do you think you're going to be alright? I mean you look like a car accident."

"I guess so. Let me take a look."

Harrison pointed to a small oval mirror hanging above a cabinet of curiosities on the wall across from the couch. The glass fronted cabinet contained three shelves. On the topmost was the skull of a monitor lizard. On the middle a collection of trilobite fossils. On the bottommost shelf an ammonite lying beside a prostrate He-Man.

Beth Ann took the mirror down and handed it to Harrison.

"I really don't look as bad as I feel."

His face was swollen. Black and blue and red. His nose was a gourd. He smiled at the black spaces where his front teeth used to be. Harrison's top lip was cut open and oozing. The bottom a lovely shade of chartreuse.

"I'm looking good," he gyred and gimbled.

"I liked you better with teeth," Beth Ann giggled.

She put her head in his lap.

"I got what I deserved. I broke up with my fiancée for you. That guy who beat me up, that was her brother. I got what I deserved. Amanda and I had been together for years. And I thought I was in love with her. We were supposed to get married this year, we hadn't chosen a date. Until I met you. And then it all changed. I broke it off . . . What were you doing here?" he asked.

"I was worried. I just took a chance and came on over. Why don't you sleep?"

"I don't want to. I want to talk to you. Look at you."

"Do you think you're safe? I mean, is that guy going to come back?"

"He won't. He's done."

"You sure? I could call my friend Buck. He's a big bruiser."

"You know someone named Buck?"

"He's a pharmacist."

"Right. No, seriously, I'm fine. Let me just relax. Talk about something else. Distract me."

"Do you want to see my underwear?"

"What?"

"Do you want to see my underwear? I just knit this pair last weekend."

"Yeah, sure," Harrison had no idea how to respond.

Beth Ann stood up. She pulled herself out of her jumpsuit. White knit panties with red letters across the front that read, NO REPUBLICANS ALLOWED. The underwear wasn't particularly comfortable. She sewed real panties inside them. Just so it didn't itch as much. And that made them seem like a joke.

She noticed Harrison wasn't really looking at the underwear, but the space where Beth Ann's thighs met her hips. The space only hinted at beneath. The curves and the hills. And the valley. He looked up at her navel, perched precariously above him.

"What do you think?" Beth Ann brought his eyes back to the underwear.

"Wonderful." Harrison swallowed hard.

"Do you need something to drink? Eat?"

"I am getting a bit thirsty," Harrison attempted to get up.

"Just lie there. Jesus, are you even feeling it anymore? I'll go ahead and look around. I'll find something."

"There's a drawer, lower left side. Next to the fridge. There's a flashlight in there. Would you bring it in when you come back?"

"Okay," Beth Ann said, walking over to the kitchen.

Harrison's apartment was small. There were few windows and very few window treatments. As far as decorating, the tone was muted. Drab gray walls. Wooden desk. Black bedspread. Lots of bookshelves, all crammed to bursting with all variety and manner of printed material. Books. Journals. Loose papers. Beth Ann looked at his home and thought, *Clearly the abode of an academic. Barely living in this world.*

She came back to the recliner with the flashlight and Harrison asked her to shine it in his eyes.

"Are my pupils dilated?"

Beth Ann shook her head.

"I probably got a concussion. I'm going to need you to spend the night here," he smiled. "When someone gets a concussion they can slip into a coma in their sleep. I've had concussions before, playing soccer as a kid. This one feels pretty mild. Just spend the night here with me and maybe wake me up every few hours. Please."

"Do you have an alarm clock?"

"Yeah, in the bedroom."

Harrison invited Beth Ann to join him in bed. She gave him a few Tylenol. He chewed them with his remaining teeth. And then went to sleep, propped up by pillows, his arm wrapped around Beth Ann's waist. Hand resting on her thigh.

Beth Ann awoke to the phone ringing but she didn't pick it up.

Harrison didn't stir.

The message machine whirred on and T's voice filled the dark of the bedroom, booming out across the void like an earthquake in the distance. Beth Ann thought about picking up the phone. Interrupting the message and explaining in agonizing detail her plan to skull fuck T and grind his bones to dust. But she didn't. She let the small drama play out.

T spoke slowly, he sounded winded. He did not mention the party. Cooper. Xavier. Jeep. No intro. He just read.

"I strolled across the gravel yard and lifted my nostrils to the sky. The smell of it was still here, despite the winter frost and the setting sun. The smell of lilacs. Of honeydew and asphalt baking in the humid sun. It was a smell of cut lawns and BBQs. And it was the aura of light playing in shadows stretched taut against the playground.

"Here was where I had been beaten up by Kurt Jackson. And there, just beyond the ring of bushes, was where the troll lived. The troll with a gleaming axe. At least, that's what Jeremy Cox told me lived beyond the bushes. In third grade it was difficult to tell. When a bigger boy told you something it was most often the truth. And a troll with a gleaming axe, grinning in the underbrush, was simply too horrible not to be true.

"On the other side of the playground, by the tetherball courts that now sat empty, desolate, was where I had seen a naked woman. She was splayed out across the pages of a *Hustler* that William Knoles had brought to school. That was sixth grade and that was before Jennifer Cole got her period and had to run out of class. That was before Katrina Mendes bra came loose and her nipple peeked out from under her tight sweater. That was before boners and French kissing. It was when I was just a kid. Still dreaming about space dogfights and hurtling asteroids. Still obsessing over action figures and movies. The woman in the *Hustler* magazine was spreading her labia. Airing her vulva for the entire world to see. And it scared the hell out of me. Because it was too open. It was too pink. Too raw. And I worried that her stomach would fall out through that hole. I was worried she was hurt.

"There were no kids at the playground now. It was winter break and the field was covered in snow. But the smell was still there. I ached to know that smell on my skin. I walked over to a swing set. It was not the one I had spent my years in elementary school on. It was new, plastic and lawsuit proof. I sat and swung.

My feet scraping the gravel and reminisced. School had been good. Wonderful. Time had erased all the hardships, all the fights. Even the encounter with Travis Jackson seemed playful in my memory. It was like a game now. Not the bloody battle that it had been then. I wondered if that was how soldiers felt when they returned to the field. I wondered if time erased the wounds for them as well.

"My soul was caught up in that place. Caught swirling some-where just a few feet above the roof of Clyde Elementary school and I'd never get it down again. But I wondered what it would feel like if I could. I imagined that my youth, a dark haired sullen boy, was still at this school somewhere. I gave him a name once. Severin, a nice name. I imagined he hung out in the basement, near the furnace where the older kids liked to smoke pot? Or maybe in the closet in the arts and crafts room, the big closet that always had a dark corner? My dark sullen boy was ambivalent. Afraid and enraptured with his own imagina-tion. He was removed. Distant as a star but intelligent and wildly creative. Even going there twenty years later, Severin was still in Clyde Elementary walking the corridors and imagining he was on the moon plotting to invade the Earth.

"I stopped swinging and looked back at the field beyond the playground. The orange sunlight played tricks on the snow. Sparkling and dancing like water on the beach."

The story ended. T hung up.

Harrison sighed in his sleep, he said something like, "That's what you get."

Or maybe it was, "That's all you get." Then he rolled over and his loose teeth rattled with his labored breathing.

25

They slept for maybe an hour longer.

Harrison dreamed of a bordello like one you'd find a hundred years ago. Something right out of a Western film. In the dream Harrison walked into the bordello and was greeted by eight women lounging around naked. There was one with short peroxide blonde hair and a tear tattoo on her left cheek that walked over to Harrison and kissed him full on the lips. "Hiya," she said. "It's been way too long. We've missed you."

A black women with enormous breasts and a red afro waved and said, "We've been wondering when you'd be back, sugar." He recognized her from a porno called *African Goddess Ass Fuckers III.*

Harrison smiled and slumped into a chair at a small card table. "Sorry ladies," he said. "You know how things go . . ."

"Sure do, babe," the blonde walked over to the bar and poured Harrison a tumbler of scotch. She sashayed back, sat in his lap and placed the tumbler down on the table hard. "Drink up," she said and kissed him again. Harrison knew her from the *Blonde Meat Eaters* series.

He could feel a warm buzzing in his pants, his penis stiffening against his thigh.

Harrison took a swig of scotch and then shook his head as he swallowed, the liquid scratching his throat as it went down. The blonde leaned into him, her fingers running over his chest and up into his beard. "What'll it be?" she purred.

Harrison smiled, took another swig and finished off the scotch. "Who was I with last time?" he asked the women.

A plump brunette with purple lipstick and bright blue eye shadow and her hair slicked back like she was in that Robert Palmer video raised her hand and said, "You were with me, Harry. Had a wonderful time too. I think you came three times." That was Kristie, she was best known for her starring turn in *Fatties on Faces VII: The Puckered Starfish's Revenge*.

"Maybe I should go with two this time? Or three," Harrison laughed.

He leaned back and the blonde on his lap ran her fingers across his lips and into his hair. "It's so good to be back," he moaned and then he jerked awake. His apartment was completely dark. Beth Ann's fingers were crawling across his swollen, throbbing face.

"I think I've gone blind," Beth Ann said.

Harrison said, "The lights are just out."

"Are you sure?"

"Yeah."

Harrison flicked the side table light on.

Beth Ann sighed hard, "I can see . . . I thought for a second . . . You look worse. How do you feel?"

"Terrible."

"We should get back to my place," Beth Ann smiled. "It really isn't safe here."

Harrison nodded.

When they arrived back at Beth Ann's, Wolfgang was still knitting. Just sitting like a junkie Buddha crafting a scarf. Or a sweater. Maybe it was an afghan. It was like he'd retreated into a special place. A quiet place. A retired place. Beth Ann and Harrison had been gone hours but Wolfgang didn't seem the least bit concerned. In fact, as they walked in, he didn't even raise his head from his knitting. Beth Ann was impressed. Whatever Wolfgang was working on had a nice stitch to it.

"So, what is it?" Beth Ann asked.

Wolfgang didn't look up, "A sweater for Carla45."

"Are you on something?" Harrison asked.

"I grabbed some pills from Cooper at the party. Took them an hour or so ago. Helps."

"Knitting fucked up, how original. Well, Wolfgang, what do you suggest we do now?"

Wolfgang didn't reply.

Harrison kicked him in his shins.

"What the fuck, dude?" Wolfgang jumped up. Eyebrows arced. Fists raised. He took one look at Harrison's beat-up face and his eyes widened.

"Amanda's big brother," Harrison said slumping onto the couch.

Wolfgang sat down and went back to his knitting. Beth Ann sat on the other end of the couch and watched. The proud mother duck swooning as her ugly duckling blossomed into a swan.

Harrison asked again, "What are we going to do now?"

Wolfgang's reply was interrupted by his cell phone.

Harrison looked at him pissed and said, "Fuck Carla45, man. We don't have time for that . . ."

But it wasn't Carla45. It was an incoming call from T.

Wolfgang answered, "Hello. Yes. Hi, T."

They all crowded around the phone.

". . . to everyone. Are you alright, Wolfgang?" T sounded out of breath.

"Yes," Wolfgang said.

"Sorry you had to see that. Seriously."

"What the fuck was that, T? I thought we were friends?"

"That was business, Wolf. And business is a cut-throat thing.

You know, it's not all numbers and spreadsheets. Sometimes we need to spill a little blood here and there. You know."

"No. I don't know what the fuck you're on about, T. Who are you?"

T laughed, "I'm just who you think I am. Hot Monster."

"But you tried to convince us that Jeep was a killer. That he was taking out hipsters. That you wanted to catch him out of the goodness of your heart. Cooper's dead. Those gangsters are dead and Rad's at the hospital . . ."

Harrison punched Wolfgang in the arm. He flinched. Wolfgang looked at him, eyes all bunched up, and Harrison shook his head and mouthed, *We can't trust him.*

Harrison mouthed, *He is a killer.*

Wolfgang paused. Face red. He was exploding with frustration.

"Who are you!?" Wolfgang shouted into the phone.

"I'm a business man," T replied. "And I'm taking care of business."

That's when the front door to Beth Ann's was kicked in.

That's when they saw T, with a cell phone in one hand and a silver crossbow in the other, standing in the doorway framed by the dim light of the hallway. His left ear glowing green from the light of the phone. He was still wearing his Riffs jumpsuit.

"They have some pretty amazing tracking software these days," T said putting the cell phone in a pocket. "Downloaded this beta from Grokster just the other night. You'd be shocked with what I can do with my cell. Really. In only a few years I'll probably be able to kill you with it."

T walked in and fired a silver arrow into Harrison's left foot.

The metal pin anchored his foot to the floor. Blood oozed up out of his shoe and Harrison could distinctly feel that his pinky toe was hanging on by only a few stringy tendons. Floating in his Vans. Wolfgang and Beth Ann remained sitting. Too stunned to move.

T padded into the kitchen. Grabbed a dishtowel hanging on Beth Ann's stove and threw it to Harrison. "That'll staunch the blood," he said.

Harrison pressed the towel down hard against his foot.

"I call this Commodore 299," T said holding aloft his crossbow. "Don't ask me why. I actually designed it in middle school and that just seemed like a cool name. It is a crossbow, made of stainless steel. And what you have in your foot right now, Harrison, is a bolt. I guess I just always thought crossbows rocked. Like throwing stars and butterfly knives."

"Are you going to kill us, T?" Beth Ann asked. She had her hands folded in her lap. Harrison thought she seemed oddly calm.

"Yeah. Sorry," T gave a smile. It looked hard with his lips just barely peeling back from his teeth. A quarter-ass smile.

"Why?" Harrison asked.

T said, "Well, it's simple really. You guys failed. You fucked up. And now I've got a huge fucking mess to clean up. I don't have much time to do it. So, don't make this too rough on me."

Harrison had a funny thought that T looked exactly like T. He hadn't become some new, evil incarnation. He wasn't all crimson forehead and sweaty laughs and mystery moustache. He was the same guy that talked at length about Animal Collective and collecting back issues of *Thrasher*. The same guy. Just now shooting him in the foot with a crossbow. That made the whole thing infuriating. T had been playing the Whole Sick Crew for years. Using them. Manipulating them. And the more he thought about that, the angrier he got.

Harrison balled his hand into a fist and thought about leaping up. Letting his pinky toe fly off in a rush of gore and beating the hell out of T. But he knew T was fast and that any attempt would end with his getting a bolt between the eyes.

Harrison decided to wait.

"T, what is this?" Wolfgang was tired. He looked weak. He

hadn't had his hand blasted apart like Rad's. He didn't have a
bolt in his foot like Harrison. But he looked the worst. He was
worn thin as bone.

"What can I tell you, Wolf? It's capitalism. I feed the machine
and it feeds me. You have to stop being human to succeed in
America. You leave all that at home and at the office."

T moved closer to Beth Ann. The crossbow only inches from
her face.

"I'm really sorry about this, honestly. But it's all in a day's
work," T said. He took a long, deep breath in.

That's when Beth Ann shot him.

She'd pulled Lil' Chris' gun out of her pocket and pushed it
into his stomach and pulled the trigger. All before he could let
out his air.

T fell to the ground beside Harrison and Beth Ann was flattened back against the couch.

The crossbow discharged. The bolt slipped into the ceiling.
Bits of plaster rained down. Then he let his breath out and with
it a stream of blood that pooled on his chin.

Harrison leaned over to look into T's eyes.

His chest rattled, a serpent of intestine bulged through the
gap in his jumpsuit. His legs lay splayed at odd angles like his
spine had been severed. He began mumbling. Oozing words.

"Ondscan . . ."

"What's Ondscan?" Wolfgang asked.

"It's a fucking enormous corporation," Harrison said.

"What?"

T smiled with red teeth. ". . . closely held transnational corporation . . . And I sold all of you to them . . . collapsing new
people . . ."

T coughed.

"The Fold," T continued. ". . . assault politics, black ops . . .
murder."

"What is he saying?" Harrison asked Beth Ann.

She shook her head.

T continued between convulsions, ". . . . hell riders. The mad motor monsters. We're The Fold. . . . sociopathic proclivities . . . killers in ties . . ."

"Jeep?" Harrison asked.

T's eyes were closed. For a second they thought he had died but then he spoke again.

"Alistair... Do you... remember meeting me, Harris...?"

Harrison did. He remembered being at a club with Cooper. He didn't think much of T at the time. The guy seemed eager to ingratiate himself. Seemed opportunistic and clingy. Neither of which were traits Harrison was particularly fond of. Both pissed him off. But T had a winning smile and he did have a cool alibi as to why he lived in a multimillion dollar mansion and drove a Mercedes. He was a success story. Someone who could afford to just hang out and talk about vinyl obscurities.

Beth Ann was biting her knuckles. She was uncomfortable being there. Watching T die. She found it exasperating and poignant at the same time.

". . . battle talk . . . Fluke . . . smile for Mother and Father . . ."

"Who are Mother and Father?" Wolfgang asked with urgency.

T was fading. Draining. Paling.

He was seeing something beyond them.

"Harrison, it's all . . . the message . . . it's all about . . . when you're young, you shine . . ."

And he died. He let out a big sigh and creased in.

26

It took Harrison twenty minutes to slowly pull his foot from the floor.

He didn't lose his pinky toe but it was just barely hanging on. Just tendon and a long, thin nerve fiber holding it together. And Harrison said the exposed nerve burned like a three-alarm fire if even the slightest draft coasted across its glistening white surface. Beth Ann wrapped Harrison's foot in towels and then searched T's pockets. She felt nauseous the whole time.

"He drove," Harrison said. "We should take his car."

Beth Ann found T's car keys and his wallet. Before they left she flipped through it and a folded paper fell out. It was a photograph.

Six people, including T, standing in front of well-groomed junipers. Everyone smiling. It looked like a graduation picture. T was the second in from the right. He was wearing a suit and tie. Looked great. Younger, thinner. To his left was Paul Achting, the comic book guru, all dimples and hair. Beth Ann had seen his photo in the news. To his right was Xavier, smiling his brightest smile. Next to Xavier was Swank, a younger, more starving artist Swank, looking dapper in a fedora and a camel-hair coat. To Swank's right was a tall, lanky guy with a mohawk. And last was Veniss standing topless, her boobs all done up like eyes, with thick black lashes painted on, a wide black smile painted on her belly.

Beth Ann showed the photo to Harrison.

Harrison looked at it and said, "Are you serious?"

"Let me see," Wolfgang grabbed the photo and turned pale.

"Are you kidding me? What the fuck is this? They all know each other? Seriously. Paul and T and Swank, all of them are here. What is this? Some sort of graduation picture? This looks like a fucking graduation picture. I'll bet all these fuckers went to school together. They were killing each other . . ."

Wolfgang looked close at the photo. Close at the guy with a mohawk.

"I know that mutherfucker," he said. "That's Fluke."

"What else can you tell us?" Harrison asked.

"You interrupted me last time. I was gonna tell you more about him," Wolfgang said annoyed. "He's a pirate radio guru and a big roller in the gore rap scene. Produced albums for groups like Gut Muncherzz, Nekkrofunk and Skull Fuckerz. That scene was too sick for me. Most of the hardcore fans I'd met who got into the stuff were freebasing ashes and into whipping and bondage gear. They were the people that you read about molesting cats and desecrating graveyards. People who ended each weekend covered in vomit and bruises. Sick fuckies. That and he hangs out in the sewer."

"So, he's the one to talk to, right?" Beth Ann said.

"What the fuck do you mean?" Wolfgang spat. "I just got through telling you that he's a psycho who hangs out in the fucking sewer. Why would we want to find him?"

"He's in on all this. I say we track his ass down. He and Jeep are the only ones still alive. We've got a gun. Let's surprise his ass. We just go talk to him."

"What if he's a killer too?" Harrison asked.

"The comic book dude. Swank. Veniss. Xavier. They were all in on this and they weren't threatening," Beth Ann said. "There are three of us. We've got a gun. Let's find him. It's time to leave. Cops will be here."

There was the not so small problem of T's body. Beth Ann didn't want it sinking into her hardwood.

"But you're the one who shot him," Wolfgang complained.

Beth Ann didn't even acknowledge that Wolfgang had spoken. She put her hands on her hips, "Will someone please help me get rid of it?"

"How?" Harrison asked.

"Chop it up?" Beth Ann suggested.

"Like we have that much time," Wolfgang said. "You're just going to have to deal, Beth Ann. We can't do anything with this body right now. I mean, for Christ's sake, he was our friend."

"At least move it out onto the fire escape or something," Beth Ann protested.

And they did. All three of them helped drag T's body out onto the fire escape and then Beth Ann draped a linen sheet over it. She threw some perfume on it too.

"Just in case," Beth Ann said.

Harrison leaned outside, pressed T's electronic car key lock. A car's lights flashed. T drove a Mercedes. Blue.

"Now we have a car. Where are we going to go?" Wolfgang asked.

Beth Ann said, "Let's see Fluke."

Harrison, his eyes swollen, lips black and runny, asked, "How about tomorrow. We can go somewhere and rest. At least let things die down a little bit more. Fuck, Beth Ann, Jeep could be right around the corner."

"Alright, I know someone in Riverdale we could stay with. Her name's Solange."

It was a long drive to the Bronx. Wolfgang drove slowly. The sun peeked over the horizon. Beth Ann said it was beautiful.

Harrison spent the drive pressing the towels on his foot. The bleeding had stopped. Now it was just a big numb throbbing mass. Wolfgang had some hash and Harrison smoked it and felt a bit better. The edge was off.

"So, anyone want to put the pieces together?" Beth Ann asked around Port Morris.

"I couldn't even begin," Wolfgang said. "This is surely the most fucked-up shit. No one could make this shit up. It's just so Hollywood."

"They're like corporate killers or something. I mean, the whole thing seemed like a battle for turf. Like T set up Jeep to stake a claim but it went bad. And all that stuff that T was mumbling about. I'd guess he was talking about the same business," Harrison said.

"What kind of business? Sounded more like espionage and Santeria to me," Beth Ann said.

"Yeah, all the shit about black magic. I think it was just nonsense. He was dying and babbling," Wolfgang said.

"Ondscan. He did say he worked for Ondscan, right?" Beth Ann said.

Harrison said, "He did."

"Remind me what Ondscan is," Wolfgang asked.

"Ondscan is one of the largest multinational corporations in the world," Harrison said. "They basically own a part of every media outlet. Every record label. Alcoholic beverage. Publishing company. Film studio. If you've got high speed Internet access, cell phones, microwaveable meals, spandex running shorts, coffee table picture books, CDs by any band with the word 'The' in their title, chances are Ondscan has something to do with it."

"So, maybe T and Jeep are like corporate assassins? They kill for Ondscan," Wolfgang grinned.

Beth Ann said, "That makes some queasy sense."

"But why would they do that?" Harrison asked. "What's the use of that?"

"To instill fear in rivals, to punish whistleblowers, to make sure deals go through, mergers and acquisitions . . ." Wolfgang replied.

"So, what did we decide to do after we rest?" Beth Ann asked. She got no answers.

By the time they got to Solange's place in Riverdale, Harrison was passed out again. Solange was a bit taken aback seeing the threesome, all clad in jumpsuits and tarred with blood, grease and fur. She asked a thousand questions a minute.

"Beth Ann, what the fuck happened? Who are these guys? Is that fur? Is that blood? Why are you wearing jumpsuits? Is this the guy?"

She led them into her shabby basement one bedroom festooned with rugs and tapestries, black lights and beaded pillows, like a cheap opium den. A large black velvet painting of Jesus cradling snow leopard cubs hung on the wall above a futon. Beth Ann hadn't been there before. She thought it looked bad. She quietly worried that Solange had gotten into something terrible. Heroin. Prostitution. Something. But she figured Solange's being a Ukrainian stripper probably explained most of it.

"What the fuck is going on? Were you in an accident?" Solange wheezed. She was wearing a night gown that emphasized her stunning cleavage. But she had thrown a ratty dressing gown over it. Beth Ann thought she looked like a supermodel in homeless clothes.

"Yes and no," Beth Ann replied.

Wolfgang made a half-hearted attempt to introduce himself before crashing on a leopard print loveseat. Harrison didn't bother with formalities. He curled up on the floor in a pile of fuzzy, furry and beaded throw rugs.

Beth Ann sat down at the kitchen table with Solange. Solange held her hands and asked if she needed tea.

Beth Ann nodded, "Thanks."

"Sure," Solange kissed Beth Ann on the cheek and got up.

Solange boiled the water on a small range. The tea was something Russian. It smelled of lilacs and vanilla. Solange placed a
steaming cup into Beth Ann's bloodstained hands and said,
matter-of-factly, "You should probably tell me what's going on."

"Yeah," Beth Ann yawned. "I suppose I should."

"Is that him? The one sleeping on the floor?"

"Yeah. That's Harrison."

"He's cute. Well, he's pretty messed up but he looks cute
under all those bruises."

"I suppose I should tell you everything. But it's complicated
and it's not pretty. It's really very ugly, Solange. Very ugly and I
don't think you'd be happy with me."

Solange said, "Go on."

And Beth Ann told her. She told her everything from meeting Harrison at the Slaughtered Lamb to running into him at
Arcadia. She told Solange how the plan came into being. The
jumpsuits. The drugs. She told Solange about Lil' Chris. Tank.
The blood. The beast. T's deception. The story ended with
confusion and exhaustion. It ended with Beth Ann sobbing uncontrollably.

"It's on the news," Solange said as she ran her fingers
through Beth Ann's hair. "The cops found the bodies at your
friend's apartment. They also found a baboon in the street.
They're out there looking for you guys. This is really, really
deep shit."

Beth Ann looked at Solange and shook her head.

She mouthed, *Please. No.*

"Yes. You should probably turn yourselves in. Now. Before it
gets worse."

"The worst part," Beth Ann said through her body breaking
sobs, "is that mutherfucker is still out there. Doctor Jeep is still
alive. We've talked about running but we can't. We talked
about turning ourselves in but then our lives will be over.
Solange, this has to end here. With us. This has to end now.
Something so fucked up is going on here. The cops don't know

shit. No one knows shit. This will all probably be whitewashed in the press by Monday. It'll look like me and Harrison and the other guys just went nuts. Took too many drugs. Went insane. Or they'll make it look like we were some terrorist gang that . . . I don't know. I just know that we're the only ones who know . . ."

"What are you going to do?"

"Please, Solange, let us stay here and think for a little while. Just a few minutes is all," Beth Ann put her head on the table. She thought about closing her eyes for a second. Just long enough to make the flashing in the corners go away.

She awoke four hours later at the kitchen table. Harrison was shaking her. Solange was sleeping, head on the table, across from her. Eyes closed. Angelic.

"Wolfgang's gone," Harrison said.

Beth Ann's ears were clogged with sleep.

"What time is it?" she asked.

"It's 10 a.m. and that mutherfucker's gone!" Harrison shouted.

27

Wolfgang stopped for a breath at Washington Square Park. He had parked T's car five blocks away. The air was too cold and his body too weak for running.

He sat at a park bench beneath the steely gaze of the NYU library. Black like a soldier's helmet against the overcast sky. Dogs yipped and yapped in the dog park. Chasing each other and snapping at their owners' hands. Despite a thousand years of incestuous interbreeding, these little runts still had the cunning of the wolf locked in their steps. Watching them chase each other around, sniff each other's butts and piss on everything, reminded Wolfgang of the party. It reminded him of Doctor Jeep spraying the room with bullets. He cringed at the memory of Faggot chewing off Xavier's face.

Thinking of Carla45's cool smile calmed him down.

Wolfgang needed desperately to see her. He needed the warmth he was sure she had. Her smile. The soft touch that must be there. Wolfgang's guts were knotted. They coiled around each other like eels at the bottom of a waterfall. Churning together. Clinging to each other for support. He knew it was only anxiety and anger. And he knew that if he didn't see Carla45 soon, didn't have her in his arms, then his guts would eat him alive.

He left the park and its yipping dogs. The apprehension of an unknown future was killing him. He picked up his pace as he rounded Astor Place. Wolfgang was done. He was so fucking done. *From now on,* he thought, *it's just me and Carla45. From now on, it's just that simple.*

Wolfgang arrived at Pasquales and pushed his way to the back where he assumed he'd find a gorgeous black woman sipping red wine at a table for two beneath a potted palm just like Carla45 had text messaged. And he did find a table for two. And it was under a potted palm. But Carla45 wasn't sitting there.

Doctor Jeep was.

He was wearing a black T-shirt with a picture of Carla45 on it. The picture of Carla45's gorgeous smile that sat on Wolfgang's desk. The very same picture that kept Wolfgang's heart beating. That kept him alive.

Wolfgang sat down at the table, his mouth open. He couldn't speak. The words were caught up in the churning of his guts. The rage billowing behind his eyes.

New Order's "Subculture" was rippling out over the smoke and laughter. The music ebbed into plates of ravioli and spaghetti. Wolfgang found it hard not to hum along to the song, while his sanity crashed down around him.

"Hello Wolfgang. Or is it WolfChant?" Doctor Jeep asked. His voice was surprisingly gentle. Almost warm. "You're wondering why I'm here and why I'm wearing a photo of Carla's face on my shirt. Those are great questions. But I'm afraid you're not going to like the truth of it."

"You sick fuck," Wolfgang felt the words mix with bile in his throat.

"I'm afraid you're the sick one, Wolfgang."

"You pervert. Have you been chatting with me? Saying those

things . . ." Wolfgang gagged. He thought about the sex talk. He thought about the countless times he'd imagined Carla45, the one on the T-shirt, kissing him, fucking him. Now that beautiful black woman's face was on Jeep's slight frame. Wolfgang gagged again.

"I'm not a pervert. I caught you in my trap."

"What has this got to do with her? With Carla45. You didn't hurt her . . ."

"Oh, no. Only met her once. She's actually a secretary for someone I worked with. I think her name is Janice or something. Heard she's a nice gal. Found this photo on her desk and made a copy of it."

". . . the things she said?"

"Me. Good actor, I suppose."

"Sickening."

"Yeah. And it's true isn't it? I know it's true 'cause you trusted me. You fell for Carla hook, line and sinker."

"Carla45," Wolfgang corrected.

Doctor Jeep laughed, "You really have no fucking idea what this is all about do you? And the worst part of it is you really couldn't be fucked to care."

Wolfgang took a quick look over his shoulder at the restaurant. There were seven people behind him. Chatting. Eating. All oblivious. He thought about how easy it would be to get up from the table and walk out. Walk away from the nightmare. But his coils of gut wouldn't let him. They hadn't gotten their fill of Carla45. They hadn't smelled her sweet sweat. Now they wanted revenge. Now Wolfgang wanted revenge. He wanted blood.

"I'm going to kick your scrawny fucking ass. I'm going to tear your tongue out and shove it so far up your skinny white ass that you'll be licking the back of your fucking throat," Wolfgang hissed.

"That's a new one. You probably could too. You seem pretty mad. But take a look under the table. This is Greedo shit right here."

Wolfgang pushed his chair back and bent down. Peered under the tabletop.

He saw Doctor Jeep's legs. Black leather bondage pants. And Jeep's left hand, the fingers coiled around a gun. A very odd looking big black gun.

"It's a functional weapon. It's a modified blaster pistol. I had a Star Wars geek design it and then I had it manufactured on spec."

Despite the dire situation, Wolfgang's interest got the better of him and he asked, "Does it fire a laser?"

"No," Jeep replied. "That would be really freakin' cool, though."

There was a pause. Both men envisioned the Greedo gun firing a laser and both men smiled at the thought of it. Jeep broke the momentary tranquility and said, "It does fire a high caliber round. Enough to open you up and spill you out. There is a silencer on it, of course. No one will hear you die."

Wolfgang's gut worms pulsed.

"You're going to just shoot me here in front of these people? What if I jump up right now and scream? You'd just shoot?"

"Yeah. This is what I do. I might get caught. Might not. But you'll be dead as a doornail none-the-less."

Wolfgang settled into his seat. He wanted to vomit.

"Do you want something to eat?" Doctor Jeep offered.

Wolfgang didn't answer.

"I had the pastrami on rye, excellent."

Wolfgang said, "What the fuck are we doing?"

"Well, it's like in the movies. I'm going to talk to you and tell you why I've gotten you trapped and what I plan on doing next. You're going to act shocked and appalled. And then you'll probably die."

Wolfgang blinked. The first time he'd felt himself blink since he sat down.

"Here's the scoop: T tried to fuck me the other night. You were there. You know how it all went down. I want you to tell me where T is."

"He's dead. Dead as a fucking doornail."

"You're kidding?"

"No."

"Who killed him?"

"We did."

"Seriously?"

"Yeah. He tried to ambush us with a crossbow. We shot him."

"T was always a bit of a romantic. Always obsessing over toys and trinkets. His whole fascination with his youth . . . Poor fucker."

"Tell me why you did this. Why me?"

"It's in my nature. Just a funny link of coincidence. Maybe even synchronicity. I wanted to kill someone with your background. Someone in a band that hadn't really broke. I killed Jakus. That was too easy. I wanted someone with an interesting background who was a bit more obscure. I tracked you across the net. Found you in the chatroom. Lured you in. T had mentioned his little group of friends. He mentioned a guy in a band. You can imagine my surprise seeing you at that party. I could barely contain myself. Even thought about killing you there. But that was just a passing thought. Really would have ruined the fun . . ."

"You weren't in the photo. The graduation photo in T's wallet."

"Aren't you the clever boy," Jeep was taken aback. "You've been playing detective."

Wolfgang smiled, "Yeah, mutherfucker, and you're so fucking . . ."

But Wolfgang couldn't finish.

There was a soft crack. Like a pistol being fired underwater. A firecracker on a mountaintop. Wolfgang felt a sudden pressure in his stomach. It wasn't gas. Not his churning guts. The look of Doctor Jeep's face was one of muted enjoyment.

Wolfgang slowly sunk to the floor. Blood spilling in waves from a gaping hole in his stomach. Doctor Jeep didn't bother staying to watch Wolfgang bleed to death beneath the table. He left the waitress a fifty and quietly exited the restaurant.

28

Harrison knew immediately where Wolfgang had gone. "He fucking went to meet up with Carla45," Harrison slammed his fists into one of Solange's beaded pillows. "And he took T's car to do it! Fucking idiot!"

He kicked and threw things.

He tried Wolfgang's cell for the hundredth time, then threw Solange's phone across the room where it landed in a pile of high-heeled stripper shoes. Harrison sat down and asked Solange for a smoke.

"I'm sorry," he said.

Beth Ann walked over to him, rubbed his shoulders. She said, "Maybe he'll come back."

"No. He's gone."

Solange went to work. She swore, on her life, that she wouldn't tell anyone. She suggested they just hide out in her place. She said, "My house is your house."

Harrison tried Wolfgang's cell every fifteen minutes. Nothing. Nothing. Nothing. Nothing. He grew despondent. Beth Ann tried to cheer him up by dancing. She put on some of Solange's more outrageous outfits. She swayed seductively and hummed Adam Ant's "Strip."

She rubbed her small breasts and sang, "We're just following ancient history . . ."

"If I strip for you, will you strip for me?" She smacked her ass and laughed.

Harrison smiled for the first time in hours.

He got up and danced with her.

They sang together, louder now, "We're just following ancient history. Ah, ha, ha."

Harrison paused to grab some lipstick from a pile of cosmetics on a dresser. He looked in the bathroom mirror and put a wide line across his face, just under his eyes.

"What do you think baby?"

"Ouch, just like Adam."

They danced and hummed. And they stripped. Soon they were naked. They lay on the floor holding each other beneath as many of Solange's blankets and pillows as they could assemble. They lay naked together in a nest of fabrics. They didn't talk. There really wasn't much to say. They just kissed and fondled each other.

Beth Ann said, "You know, Solange is my ex. Did I ever tell you that? I mean, I know we've only known each other a few days."

"No. Bisexual, huh?"

"Yeah. I guess. It really wasn't like that."

"A few days ago, I would have found that really sexy."

"A few days ago?"

"Yeah. Now I don't want to think of anyone else having you. Touching you."

They kissed. Beth Ann was gentle on Harrison's battered lips. Her tongue avoiding the gaps and scabs in his gums.

They held each other until Harrison got up to pee. When he came back he sat down across from Beth Ann and smiled to her.

She tried to speak.

He shushed her. "Don't say anything."

"I need to," Beth Ann said. "Sorry."

"What?"

"What the fuck are we going to do?"

"Nothing. We'll just live here with your ex-lover and fashion clothes from these blankets and pillows and shit."

"No, seriously, Harrison."

Harrison shrugged, "We're going to leave."

"And then?"

"And then we'll get coffee. And maybe smoke. I don't know. Honestly, Beth Ann, I have no fucking idea what we should do next. We can run for our lives. Hope the cops or the killers don't get us. Live like fugitives and hope to make it to Mexico or Liberia or something. Or we can find that Fluke guy. And maybe force him to help us stop all this."

Beth Ann nodded.

"I think I know how to find him," Beth Ann said calmly.

"Wait! You do? Why the fuck didn't you mention that earlier?"

"I wasn't sure if that's what we wanted to do. I mean, the guy I know who might know Fluke, he's a friend. I didn't want to drag him into this, I guess. I just don't want anyone else to get involved. To get hurt. We've already dragged Solange into this. I couldn't live with myself if anything happened to her. That's why we need to stop this now. Kill all these mutherfuckers."

"Okay," Harrison said, "I don't care if this guy is a maniac like T or Jeep. If he sleeps with a bazooka and scalps his fucking victims. You're right. We've got nothing else to lose. We need to end this shit. We can't just hide in these fucking blankets for the rest of our lives."

Beth Ann pulled on some of Solange's down-time clothes. Sweatpants. An orange sweater. Harrison found some men's jeans. A black T-shirt that read MATH IS FOR GIRLS. They stuffed the filthy jumpsuits into a duffel bag and then walked through freezing drizzle to the 225th Street station.

"So, who is this guy?" Harrison asked, breathing hard in the ice air.

"Just a friend. His name is Jorge. He's a sludge diver."

They stopped and got coffee at a little joint near the station. Beth Ann called Jorge and gave Harrison a thumbs up. "He does know Fluke. And he's looking forward to meeting you. You guys have a lot in common."

"What? Was he your lover too?"

"No. You'll see."

29

They met up with Jorge at a pizza joint on Roebling an hour and a half later.

Jorge was tall. Thin. As gangly as a spider, with a large fro of black hair sitting atop his pencil head like a dark cream puff.

"What's going on, Beth Ann?" Jorge asked kissing Beth Ann's cheek. He had a thick Puerto Rican accent.

Beth Ann introduced Harrison. She told Jorge they were in serious shit and she needed to get ahold of someone called Fluke.

"Yeah, like I told you before, I've heard about him. He's technically not in the sewers. He lives in a treatment plant here in Brooklyn. I have no idea what he does down there. This is all from a friend of a friend," Jorge said. "I won't ask you about your dirt. But let me tell you, if I bring you to this guy you're gonna owe me big time."

Beth Ann smiled at Harrison.

"What's that mean?" Harrison asked.

"Well, that's what I was going to tell you. See, Jorge here is what you'd call an amateur anthropologist. He's obsessed. But he also happens to be a sludge diver. The only guy who can get us into the sewers. Or wherever it is that Fluke hangs out. Jorge spends his week toiling away as a scuba instructor on Long Island but he spends his nights and weekends sludge diving. He's a fucking professional."

Jorge smiled, "I wear a specially designed wet suit. Comes complete with a full Captain Nemo helmet. I dive at water treatment plants. Sewage treatment plants. Toxic waste dumps. Runoff ditches. The water that me and my crew submerse ourselves in is really nasty. Rotten. Most of it cut with enough feces that it's nearly solid."

When Harrison asked, Jorge could not say how exactly he got into the "field." He just said he was attracted to the taboo of sludge diving and the sheer dicey-ness of it.

"You need bigger balls than the average bear, *puta,*" Jorge said. He added, "That means whore."

Jorge, Harrison learned quickly, only cursed in Spanish. And he had the annoying habit of translating every cuss word he uttered right after he said it.

"Yeah, it's a fucking adventure, man. It's like going to the moon."

"Sure. Whatever gets you off, Jorge," Harrison jabbed.

"It does. But I'm not just an action guy. I read a lot. I like to challenge the mainstream. I like to mix it up and question authority. Human evolution is my particular interest."

Just as Beth Ann had hinted at, besides the sludge diving and cursing in Spanish, Jorge was infatuated with quack anthropology. He religiously read *Fate* and *Fortean Times.* Studied works that Harrison recognized immediately as New Age bullshit. He ascribed to theories of human evolution that were so outlandish the very mention of them made Harrison's bowels quake.

"Let's get to why we're here," Harrison said desperate to avoid a conversation.

"Ah, ah, ah," Jorge waved a finger, "I can get you to this Fluke dude but first I want to talk to you about some theories I have. Let's do a little quid pro quo here, bro. I'll agree to help you out. But you've got to listen to what I have to say. And you've got to *listen* seriously. Really think about it and not just blow it off."

"I'm not sure we have time for this. Maybe we can talk about it after we get back from seeing Fluke?"

"What's the rush?"

Harrison looked to Beth Ann to back him up. She just shrugged.

He got up and pulled her aside, "Are you fucking kidding me? You're going to make me sit down and talk to this fucking guy about craziness?"

Beth Ann glared at him and said, "This fucking guy is a friend of mine. This is the only way we're going to get into a fucking sewer. This is it."

"Did you at least mention to him that I'm not an anthropologist and that I am an extreme rationalist?"

Beth Ann nodded.

"Alrighty then."

Harrison took a long deep breath. Let it out through his nose. He sat back down and turned to Jorge, "This is going to be really painful isn't it?"

Jorge nodded, "You bet, *pinche pito de pitufo.* That means Smurf dick."

"Seriously though, if you even start in on that bullshit about aquatic apes I'm gonna throw a beer at your head."

"No aquatic apes. This is even better," Jorge's eyebrows danced.

"Great."

Harrison settled into his chair, lit a cigarette and took a deep drag. Jorge slicked back his hair as though he were a racecar driver jumping into the hot seat.

"Have you ever heard of Oscar Kiss Maerth?"

"Kiss-my-ass?" Harrison joked.

"Come on, man. I'm trying to be serious."

"No, I haven't."

"Well, you probably should know him. He wrote a huge fucking book in the 1960s called *The Beginning Is the End.* I think you'll appreciate this hypothesis."

"Yeah, I'm sure I will."

"So, the story is simple: We're in a state of evolutionary decline. Devolution if you will."

"Like Devo?"

"Exactly, that's exactly right. Where did you think the band got its name? Its ideas? That whole thing was a bunch of art students trying to shock people and be different. So they grabbed a copy of the book and ran with it. They decided to just make it crazy. That was the '70s man, punk rock and all. *Jocko Homo.* It was all devolution . . ."

"So what is it? Just break it to me straight, Jorge."

"The idea is cannibalism. That's the key. We never evolved from apes to ape-men. That's just absurd . . ."

"And the fossil record?"

"Those aren't ancestors. Those are contemporaries."

"Ridiculous. But continue."

Jorge paused. It was a pregnant pause. A pause that needed, no, demanded an apology. Harrison had crossed the line. He had insulted Jorge already and now he had to pay. The pause was long and bad. Silence flooded in making it that much more difficult to resume. For the apology to stick.

"Sorry," Harrison said.

That wasn't going to work. It was too easy.

"Look, really, I'm sorry. I'm being an asshole. I'm interested. No, really, I'm interested. Please."

Harrison knew it always took a please.

"Alright. But this is the last time," Jorge said. "I'm only going to start once again and then if you interrupt with some snide ass comment I'm going to stop. And you can forget Fluke. Clear?"

6 SICK HIPSTERS 225

"Crystal."

"So, Maerth's book suggests that humans didn't evolve from apes but started over a period of millions of years to devolve into people. I can't really recall if it's millions of years. It may have been thousands, but the point is that it is what happened. And how? I'm sure you're just itching to know."

Harrison nodded. Not the right place for a joke.

"Cannibalism. But more importantly, eating brains. Eating gray matter is what leads to devolution. Apes started eating apes. They became lunatic geniuses. Mad with hunger—for power and destruction—and one thing led to the next and they were splitting open skulls and emptying the content into their gullets. Disgusting and altering.

"The eating of brains caused a whole host of changes to result. The bigger brain. The fur loss. The so-called intelligence. It's all on account of an addiction for consumption of brains. And their offspring were addicted to brains too. And it went on and on and devolution continued until the apes became men, and the men were the baser of the species. According to Maerth the social classes as they are set up today are a direct result of this. Everything results from brain eating. Even smelly armpits. Genesis' story of the Tree of Knowledge is not about an apple. It's about the skull. Eve ate the brain . . ."

Harrison had to interrupt there, "What evidence is there for this?"

"Maerth says that there are many skeletons. Skeletons with their heads removed and skulls opened and brains obviously removed hungrily . . ."

"Removed hungrily?"

"Yeah, that's what the evidence suggests."

"You're just not thinking clearly, Jorge. This whole thing. This whole anthropology thing is science. You're talking about paleontology and anthropology and anthropophagi and you can't just read this stuff and assume it's true. I'll admit, Jorge, it's a fascinating idea. And I can see how it could be compelling.

"The idea that we're not the highest evolved life form around is not a new idea, and it doesn't take apes to show us our faults. Men are impulsive. Violent. Racist. Nasty beasts. And just because we've invented God to convince us that we're actually not that far from divine, doesn't mean that we don't act hideously most of the time. Maerth is just picking up the sentiments we've always had. Look at insects. They function in societies as functional as humans. Why not say that we've devolved from them? It's just as ridiculous."

"I knew you were going to shoot it down."

Harrison felt bad. He felt like the bully at school who popped the little kids' balloons and stole their lunch money. But when it came to science he couldn't let someone get carried away with ridiculous assumptions about the world.

"I'm sorry, Jorge. But I wanted to be honest with you. It's really a crazy fantasy idea. I feel totally bad for shooting down your devolution thing. I really did listen, but the fact is there really isn't evidence for any of that."

"Sure, *puto*," Jorge said before turning to Beth Ann. "This guy seems to know his shit. I approve."

Harrison said, "Now how about Fluke."

Jorge sighed, "I said I heard of Fluke. But I haven't heard 'bout him in a while. But I really doubt he's moved."

"Great, we'll take a chance. Where is he?"

"The Newtown Creek Treatment Plant."

"And chances are he's there now?" Harrison asked.

Jorge said, "Sure."

"Good," Beth Ann said. "Let's do this."

30

Beth Ann and Harrison soon realized that doing "this" involved a great deal more than just walking over to the plant and rapping on the door.

They ate a dinner of steamed mussels and talked about the intricacies of sludge diving over a dessert of frozen yogurt and chocolate malt powder in Jorge's small apartment on 13th. Jorge had to clarify that it normally took years for someone to be ready to sludge dive.

"This is not going to be like a tropical dive. You're going into a river of shit and piss. A river of bacteria and intestinal parasites. This is toxic waste, my friend. Let me tell you what happens when a plant worker falls into the soup. They rush his ass to the ER and scrub his body raw, literally scrubbing away the top layer of skin everywhere. I mean in his ears. Between his toes. His ball sack. His eyelids. They call it being, 'baptized.' It's that toxic."

"Hence the wet suits," Harrison said.

"They aren't just wet suits. Shit, *cabron*, these are heavy-duty rubber suits. With leather over layers of rubber. This is the stuff they wear when they clean out nuclear power plant cooling tanks. Just letting you know what this is going to be like. You won't see anything. Just the filth a few inches away from your headlamp. It will be like swimming in mud. The going will be rough. You'll be sore as fuck tomorrow."

"How much these suits cost?"

"About 10K apiece."

Harrison was shocked, "Where'd you score the cash for that?"

"I have side jobs," Jorge made the universal sign for cashing a roach.

Harrison and Beth Ann slept, curled together like puppies, on Jorge's couch. At midnight Jorge roused them and they took his beat-up 1972 Chevy Cheyenne pickup to the drop-off point. Jorge parked on a side road a few hundred feet from the plant, pulled out blueprints and laid them on the dash.

"You've both done this before, right?" Jorge asked.

"What, scuba dived in a sewer? No," Beth Ann answered.

"No, scuba dived, *maldito,*" Jorge rephrased.

Harrison looked at Beth Ann, she gave him thumbs up. "Bermuda. Spring break in college," she said.

Harrison said he'd scuba dived with his folks in Australia. It was their one international family trip. Ten years ago. And he added that he sucked at it.

"Alright," Jorge said, "here's the pipe we're going to enter in on. When this sewage pipe enters the plant there is basically a grate. Bars that go across the pipe. That's how they catch rags and shit that floats down. We're gonna have to cut through it. Cutting pipe is always a sure sign of infiltration and we could get in some huge trouble. But sounds like we don't have a choice. Other than calling the police and letting them come . . ."

"And what would be the fun of that?" Beth Ann smirked.

". . . right, we wouldn't want to do that. It's much more fun breaking and entering. Anyway, after we cut through the pipe we'll swim into the plant where the pumps lift the water out for the settling tanks. That's where we'll get out and find your man."

"Have you actually been?" Beth Ann asked.

"It's been years." Jorge bulldozed on, "Now, every plant has night staff. There will be security guards and workers. But it'll be a skeleton crew. My pal Tommy Mantlo works the night shift there. I gave him a call while you were sleeping and told him what we were doing."

Harrison threw his hands up in disbelief, "You told someone what we were doing? What the fuck, man!"

"Don't worry," Jorge took offense. "I told him that I was training you. That we were just gonna swim in. He offered to move the catch bars for us but I told him not to bother. I don't want him in trouble, too. Better that it look like a break-in. Anyway, he told me that there would be a crew of three dudes there and that they'd be spending most of their time patrolling the grounds outside the plant. They check on the inside a quarter after, and it takes them about twenty minutes to do the full loop. So as long as we're in and out of the water before the hour we should be fine."

"How do you think Fluke got in there? With armed guards at the gates and all," Harrison asked.

"Money, *vato.*"

"And what about leaving?" Harrison asked.

"Same way we came in."

"You're coming in, Jorge."

"I'd rather not. I'll just show you where to go."

"Bullshit. No, you're coming."

Jorge sighed.

Harrison asked, "It's easy, right?"

"Right, right. You ready?"

"I suppose. Let's smoke a cigarette first."

Beth Ann and Harrison stepped out of Jorge's truck and stared out at the treatment plant just a few blocks south. Sparkling in the crisp night.

"Oh yeah, I got these suits wired for sound," Jorge called from the truck. "I've sewn a cheap little MP3 player into each one. When you turn your helmet on, the MP3s will play. I've loaded them with some sweet funk. You'll love it."

Harrison paused, "I should tell you that we'll be bringing a gun."

"What?" Jorge coughed.

"A gun. This won't be your usual dive," Beth Ann said.

"Right, *pendejo*. That means asshole," Harrison added.

Jorge looked really nervous. He looked nervous suiting up and he looked nervous getting in. It was like he suddenly realized that this wasn't just a nasty extreme sport anymore. That Harrison and Beth Ann were in on this for more than sick kicks. And his nervousness threatened to spread like contagion.

"He's making me anxious," Harrison said as they suited up in the middle of the street like ghetto astronauts.

Beth Ann kissed him. "Just keep cool, babe."

They entered a manhole in the street roped to each other. There was very little light in the pipe, just a diffuse haze from the open manhole above. They walked for a few yards along a concrete platform splattered with years of sewage and then entered the brown stream where the platform ended. The stuff was up to their hips at first. Then shoulders. Then masks. Both Harrison and Beth Ann took unnecessary deep breaths and then submerged into the deep end of the shit pool. They flicked on their helmet lights and music—Jorge's '70s funk sputtered to life in the helmet's cheap speakers.

Harrison quickly realized that sludge diving was not like scuba diving.

The pipe was narrow, they had to crawl on their hands and knees and there was nothing to see. Moving through the fast slime was more akin to sleeping than swimming. He knew he was crawling forward but he didn't really feel it. Through the tight glass plate in his helmet he saw only his own reflection and green-brown ooze, a thick broth that tumbled and turned like sand in surf. Never settling out but never fully mixing either. It was like being in a warm womb of death. He knew that if one drop were to penetrate his wet suit, beyond the protective eye and headgear, the gloves and flippers, he'd probably catch Ebola. Or that flesh eating bacteria infection. Maybe even AIDS.

And the sound. It wasn't the sound of the sea or the rushing water of a brook. It was an unnatural sloshing that reminded him more of wading into a swamp knee high with muck. It sounded like chewing thick gum with clean teeth. The music helped to glaze over that. Jorge's taste was eclectic but Harrison found himself nodding along to it. Jazzy. Slippery with fuzz guitar. Cooing female vocals. It made the dive entirely surreal.

It took roughly ten minutes for Jorge to burn through the bars. Harrison found comfort in getting close and watching them melt apart as Jorge created a perfect square in the grate and then slipped through into the dimness beyond.

Harrison followed through slowly. He caught up with Beth Ann and Jorge and they could see light in the shit above, streaming down in golden, piss yellow rays from a halogen bulb. Shallower and shallower until their heads broke the surface.

They were in.

Jorge reached down and helped them out onto a concrete platform beneath the clinical glare of halogen lights. Harrison looked at his watch. It was 1:13 a.m.

It took several minutes to wipe clean the suits. Several minutes before they could take off their helmets. Several minutes before they could breathe clean air. But when they did it was as if they were taking their first breaths. Born again from a river of feces.

Leaving the suits in a neat pile, Jorge led them down a concrete tunnel lined with pipes and halogen lights. Harrison figured it never ever got dark in there. People who worked with excrement all day probably needed all the light they could get. The tunnel ended at a staircase. They took it down a few flights to a subbasement labeled, Q12. And that's when they started to hear the buzz.

The sound of static.

"This is near where I saw him the first time," Jorge said. As if Fluke was some monster. The way Jorge said "saw him" made it sound entirely possible that Fluke really was a giant parasitic worm.

The static sound continued for a few hundred yards down a corridor much like the one before the staircase. Industrial. Barren. A few more twists and turns through a labyrinth of look-alike tunnels and they arrived at a steel door that was painted with broad yellow and black stripes like a flattened wasp.

"A little birdie told me he lives in here."

Jorge knocked twice on the door. Silence. Thirty seconds passed. Jorge frowned, knocked again. Harrison looked at Jorge.

Jorge said, "Why the fuck you looking at me?"

Beth Ann said, "Step aside."

She pulled a bobby pin from her hair. Harrison hadn't even realized she had bobby pins in her hair. There was so little hair there.

It took her three minutes to pick the lock. Then she pulled on the door handle; there was the sound of straining hinges and it opened.

And they walked into a library.

For Harrison it was as if they'd wandered into an episode of *The Twilight Zone.* A library, like one you'd find in the estate of a retired Nobel laureate, in a sewage treatment plant. The kind of library in all the movies about lonely older millionaires who find true love with the down-and-out prostitute they mistakenly brought home. The single-mother secretary that they met on the subway. The kind of snooty library with embossed books. Mahogany shelving. Leather chairs. Fringed reading lamps.

"Welcome." A tall, thin and naked man stood just inside. It was the man in T's photograph. He'd shaved off his mohawk and lost the G.G. Allin straight razor posing. He was holding a shotgun.

Beth Ann didn't fuck around. She whipped Lil' Chris' blaster right out and said, "You Fluke?"

He smiled. Nodded.

Harrison was already sick of the guns. The thought of a standoff in a library in a sewage treatment plant just bored him to death. *Fucking ridiculous,* he thought.

"Let's not start shooting," Harrison said stepping in between Fluke and Beth Ann. "We came down here to talk, right? Then let's just ask Mr. Fluke here a few questions and hopefully we'll all leave the same way we came in."

"Shall we?" Fluke asked. He motioned for Beth Ann to take a seat at a small table. She did. Fluke backed his skinny ass into a big leather chair across the room. He was gracious enough to cross his legs so they didn't have to stare at his shriveled ball sack. He kept the shotgun pointed at Beth Ann. She kept Lil' Chris' gun trained on him.

"I've only heard rumors about this place . . ." Jorge said looking around.

"I don't know you," Fluke said. "Didn't get your name . . ."

Harrison interrupted, "What is this place?"

"This is my place. My classroom. As good a place as any to hide from prying eyes," Fluke answered. "Harrison Gelden. It's really fantastic to finally meet you. You know, I've followed your work ever since that piece you did, I think it was called, 'Hauterivian . . .' it was 'Hauterivian' something . . ."

" 'Hauterivian Bearded Bivalve,' " Harrison said.

Fluke laughed, "Indeed. It was brilliant. Clearly the best thing in that whole issue. God, Bonersette Holmes' piece was absolutely terrible. To think that people consider his work on the level with yours. By the way, you look like shit."

Harrison tried not to let his distress show. He took a deep

breath and said, "Yeah, Bonersette sucks and, yeah, I look like shit 'cause I've been through hell getting here. Fluke, please tell me how the fuck a withered ass mutherfucker living in a shit plant knows about my sideline as a pornographer? I mean, I thought I was freaked out enough coming down here— freaked out enough after the fucked up night I had last night— but this is as close to shattering any reality I've been clinging to as I've gotten."

Fluke laughed again. "I'm not surprised. If you came down here and told me that you liked the stuff I used to DJ under the name of Twigless back in Syracuse in 1995, I'd be incredibly freaked out too. I know everything about you because I just happen to be a fan. I suppose you could say it's chance, but you and I know some of the same people. T turned me on to your stuff. He knows your secret, of course. He just didn't want to tell you he knew. He's saving that for later. But that's just the nature of this fucked up game, isn't it?"

"What game is that?" Harrison asked.

Beth Ann echoed, "What game, Fluke?"

"I love it. The meek paleontologist. His fierce paramour. It's amazing what love can do, isn't it Harrison? You've been through hell and if it weren't for the woman at your side you'd probably be some blubbering mess right now. But look at you, all gung ho to come down here and ask me for the truth. That's brilliant. Alistair told me you all might be a bit on edge. A bit pumped up. Too many energy drinks? Too many lines? I've got a fucking shotgun, you dumb cunts."

"Cut the shit, Fluke," Harrison spat. "There are three of us here. You shoot Beth Ann and by the time you load another shell I'll have my thumbs knuckle deep in your eye sockets. And Jorge there, well, he'll be boring you senseless with talk of cannibal ape men."

"Fuck you, *puto*," Jorge said flicking Harrison off.

"Really? You'd be fine with me shooting her?" Fluke smirked.

"No. I wouldn't be fucking fine with it. But I'm pretty god

damned numb right now. So, I might have a bit of a delayed re-action." Harrison turned to Beth Ann and said, "Sorry, babe."

Beth Ann blew him a kiss.

She turned back to Fluke. "Start talking, fucker."

"Alistair tells me that you were caught up in a turf battle. That he and T had a time of it and that T had roped you into doing his dirty work. All politics. Is that right?"

"Yeah," Harrison replied. "And T's dead now."

Fluke looked surprised, "Really? Death of Hot Monster, huh? Interesting."

"You're next," Beth Ann smiled.

"Ouch," Fluke chuckled. "She is quite the bitch isn't she?"

"When she needs to be," Harrison said. "Fluke, tell us what The Fold is."

Fluke nodded. Bald head bobbing. He let out a sigh and ran his fingers along his scalp, "You want to know everything, Har-rison? I wonder if you can handle even a tenth of what I'm going to tell you . . ."

"Just get out with it, you gabby prick," Beth Ann said.

Fluke cleared his throat, "Most of it is economics. Problem is you don't see it. You think you're fucking the man, fighting the system, but you're not. You're part and parcel of it. Every move you make is bought and sold. Everything you buy goes to some larger pocket and a hidden hand directed you to it. You don't shop in chain stores. You pride yourself on buying indie, but that's all myth. A myth that the large corporations allow you to buy into. A myth they've created just for smarties like you. The only way to truly fuck the man would be to live at the bottom of the sea.

"But economics can't explain it all. You're dealing with something much more abstract. The Fold. That's the name for the whole project. It's about viral marketing. About under-ground promotion. Black ops. Voodoo sales. Ondscan wants to grow a new generation of consumers like you that don't want to buy what they sell. Not really intuitive is it? The Fold is how they do it. Ondscan is completely hands off though. They give the money—under the table of course—and let things play out. Let The Fold do its thing. Plant moles in subcultures—Veniss, Paul, Swank, Xavier, T—and then let them sow the seeds under the guise of rebellion. They are the underground elite and when they speak, people listen. An ingenious ploy to wrap new clothing around the same, tired king."

"And Jeep?" Harrison asked.

"He's the next stage. The eventual. He wasn't in our 'class.' He came later. He knew us but he was trained differently. Fact is Doctor Jeep isn't a person. He's a walking, talking jingle with a gun. He's a memeoid. The absolute fulfillment of a fad."

"You've already lost me," Beth Ann said. "What the fuck is he talking about?"

She looked at Harrison and Harrison shrugged.

Fluke laughed.

"Memetics. It's geek speak for little packets of cultural information that move around our minds and societies, much like genes are transferred from parent to child. Fashion. Pop music. Melodies. Slogans like *Don't worry, be happy* or *All your base are belong to us* or *Skate or die.* All are memes. They move like viruses unmoored from their original hosts. They move and create, spawn, culture. Culture isn't a construct. It's a biological certainty. I'm sorry if that's a bit complicated.

"Simply put, it is evolution. The beak of the finch evolves towards function. If the bird eats grubs that live in tiny holes in the bark of trees, it evolves a long, thin beak to get them. Language evolves the same way. If a word is out of fashion and can't fit into the small cultural holes it's designed for, it either vanishes or it evolves. Look at the way slang has just taken over. The word 'dope' is a particularly adaptable and robust meme. It went from drugs. To denoting idiocy. To meaning 'cool.' But a meme isn't the word. It's the meaning behind it. We are infected and then we spread them. You hipsters are the most contagious mutherfuckers on the block. All your elitist memes. You like Patsy Cline and not P Diddy. You like Harmony Korine not Ron Howard. And you try and convince everyone you know to think like you. You're infected. Contagious. Driven by your memes.

"You have to understand this battle," Fluke continued. "You're not up against a monolithic entity, a bear running at you from the forest. You're fighting for survival against a wave of fads and Doctor Jeep, even T and Swank and Xavier, all represent the same movement. In their cases it doesn't really matter what the meme is, just that it's powerful and replicates fiercely. The Fold has tapped into this. They've tried to mold it to their marketing strategies. And Doctor Jeep is the end result. He's a memeoid. A person who lives only for the meme. For the idea. Just like a cultist or a suicide bomber. In the end, his life, our lives, don't matter. His existence is only to enact the meme."

Harrison asked, "What is the meme that he's carrying?"

"That's the brilliant part. It's everything cultural. He's supposed to be the most elite cultural entity that has ever lived. He's a warehouse of virtually every hip, underground meme imaginable. And he's blossomed by killing other memes. Consuming and absorbing them. Lovely image, isn't it? Fact is Paul, Swank, Xavier, were dinosaurs. Just meme mules. They were born to die. Hell, they'll be twenty times more popular, more influential, now that they're dead. They only had slight inklings of what they carried. What The Fold's memetic engineers implanted in them . . ."

"Mother and Father?" Beth Ann interrupted.

Fluke nodded, "Yes. Father is a memetic engineer. He's got a 'lab' at Ondscan in midtown. Does meme splicing and meme design. It's really just an office staffed by overeager cronies. Marketing people who have a taste for pain and suffering. Mother is a retired schoolteacher. She helps Father come up with his dastardly plans."

Fluke laughed and then grew silent.

"This is all paranoid conspiracy bullshit," Harrison spat.

Fluke looked at Beth Ann and shrugged his shoulders.

"This guy is fucking nuts," Jorge said. "How can you believe any of this? Isn't he part of the whole thing?"

Harrison walked over and took the gun from Beth Ann and stepped up behind Fluke, pressed the barrel into the back of his shaved head. Fluke didn't flinch. Didn't raise the shotgun.

"And how do you fit into it all?"

Fluke sighed, "You two are really incorrigible aren't you? I train The Folds' less than brilliant minds. Their newest recruits are sent here for, essentially, a liberal arts education. I use anarchist and green teachings. Works by Jesus Sepulveda. Chellis Glenndinning. Ward Churchill. I use them to subvert their preconceived notions of free enterprise and even reality. Once they are converted anarchists, ready to rage at the immateriality of the world, I help them channel that into pure capital. I take suits and make activists. Then turn them into free-market monsters."

Jorge said, "I've read Sepulveda. You couldn't possibly twist his shit into pro-business propaganda."

"No, I don't. And I couldn't. You are right on that. But I can, and I do, show them the reality behind words. Even Sepulveda's. You're still under the impression that everything falls into a right category or a wrong category. But what they come to realize here is that there is only a right. Nothing is forbidden."

Beth Ann said, "Tell us how you got here, Fluke."

"Gore rap, right?" Harrison asked.

Fluke nodded, "It began, as everything does, as a cult phenomenon at the very fringes of the very fringes. In college I discovered an underground of acne ridden misanthropes who were tape trading DIY gore rap on the west coast. It's terrible shit. Simply wretched. No purpose other than to sicken. And that's the simplistic beauty of it. That's why I knew it would sell. I was drafted into this black ops marketing division and given the opportunity to turn gore rap into a bonafide cultural commodity. My design was effortless. My sales pitch undeniable. I kept it underground. Left the illusion that it was totally autonomous. Sold it to every teenage boy with a hard on for pain. And to this day, gore rap looks subversive. But it's not. It is bought and sold, written and rewritten, by white men with MBAs."

Jorge was shaking his head, "I don't believe this fucking guy. You don't believe him do you?"

Ignoring Jorge, Fluke continued, "I spread contagion via illegal broadcasts."

"What broadcasts?" Harrison pushed the barrel harder into his goose flesh.

"Remember the riot in Bushwick last summer? When it was rumored that a Hassidic Jew ran over a black grandmother and then fled the scene? Or when those Vietnamese kids were beat to hell by that mob of Lebanese men after it was rumored that some teens gang raped a Lebanese mother? Or on a more global scale, the early reports that Gore won the 2000 election . . ."

"Sure."

"I was point person on those operations. There was no black grandmother run over by a Hassid. No gang of Vietnamese rapist teens. Gore lost by a landslide. Forget the shit about pregnant chads. Just stories. Urban legends. I created them. I broadcast the stories. That was my disinformation packet. My meme."

"Why?"

"Because we have a vested interest in keeping minorities on their toes. Because we need blacks and Arabs and Jews to live in fear. They make better consumers when they don't know if tomorrow will be their last day on this planet."

Harrison desperately wanted to shoot Fluke. It would have been so easy. He wanted to just pull the trigger and end this miserable man's disgusting existence. Jorge shook his head and whispered, "Don't."

Harrison clenched his teeth. Let his jaw muscles tense. He

felt alien. His reaction to Fluke so emotional. So gut. Harrison said, "I want you to tell me what comes next. Where is this going? I don't need to hear about memes or any shit that you make up. Jeep's not just killing off memes anymore. He's a maniac with a fucking gun and he's after us."

"Collateral meme damage," Fluke said.

"Fuck you," Harrison pressed the gun harder. "But how do we stop him?"

"You kill him."

"And it will be over? I mean, we'll be able to just go back to our lives? Whatever those will be."

"No, of course not. You're here with me. I've told you what you probably already had an inkling of, filled out the spaces between the spaces, and unfortunately that makes you really, really dangerous. Mother and Father will stop at nothing to destroy you."

"I'm not with these guys," Jorge chimed in. "I just led them here."

"If we stop Mother and Father? Then?"

"If by stop you mean kill. Then, yes, it's just like any hydra. You can't just cut off the heads. You've got to kill the body."

"And Ondscan won't just send a mob of goons after us?"

"You haven't really heard me have you? Ondscan, the big company, doesn't really know what The Fold does. It's under the radar. Black ops. Mother and Father are the only link."

Harrison looked at Beth Ann. The thought of more killing, of more blood, was exhausting. She looked as though she felt the same way. Down in the filth of the world. Talking to a guy named Fluke about secretive corporate head games and killing. Harrison was desperate for another shower. He walked back over to Beth Ann and handed her the gun.

"Give up?" Fluke said chewing his nails.

Beth Ann pointed Lil' Chris' gun at Fluke and kept it there, extended, her hand as still as bone.

Fluke was silent, cradled the shotgun in his lap.

Harrison made his way to the bookshelves and browsed. He flipped through a copy of Danny Casolaro's unexpunged *The Octopus*. A photo album of Dash Snow Polaroids. Tim Lucas' *Throat Sprockets*. All gems.

"You can't really live in here. I mean, seriously?" Harrison asked.

"There's a kitchenette over to your right. And a bathroom just off that."

Harrison peeked around the corner to his right where Fluke had a decent kitchenette. Toilet. "Why bother with the toilet?" he asked. "You can just shit upstairs right into the river."

Fluke chuckled, the shotgun shaking slightly.

"Let's get back to business," Beth Ann said. "Tell us where to find Mother and Father."

"I think I should tell you that Alistair will be here soon. He's been really eager, almost rabid really, to have you two. Alistair's the type of guy who enjoys checking off boxes."

"He won't be checking these boxes," Harrison said distractedly as he flipped through a copy of William Gerhardie's *Doom*.

"Oh, yeah," Fluke replied. "You going to be the one to tell him that? Are you going to grow some big testes all of a sudden? Break out of your porn ghetto and kill the baddie? Save the girl? I just don't see it."

"I never read any of his stuff," Harrison walked over to Fluke, held up the copy of Gerhardie's book. "What's it like?"

Fluke smiled, "Ah, he's one of my absolute faves. A real guilty . . ."

Harrison was on him in a flash. So fast it even surprised Harrison. It was almost cat like. Harrison chalked it up to nerves and sleep deprivation. He had once heard anecdotally from Rad that people can get to a point after enough trauma that their body acts on instinct. It just plugs away, jumps at the slightest synapse firing. Harrison ripped Fluke's shotgun from his knobby hands and stuffed it into his face, Fluke's hawk like nose smashed against his left cheek.

"You're going to tell us who the fuck Mother and Father are. Now," Harrison growled.

"No . . . Not like this . . . No . . . ," Fluke said, his voice echoing in the barrel of the shotgun.

"Fine," Harrison pulled the gun from Fluke's face.

He pressed it against Fluke's left knee and fired. The knee cap exploded in a red and white shower of cartilage. Fluke screamed, grabbed at the hole where his knee had been. His left leg flopped to the tile floor, twitched once and then lay still.

Harrison pushed the shotgun back into Fluke's face, "Who are Mother and Father?"

Fluke shook his head, gritted his teeth. He was trying to staunch the blood spilling out of his leg. His fingers clutched at pink meat but the blood just kept pouring. He was a few shades paler than before.

"Harrison, you need to listen to me . . . This isn't the way it was supposed to . . ." Fluke said.

Harrison pumped the shotgun, put it to Fluke's left wrist and pulled the trigger again. Fluke's left hand flew off and even more of his leg disappeared.

Fluke howled.

"Fuck! Harrison, you have to fucking stop . . ." He looked wildly around the room at Jorge and Beth Ann.

Harrison put the shotgun on Fluke's right kneecap. "You still have one leg left. One hand. That's totally manageable. Two legs, that's another story. Tell me their goddamned names."

"They'll kill me," Fluke cried.

"*I'm* going to kill you, mutherfucker!" Harrison shouted. "If you don't tell me what I need to hear and do it quick, I'm going to blast your limbs off first. Now fucking talk!"

Harrison looked to Beth Ann, she was grinding her teeth. She looked like she was about to burst into tears. And yet she kept Lil' Chris' gun trained on Fluke.

"Don't do this . . . Don't . . ." Fluke mumbled.

Harrison bit his lower lip and moved the shotgun down and

pushed it deep into the muscle on Fluke's right thigh, "I'm going higher up this time. You don't answer and I take part of your hip and maybe even one of your balls with this shot."

Fluke was sweating rivers. His eyes all bloodshot.

"You need to talk, Fluke. Tell me what you know or God help me I will take you apart right here."

Fluke broke, "They live on Long Island, in Port Washington. Hook is the last name, Tammy and Bernard. They are in the phone book."

"Can I trust that?"

Fluke nodded.

"Really?"

Fluke nodded furiously.

Harrison pulled the shotgun away. He backed up and smiled to Beth Ann.

Fluke flew to the floor. His skin was the color of white paper. White in a sea of deep red. A twitchy smile spread slowly across his face, "Harrison, you have no fucking clue what's going on. You just fucked everything . . ."

There was a cymbal crash. Fluke stopped midsentence. A small red hole opened on his forehead. He looked stunned and his body sagged. He was dead before his head hit the floor. Lil' Chris' gun was smoking in Beth Ann's hand.

"What the fuck? I can't believe you just did that. We could have gotten a lot more info out of him," Harrison shouted.

Jorge wretched loudly.

Beth Ann muttered, "I don't know why. I mean, you just went crazy on him. You were tearing him about like a bug. I just . . . it just happened. He was so . . ." She was shaking, the gun loose in her hands, and Harrison couldn't tell if the water steaming down her face was from tears or sweat. Pain or anxiety.

She handed Lil' Chris' gun to Harrison, "Please, I don't want this."

"Hey guys, can we get the fuck out of here now?" Jorge said, a long string of saliva hanging from his chin.

That's when they heard footsteps. Boots running.

"The guards," Harrison said. "We've got to get the fuck out of here fast. Any other ways out, Jorge?"

"And leave my gear? You're fucking kidding me!"

"No. I'm not. Is there another way out?"

"Man, I can't just leave these suits here."

"Jorge, is there another way out?!" Beth Ann shouted.

"Yeah. Yeah. There's a service tunnel that leads out opposite from the way we came in. Fuck me though," Jorge was biting his lower lip.

The service tunnel was down a level lower. It was narrow. They had to crouch as they made their way down the tunnel. And it was lit only by a single dangling bulb every few hundred yards. The dark places in between were like pools of unfiltered night. The tunnel ended at a grate, a hanging metal ladder leading upwards and out onto the desolate scrubland surrounding the plant. It was a hike back to Jorge's truck. A hike through a wilderness of abandoned construction materials and burnt out cars. Harrison looked at every blackened hulk they passed and imagined each held a body. *New York's like that,* he thought, *you look around isolated places and immediately think about hidden corpses.*

"I can't believe I left my suits there," Jorge said every five seconds.

It took them a while to navigate the icy flood plains surrounding the plant. After about half an hour of stumbling through slush and pale weeds, they got to Jorge's truck. Jorge let it heat up while they rubbed their faces and blew smoke into their ruddy hands. When the truck was suitably warmed with plumes of exhaust they drove out.

"Are you going to kill someone else?" Jorge leaned over and asked Beth Ann.

"Yes. If we have to," Beth Ann said, calmer now.

That was when Harrison really noticed a change in her, a steely determination that hadn't been there before. He knew

that she could have gone blind that minute and it wouldn't
have fazed her. Maybe it was lack of sleep. Maybe it was love.

"And that whole scene down in the plant? What was that
about?" Jorge was chain-smoking. "What the fuck was that really
about?"

Harrison said, "Corporate affairs, Jorge. Business deals gone
sour. It's about changing the world. About pulling back the curtain and getting a good look at the wizard. And he's not a
plump old dude with a white moustache and a purple suit. He's
a fucking hipster with a charge card and a degree in marketing.
He's back there plotting out the course of your life, your inter-
ests, your every whim and desire. He's back there building a
better you."

Jorge kept smoking. Kept shaking. "I'm not following," he
said.

"It's simple really," Beth Ann put her hand on Jorge's shoulder. "We fucked with a killer."

31

That's when something hit them.

The truck lurched, spun hard right and went off the road. It landed in an ice-filled ditch. Jorge and Harrison hit the dash. Cigarettes doing smoky pirouettes. Beth Ann slammed against the window. Glass shattered. The injuries were limited, reasonable. Whiplash. Spinal compression. Harrison had a metallic taste in his mouth and he thought, at first, that he'd swallowed a seat belt buckle. But it was just blood and a few more loose teeth. Beth Ann had a nasty gash on her forehead. Jorge seemed fine. Before he asked Beth Ann or Harrison how they were, before he even turned to look at them, he lit another smoke.

"What the . . . ?" Beth Ann asked rubbing the gash on her head. She rubbed the blood all over her face. Looked like Sissy Spacek at the end of *Carrie*.

Harrison reached over Jorge and opened the driver side door. He pushed Jorge out and stepped over him into the long grass and snow in the ditch. The vehicle that hit them was stopped on the road above. Lights on. Driver sitting behind the wheel.

Harrison palmed Lil' Chris' gun and hiked out of the ditch and over to the big, black Jeep sitting on the road above. He approached the driver's side and Alistair Banister, smoking a clove, looked up at him.

"Hey there," he said.

He had a gun resting on the dash.

"Why'd you run us off the road?" Harrison asked, not realizing that it was perhaps the most ridiculously stupid thing he'd ever said.

Alistair snickered, "I didn't see your truck."

Then he took a long drag of his clove and Harrison slowly brought Lil' Chris' gun level with Alistair's head.

"You gonna kill me first?" Alistair asked.

Harrison nodded, finger wrapped around the trigger.

"You talk to Fluke? He down there in his pit?"

Harrison nodded again, "He told us how to find Mother and Father."

"Really? How generous of him," Alistair said.

"Well, the gun helped."

Alistair looked up at Harrison, grinning like a death's head. "You don't know what the fuck is going on. Do you?" he asked.

"I think I have a pretty good idea now."

Alistair put his right index finger into the barrel of Lil' Chris' gun. Still grinning, he said, "And you think you can stop all this?"

Harrison mouthed, *Yes*, and pulled the trigger. That fact that Alistair's finger was blown to globules didn't seem to register on Alistair's face. His hand snapped back and the car was sprayed with gore. But he just kept grinning. His face dripping. Looked at his mutilated hand, at the place where his index finger had been, and then looked up at Harrison and shook his head.

"You made a big fucking mistake there."

Alistair was fast. He had his gun off the dash before Harrison noticed. His hand just darted like it wasn't attached to his body. Moved like a fly from an approaching shadow. Alistair pointed the dark gun in Harrison's face but his trigger finger was gone. The blackened stump twitched obscenely. He was trying to shoot. Pulling at the trigger with no finger. Harrison figured Alistair was so fucking twisted—or on such a brilliant cocktail of drugs—that he was probably just operating on autopilot. Some sick instinct.

Harrison put Lil' Chris's gun to Alistair's forehead, pressed the barrel down hard so that a little ridge of skin bowed up around it.

"Harrison!" Beth Ann screamed from somewhere nearby. He didn't look to see. His eyes were locked with Alistair's.

"Go on . . ." Alistair whispered.

"Why are you doing this?" Harrison asked.

"Harrison!" Beth Ann was getting closer.

"It's just what I do, Harrison. Now go on . . ." Alistair's eyes were black grottos.

"And if I don't?"

"Then I'll just keep coming after you. You know that. And if it's not me, it'll be someone else. And then someone else after that."

"Why?"

"Harrison," Beth Ann was behind him. Her hands light on his side.

Alistair said, "You're one of us, Harrison. You're one of us . . ."

Harrison pushed the gun harder. Deeper. Red heat spread from the spot.

"No," Harrison said, "I'm nothing like you. You're sick."

"Do it, Harrison," Beth Ann whispered. She had her face nestled into the small of his back.

"Kill him," she said. "End this."

"Then he'll be right," Harrison pushed the gun deeper. Alistair didn't flinch. No pain in his eyes.

"That's just a cliché," Beth Ann squeezed hard. "That's just what they say in the movies. In the comic books. You'll never be like him. You'll be better. Isn't that what we wanted in the first place? When it comes down to it this is what we set out to do, to kill a killer."

Harrison took a deep breath in. Held it.

Beth Ann whispered in the small of his back, "This is what we need to do, Harrison. This is what you need to do. If you don't end this here . . . If you don't end this now, he's gonna be on us for the rest of our lives . . ."

"Why?" Harrison whispered back.

"Why!" He shouted into Alistair's smiling blood bedecked face.

"I will hunt you down. I will spill your guts," Alistair said through bloody teeth. "I will skin you and then skin your girl and then skin any children you might have. I will fuck you where you breathe."

"Do it," Beth Ann prodded.

"Do it," Alistair jeered.

Harrison thought about Beth Ann being dead. He thought about that scene in *The Abyss* where the only way for Ed Harris and Mary Elizabeth Mastrantonio to get out of a crippled sub is for Mary to drown and Ed to swim her back to the mother ship and then resuscitate her. He was thinking about that scene and how long and hard it was to bring Mary back. How everyone stopped trying but then Ed got a second wind and pounded on Mary's chest and brought her back. How they hugged. And that's when Harrison pulled the trigger and the gun jammed.

Or maybe it was out of bullets.

Or maybe the safety was on.

Or maybe it was karma. Pure unadulterated karma. That or black magic. Ondscan evil. Something entirely metaphysical. Something superstitious.

"Nice shot, asshole," Alistair laughed.

Harrison pulled the trigger a second time and it worked.

This time Alistair's brains evacuated his head at about a million miles an hour. Gray matter punched through the passenger side window and Harrison thought he saw an eyeball skitter across the dashboard. He pulled the trigger again and the second bullet ripped through the husk of Alistair's head but nothing came out. He didn't shoot a third time. Alistair's wrecked head slumped forward. His index finger kept jetting blood but slower.

Harrison dropped the gun into the snow on the road.

Beth Ann was crying, sobbing into his back.

Jorge walked up and looked into the car. Looked at Alistair and then looked at Harrison, eyes as wide as the sodium moon above them.

"You just massacred that guy," he said.

"Yeah, I guess I did," Harrison replied.

Jorge said, "I don't want to know."

They dragged Jeep out, left his body steaming in the brown snow at the side of the road. Harrison was collapsing inside. He felt haunted. It wasn't so much the image of Jeep's skull splintering as it was his disheveled body. Harrison was struck by the weight when they had hauled it out—Jeep's empty head a cantaloupe rind. It was uncanny but part of Harrison felt like the corpse should have been lighter. With Alistair gone it was merely a sack of bones and blood. It was like a man shaped jellyfish. That weight struck Harrison. And he started thinking about what a soul weighs. *Light as air? Tangible?* He couldn't believe he was thinking about souls. He didn't believe in souls. No time to get irrational.

They piled into Jeep's truck. Jorge in the backseat because he was shaking too bad to drive. Harrison at the wheel. Beth Ann beside him. As they drove away from the plant Harrison watched the sky. Early morning sunlight and thin, gauzy clouds and tangled trees that broke it. He thought he saw the left hand of God in those slender clouds. He admitted to himself that he hadn't slept well in the past week. He admitted he'd been in a war zone. Attacked by friends. Professional killers. Swam in a river of shit. Tussled with a fucking baboon. That all seemed a bit pedestrian compared to the left hand of God. He was just an actor in the play. A bit part trying to figure out his fucking lines and not embarrass himself.

But there was a hand pointing down at him. The index finger all cumulous and gray, pointed at the car, as though it were picking them out for the cops or the angels. Harrison wanted to try and swerve to get out of its way. As though maybe an arm would form and it would reach down and pull them up into the sky. He started to sweat thinking about the end of the world and he had to slap himself a few times to be sure that he was really awake.

The hand drifting above them kept perfect time with the car. Kept perfectly aligned.

Beth Ann was staring at him and reading his thoughts.

"I know," Harrison broke his reverie, "I'm going fucking crazy."

Beth Ann looked solemn. Her eyes deep pools. Deeper than ever. When Harrison turned to look back at the sky, the hand was gone. Dissipated into a thousand wisps of cool water. He sighed with relief.

Harrison said, "I just thought I saw the left hand of God."

"What?" Jorge was suddenly in on the conversation. Piping in from the backseat.

"Nothing. I'm just really tired," Harrison said looking in the rearview mirror.

Beth Ann put her hand on the back of his neck and squeezed. He felt better just having her touch him. Just knowing that she existed. Just knowing he existed.

32

They stopped by Jorge's apartment. Beth Ann and Harrison went in and showered and then borrowed some of Jorge's clothing. They kept the filthy Riffs jumpsuits and tossed them onto the back seat.

"You sure you don't mind us borrowing the Jeep, seeing as we kind of helped ruin your truck?" Harrison asked.

"No, *puta,* I'll see you guys in jail."

"Thanks Jorge. We won't be going to jail," Harrison said as they pulled away, "You call the fucking police and I'll come back here and blast your skull apart too."

Jorge laughed.

Harrison and Beth Ann stopped and got coffee. A Starbucks in Queens crowded with early risers. Beth Ann didn't speak, she kept her head down, eyes closed in the steam that curled off the coffee. Harrison asked her if she was alright. She said she couldn't remember the last time she knit. She mumbled something about needing to sleep. About wanting to be alone.

But most of all she wanted to knit. She wanted to feel her

needles in her hands. Hear the clack a clack of them working hard for her.

Harrison called his message machine. There was one message. It was one of T's dispatches from the future.

"Fuck. Beth Ann, here listen to this."

Beth Ann moved close to the phone. She nodded that she could hear.

The message's time stamp said T recorded it just before coming over to Wolfgang's. Beth Ann imagined he sat out in his car just outside the apartment and read the story while he smoked a cigarette. Then, when the tape stopped, he came up and shot a bolt in Harrison's foot.

"He left one at your apartment, too. Something about a playground. Something about his memories of childhood," Beth Ann said. "You were sleeping. Then he came to kill us."

The message began, "Hey, Harrison. I just need to read you something I just wrote. I know. I know. Where do I find the time? I think you'll get a kick out of this. I need to read it. Like a cancer or something. This just has to get out now. It's not about Alistair. It's not about tonight. Honestly, man. Please just listen to this. Next time I see you, I'll tell you what it all means. Sorry if it sounds stilted. It's still rough."

There was a pause, maybe five seconds. Harrison could hear T unfolding paper. Rustling. Harrison figured T kept this story folded up in his back pocket. This was a good one.

"A year ago I set up a reenactment of a memory. It was an early memory. From when I was six years old, 1981, and I was with my mother in Florida visiting my aunt. It was January, perhaps the remaining days of December, and I remembered going to the pool at my cousin's house and floating on my back, staring into the sky, while I listened to the radio. The pool had underwater speakers. I distinctly recalled hearing only one song, a dazzling song that lulled me to sleep. I did not know how long I slept. Floating in the sunlight. But I was awakened by my mother's calls for lunch. And I found myself burbling and gurgling under the water. I was at the bottom of the pool.

"I had slept and sunk but had not panicked. It was as though I had retreated to some primal state, a uterine state, which called to every molecule of water in my body and simply let myself disperse. The song was the key to recreating the scene. When the memory came back, two years ago, I was in the shower with a girlfriend. She was massaging me and the memory hit like a bullet. I recoiled, the girl knocked her head and she wound up in the ER. A few stitches and a breakup later, the song was still seared into my every thought.

> *Goodbye my friends, Maybe forever*
> *Goodbye my friends, the stars wait for me*

"A chance conversation with a taxi driver, a man roughly my age who was quite an AM radio aficionado, revealed the title of the song. It was 'Time' by the Alan Parson's Project. I bought their album, *The Turn of a Friendly Card,* on vinyl and when I heard the song again a warm, electric shiver crept slowly up my spine until the hair on the inside of my ears stood up. I was able to travel to Florida last January. I had not spoken with my aunt since the late '80s and I was awkward and bumbling when I called and invited myself over to visit. Miraculously, she lived in the same house. The pool was well maintained and unchanged and the underwater speakers worked. Even better, she had found a way to hook up a CD player to the pool sound system. After a disastrous lunch, during which I managed to insult my aunt in a stupefying variety of approaches, I was able to retire to the pool while my aunt napped. I had burned a copy of the song and put it on repeat on the CD player and then climbed into the pool and began to float out under the warm sun.

"At first the sensation was graceless. I distinctly felt as though I was trying too hard, as though I was pushing a square peg into a round hole. But I concentrated on the music and the strained feeling quickly subsided and before long time evaporated and in my mind I could not tell if I was six years old or twenty-nine. I could not feel my adult body and my adult mind had blurred in the face of overwhelming memory. I slipped into a peaceful slumber, exactly as I had done when I was small. And for the first time in nearly twenty years I was filled with light, bouncy, almost carbonated joy that swelled in my lungs and pulsed through my membranes. It was the light of vigor, of innocence, of freedom.

"I awoke, as I had before, at the bottom of the pool. The song playing. The light filtering in. But this time I awoke to the sound of my aunt screaming. I swam to the surface to calm her. I didn't attempt explaining my near drowning. I simply told my aunt that I'd fallen asleep, exhausted as I was from the long flight, and that I would be fine. I also told this to the paramedics and the police. And I never forgot the feeling of that day. When I returned to Pennington I knew what I needed to do, it was a high like a drug. I needed another fix. So I cannibalized my memory, old letters, notebooks, photos, and 16mm film reels. After several subsequent successful reenactments, I found that the sensation of my childhood grew increasingly tangible. Before it had simply been a tinge of nostalgia, now it had grown into a haze of emotion, a delirium of awareness. It was as though the very air around me was alive with a nostalgic char . . ."

The tape ended.

Three minutes had passed. A wave of sympathy washed over Beth Ann. T was clearly just a fucked up kid stuck in a man's body. He was like Fast Eye, something more than human, trapped here in an uncaring world. A brutal society that didn't give half a shit about childhood fantasies.

Beth Ann went back to staring into her coffee.

33

They went to Long Island, to visit Mother and Father and shut everything down.

Took the LIE to Shelter Rock Road and then up to Port Washington by way of small, curvy streets. When they got there they stopped at a gas station and looked up the Hook, Bernard, residence in a phone book and then parked across the street from their home and smoked cigarettes.

The Hook dwelling was a colonial style estate home that backed onto a preserve. It was blue. Two stories. Fairy tale shutters. Detached garage. White picket fence. It was a true vision of suburban living. Beth Ann imagined kids and dogs prancing in the front yard while Mother and Father watched from the front porch. All smiles and waves.

"What's the plan?" Beth Ann asked. The first time she'd spoken since Starbucks.

"We'll wait and watch."

"How long?"

"Until we get it down."

"What?"

"The routine. We're going to stalk them. You take Bernard and I'll follow Tammy."

"We've only got one car."

"You take the train. Act like a weird homeless junkie or something. Look . . ."

Father, Bernard, came out of the house with a spring in his step. Harrison thought he looked familiar. But then again every midtown suit looked familiar. They were all too well groomed. Too efficient. Too sanctimonious. Bernard made his way to the Lexus SUV parked in the driveway and sped off. Harrison and Beth Ann followed him to a railroad station a few miles from the house and Harrison dropped Beth Ann off, told her to be careful and not follow Bernard too closely.

"I need money for a ticket," she said.

Harrison gave her a twenty.

"See ya." She kissed him on the forehead and left. It was touchingly domestic.

After following Tammy for a very dull day, Harrison drove to the train station and waited for Bernard and Beth Ann to come back from the city.

He went through Jeep's CDs while he waited. Jeep had a decent selection. Bonk. Black Sabbath. Mean Reds. *Back to the Future* soundtrack. Looking at the cover of the Bonk disc made Harrison think about Mandy. She was a short punk rock girl he'd meet in college. Fresh faced and emotionally scarred. Mandy was a cutter like Rad and she had a crush on Harrison.

She gave him a mix tape once. "The Palm" was complete with a hand drawn cover. It depicted a little girl holding her hand up and on each of the fingers was written words. The thumb had "The Palm," index finger "Explor-," middle, "ations," ring, "of," and pinky, "reality." It was cute. Simple. Harrison found it endearing. On the inside was the track listing and Mandy's home phone number with an XXO and a little scribble of something that looked surprisingly like a vulva. Harrison thought that was kind of cute too. But the more he looked at it the more creeped out he got. Girls that had crushes on him in college always seemed to walk that fine line between cute and creepy. It was totally purposeful.

Harrison had normally found punk rock girls unattractive. Most he met were either overweight or too hard cut. They were either fashioned from putty or from marble. He liked a soft look and this girl Mandy had it. She was short, pudgy and wore a school girl uniform. Pigtails and black lipstick. She was soft-spoken. Had an air of naivety. Her scent was peppermint and cough drops.

She and Harrison spoke at length about punk and their parents, their problems, their family pets. He spent the night with her once but they never touched. Just lay in bed and listened to her snore. And Harrison noticed the cuts, long and fresh, along her arms in the morning when she was getting dressed.

"It makes the pain go away when I cut. I carry my kit with me everywhere I go. I call it Baal, the other god of the Bible, the god of human sacrifice. Sacrifice sounds like scarify to me so it makes some poetic sense. Baal contains a few fresh razor blades, surgical scissors, needles and a scalpel. When my life gets crazy, and shit always seems to be hitting the fan around me, I find a quiet place and I begin to cut and the emotional turmoil that's making me sick just seems to seep away. It's like the eye of the hurricane. It's peace. That sounds sick doesn't it?"

But it didn't.

"How long?" Harrison asked her, pointing to the scars.

"Nine years."

"Those scars are complicated, detailed."

"Cutting helps me focus."

He listened to the mix when he got back to his dorm room. Most of the tracks were standard mix fare. Stuff that he had come across before. But there was a hidden track. A thirteenth song. Unlisted and not even hinted at. The first time he heard it he was fascinated. The song was brilliant and entirely new. Harrison memorized the lyrics. Would nod along to the song on his way to class. Hum it while he folded laundry. And yet, though he was often tempted, he never looked up the song. He wanted that thirteenth track to remain a mystery, a gift that could not be easily repeated. It was the unspoken bond they shared.

Sitting in Jeep's car, Harrison suddenly, desperately wanted to know what the thirteenth track was. He'd lost the CD sometime in grad school and Mandy was nothing but a few loose threads of memory. She was a smile in a halo of sunlight. Thinking about Mandy, about music, about the randomness of life, Harrison started to feel panic well up in his gut once again.

His heart racing. Sweat boiling up on his forehead. Harrison needed a quick release. A bullet from God with the title of that song. But it wasn't going to come. He didn't even recall the tune anymore. The lyrics were lost. The whole thing fucked. And that got him thinking about the mirage of pain hovering over the asphalt of his life. Shimmering like heat. And that got him thinking about Jeep. About how he'd killed him. Erased him. And the thought of nonexistence mixed with his sleep deprivation coalesced into something akin to an anxiety attack. Panic at knowing that when it's all been said and done, when we're buried and gone, the memory of us, the slight inconsistencies that defined us, will slowly, inevitably fade away. Harrison wanted to put his fist through the front windshield. Feel something that would last. That's when Beth Ann knocked on the passenger side window.

"What's going on?" she asked getting in the car. "You alright?"

"Just having a panic attack or something."

"Or something?"

"I just want to end this. Get this done and get on with our lives. I want to know the lyrics to that fucking thirteenth song," Harrison said.

"Are you alright? What thirteenth song?"

"Never mind, I just want to get back to seeing my life again. I should have slept with Mandy. I should have fucking looked that song up. There were so many things I should have done. I just want my life back . . ."

"So do I," Beth Ann kissed him on the forehead and got a sweat gloss on her lips. "You sure you're alright?"

"No. I'm not fucking alright. My nerves are shot. I killed someone. Alistair doesn't exist anymore. I blew his existence right out of this fucking world. I think I feel guilty about it."

"Don't. He was going to kill you and me."

"I know. I know."

"Then let it go. There's nothing you can do now."

"I won't forget," Harrison closed his eyes. Centered himself.

"Let's talk about today. How'd it go?" Beth Ann asked.

"Fine. You?"

"Easy."

"Did you get hassled?"

"No."

"Me neither."

"So, what did she do?"

"Went shopping at the mall. Played with the kids. Nothing special. And him?"

"Got a new suit. Saw a movie. He gorged on mussels at a Belgian fry place on Houston and made a lot of phone calls."

"Interesting," Harrison smiled.

Beth Ann asked, "Now what?"

"Now we sleep."

"Where?"

"In the car. We'll find some quiet side street and crash and then tomorrow we'll do it."

That night they slept like drunken goldfish.

Beth Ann told Harrison she had seen that before. When she was in school, at a party. Someone poured a few shots of Schnapps into a goldfish bowl. After fifteen minutes of swimming in that concoction, the poor fish began to drift. It swam slowly and sullenly. Bouncing against the curved glass walls of its home as though it were shedding the ghost. It died later that night but it was a death so painless, so subtle, that it was like the fish drowned. Beth Ann didn't need the Schnapps. Harrison watched her drown in a nullifying sleep on the driver's seat of Doctor Jeep's car, her arms and legs splayed out against the door and the hand rests.

Beth Ann woke up first when the sun smashed into the car, burning with a slow intensity. She woke Harrison and he groaned, the bruises on his face having turned, almost overnight, from deep ochre to yellow.

"Good morning," he smiled.

Beth Ann smiled back. Her neck was super stiff.

"Let's get our jumpsuits on," Harrison said.

They did and Harrison got out to stretch and piss on one of Bernard and Tammy's neighbor's lawns. When he got back in the car he leaned over and gave Beth Ann a morning kiss. His lips smelled of rot. His eyes were red.

34

Form follows function.

That was the one thing Harrison Gelden learned as a paleontologist that really, seriously made any sense. He saw it applied to everything: the corkscrew pecker of the pig, the winged fingers of the bat, the spiral of the ammonite shell. They all had their shape—their style—because their shape defined them; it allowed them to be piggy, batty, or ammonitey. And Harrison found people were the same way. The midtown exec was lean, agile for maneuvering around traffic and through corporate takeovers. The junkie gaunt and weak, frame was built for abuse. Form followed function. Naturally, Harrison also saw variations on the theme. It was all about ability and necessity. Fat, cushy execs. Angular, toned junkies. But he also decided early on that it was very difficult to transform, to match an old form to a new function or to switch functions midstream. For Harrison, that was why smokers couldn't quit. That was why things went extinct. And it would only make sense that someone like Harrison, someone who spent the better part of his life squinting at trilobite fragments in underlit museums, couldn't really make the transformation from gangly curator to cold blooded assassin.

But there he was in the suburbs. Bored to tears in Port Washington, Long Island, amidst rows of manicured lawns and white picket fences, smiling jock students in baseball caps and overweight women in pink walking dogs with argyle fleece vests. Harrison was there in hell trying to save humanity, trying to salvage the last scrap of dignity from the sick culture that surrounded him. He was there in the suburbs to break up a family, kill someone if he needed to.

Harrison Gelden, PhD, six foot two inches, auburn hair and a clipped beard wearing a filthy, orange jumpsuit and falling asleep on a jewel toned Drexel sofa with his feet, also filthy, propped up on a Silkeborg teak coffee table. He was so tired his vision had gone blurry. Losing his spunk fast. Sitting next to him, also in a soiled orange jumpsuit, was the woman he loved. She was tough as nails. But on that marvelously expensive and deceitfully clean sofa, Harrison thought Beth Ann looked haggard and gloomy. She wasn't herself. She wasn't well. Across from them, in a Louis XVI adaptation arm chair, sat a dapper and well coiffed woman with a Glock 9mm. Her name was Tammy Hook. And she had her gun pointed at Harrison's kneecaps.

Harrison and Beth Ann had broken into Tammy's house and hid out in her kitchen. They knew from Harrison's scouting that when she came home she'd head there first, for a glass of merlot and a cookie. If it had been any other day she would have plopped down at the granite island and enjoyed her decadent snack while catching the last half hour of her favorite soap. But it wasn't one of those days. Instead of her soap, a cookie and a slight buzz she got Harrison and Beth Ann.

Harrison smiled and asked Tammy, "Are you Mother?"

Tammy screeched and went for the Glock in the fleece-lined brown leather holster on her left thigh. It was a made-for-cable-TV moment, the three of them standing there and Harrison really wasn't sure how it was going to play out. But he knew

Tammy was sure. For those few seconds it was her show. It was the Tammy show until her husband, Bernard, waltzed in with an assault rifle.

Sitting across from her, Harrison could see that Tammy wasn't in control of her life. It was really the Bernard show at home. Her show was just one act. Just her pulling the gun. The rest came down to Bernie. And Bernard, graying going on 50, was the real corporate deal. He was pinstripe suit and thick tie. Laptop and briefcase. Cigars and Cognac. He was called "sir" on the street and his fingernails, Harrison noticed, were immaculate. But Harrison also sensed that beneath the sheen Bernard was something else, something much more intimidating.

Harrison and Beth Ann were lead into the living room and seated. Bernard took a Featherstone side chair, assault rifle in his lap, beside Tammy and scratched at the nape of his neck.

He began with cult movies.

Called them midnight movies.

Said he loved the stuff. "If I weren't an exec I'd be a film critic," he said. He thought it must be great to be a film critic. He spoke at length about something called *Accion Mutante.*

". . . Spanish movie from the early '90s, takes place in a future where everyone is beautiful, everyone is nice. But there is a resistance, in particular a group of crippled terrorist retards fighting against the status quo. This gang consists of Siamese twins, a quadriplegic, a hunchback Jew, a deaf giant, and their leader is missing half his face. These fuckers are running around shooting up all the sperm banks, health clubs, salons, the whole bit. They kidnap a bread heiress, this socialite bitch . . . . I'm telling you, it's a fucking riot. You've got to see it. Too bad it was never released here in the states . . ."

The room was too hot. Stuffy. Harrison was sweating profusely.

Bernard, seemingly oblivious to the heat, wiped his eyes and rambled on, "These films are so fucking crazy, so goddamned outrageous, sometimes I find it hard to imagine anyone could get them made. I mean you should see *El Topo* and *The Holy Mountain.*"

Bernard's voice rose, his eyes bugged out and scratched at his neck. He leaned back in the Featherstone chair. Tammy looked over at him and eyed the chair. It was obvious that she hated him leaning back in the chair. Harrison guessed it cost something like $1,500 and Bernard's treating it like shit made Tammy furious. But she said nothing.

"You filthy fuckers watch many movies?" Bernard asked.

"No," Harrison lied. He loved movies, watched tons of them, especially bizarre, obscure and bad ones.

"Art films? Drug films? Political films?" Bernard continued, scratching at the back of his neck more and more aggressively. His neck was splotchy with red flowers of inflamed skin. Harrison half expected his leg to start kicking.

"No, I haven't seen much. I mean, maybe a few Godard films in college."

That was another lie, Harrison was a film major when he entered college, switched to paleontology his junior year.

"What about you, Beth Ann?" Bernard asked.

She said, "I'm going blind, I don't have time for movies."

Bernard laughed loudly and threw his hands up in mock desperation. It was entirely too melodramatic but Harrison was glad that at least Bernard had stopped scratching. Bernard said, "You're killing me here, you guys. Look, you've got to get out more and see some movies. Life isn't just about dope and sex and fossils. You know that right? And why not see some good flicks before you *do* go blind?"

"Sure," Harrison replied.

"When you get around to joining the rest of the human race, why don't you stop by the Brooklyn Heights Cinema over on Henry? They always have a good run of obscure films at midnight in the winters. Honestly."

Bernard gave an open-face palms shaking signal. His way of

saying, I got nothing to hide bro. Tammy nodded in agreement.

Harrison shrugged and gave his drooping lip signal for, okay, whatever fuck-o.

"So," Bernard pulled a stick of gum from his jacket pocket and crammed it into his mouth, "I'm like you guys, I thrive on difference. We're cut from the same cloth, with the exception that you're over there and I'm over here."

Then he leaned in, the chair creaked and Tammy groaned.

"Movies are literally my life. I mean, I don't work in film, per se, but . . ."

Harrison wasn't listening. Just thinking about Bernard's horse mouth. His thick, fibrous lips stretched taut over massive buckteeth. Teeth that could bite through a book. Teeth that no woman would want near any sensitive parts of her body. And the gum. Harrison knew the poor shit never had a fucking chance against those huge buckteeth. It probably lasted maybe a minute or two before it liquefied, became stringy bits that were more saliva than gum. He always hated when gum reached that point, when it was too soft to chew, when it lost all elasticity.

"So, *Accion Mutante* ends with our crippled champions killing each other off. See, they don't want to split the ransom money for the socialite they've kidnapped. It's enough that she's fallen in love with their leader, a bit of Stockholm syndrome. You know, when the victim starts identifying with the attacker. I hear it usually happens in long standoffs . . . Sound familiar, huh?"

Harrison snapped back. Shook his head. He hadn't been listening.

"It's your story, man. That movie has you written all over it. You thought you were a bunch of subversives. Gonna come here and fuck us. But you lost. You lost your cool. Maybe you just didn't prepare. Maybe you just didn't have the skills. Looking at you, I'm really beginning to doubt that you're a scientist."

Harrison smiled, "I'm a paleontologist. Not widely regarded but I hold my own. I suppose I don't seem the scientist type to you 'cause I'm not wearing thick glasses and a fly fisherman's vest. Form follows function."

Bernard shook his head. Coughed up a wad of phlegm that he swallowed hard on. Tammy looked disgusted. She looked at Harrison and Beth Ann and her face said, *He never acts like this around the children.* Her face said, *I've taught him better than this. He's just doing it to look cool for you.*

Bernard said, "Whatever, Harrison. You're in my house, sitting on my couch and you thought that by coming here and killing us that you'd make it all stop. That you'd put an end to the insanity. But you're way over your head here. You don't have the faintest idea what you're fucking with." And Harrison knew Bernard had a point. He and Beth Ann really didn't know what they were doing there. They tried to put the pieces together, to assemble the puzzle. But it was like one of those 3-D, pictures-on-all-sides puzzles. Harrison figured he needed a degree in theoretical mathematics and the ability to converse in Klingon to figure all the twists and turns. And he was just a paleontologist.

Bernard stood. Nodded to Tammy to lift the gun. She pointed it at Harrison's chest.

"I'm going to go and make myself a drink. Be back in a few minutes."

Before leaving, lips quivering and specked with saliva, Bernard said, "I'll bring one of my favorite films downstairs. Think you'll really get a kick out of it."

Harrison looked at Tammy. Tammy smirked. Beth Ann was quiet, staring into space. And Harrison hoped that she'd remain that way. Remain cool.

On the coffee table in front of them were pictures of Harrison and Beth Ann, of their friends, of their gang. Printouts of emails, documents. Harrison glanced at them, caught his familiar smile in a photo taken at his apartment, a line of an email he'd sent his parents, a blog entry from T, one of Cooper's poems. He looked at them, splayed out like the corpse of his life, and he suspected they'd always been sitting right there.

His mind drifted back over the past seven days.

Seven days that stretched into a lifetime of highs and lows. Seven days of delight and brilliance, of pain and disenchantment. Seven days that carried him from the dusty halls of academia to the consecrated halls of murder.

Bernard returned with a glass of scotch. He plopped down right across from Beth Ann and Harrison, the chair giving a little under his bulk, and he put his left arm around Tammy, the assault rifle still tight in his right hand.

He was beaming.

"I forgot to bring you down a video. I was going to bring *The Truth According to Satan* but I forgot. Sorry. I do have something, though. You'll want to look at this." He handed Harrison a sheet, a printout of an email.

"T emailed this to me a few hours prior to the regrettable party that you Riffs held earlier this week. It's short and I think you'll find it illuminating."

Harrison asked Tammy if she thought he'd find it interesting.

She shrugged, winked and then settled back into her complacent stare.

Harrison read it. The email began: "Dear Mother and Father."

Harrison looked up at Bernard and Tammy sitting so patiently. A perfect suburban couple with drinks and guns. They were the epitome of everything he ever hated about the country. The epitome of everything that exists outside of Brooklyn and thinking that he might die there in the suburban wasteland gave him palpitations.

The email continued:

The whole thing is just falling apart. I'm sure both of you can see that now. When Fluke decided to leave the front, to return to the barracks, I knew that the dream had ended. And now the frenzy marketing. You're killing this.

I know the boys over in strategic planning have modeled it all out. Countless ways. Up and down. They always come up with the same scenarios. They factor in insanity. Megalomania. Addiction. Depression. It always comes out the same. We always win. Why would you want to change the template? The design was flawless.

Phase 1 was where we needed to stop and stay. We were getting so much done. All the people I've slowly molded and embraced. They all trust me and I got them seeing the same future. We were building a product like none that has ever existed. It was going to be so evolutionary in scope. A brand that has seeped into the genes. That is expressed in every generation and grows and adapts. It was a beautiful thing. We sowed Ondscan into the very soul of America. It went way beyond Father's talk of viruses. It was a functioning part of the whole. Not just an infection.

I guess that's the whole problem, right? It's not good enough to be a part, an essential cog. No, Ondscan has to be the whole. So you let Alistair loose with his frenzy marketing idea. When he brought that shit up in training everyone scoffed at him. Remember? Father, you yourself called the idea impractical. And we were already a rogue unit. You can't turn rogue *rogue!* Now, Paul and Swank are dead and our work is slipping out of our fingers.

Well, I'm not going to let you ruin all of this for the bottom line. It is evolution; Alistair is a mutant. Not the next generation. Xavier and I are going to end this. And if it means destroying The Fold we will. I'm sorry.

Harrison handed Beth Ann the email. She was awake and read it fast. Said nothing. Placed the printout back on the coffee table.

"What do you want me to say?" Harrison asked Bernard.

Bernard pursed his fat lips, "You know it all?"

"I think I can see the forest for the trees."

"Illuminate me, if you don't mind."

Harrison hated games.

"Alright," he said. "Ondscan wants to be on the forefront of globalization, of the culture wars for the wallet of humanity. Ondscan puts money into a black ops marketing program. One that will take fucked up, sick people who have an edge with sub-cultures and make them business savvy wheelers and dealers. But I'm sure it's extended beyond that. Way beyond that into every little fuck-the-man subculture in America. Maybe even beyond that, too. You train these people to infiltrate every media outlet they can, to slowly cultivate a population that will buy all your shit, and you sit back and count the beans. Is that close?"

"Close enough," Bernard turned to Tammy and Tammy nodded.

"And I'm guessing that it all went wacko on you. You lost control. Alistair flipped out and started killing..."

Bernard shook his head.

"So what then?" Harrison asked.

Beth Ann remained silent. Harrison hoped it was a clever distraction. He wanted to ask her if she was hurting. He didn't.

"Alistair didn't lose control, Harrison. You read T's email. It was Phase 2. Alistair had this big idea that if Phase 1 wasn't successful enough then we'd move to Phase 2. Frenzy Marketing is what he called it, but it pretty much boils down to serial killing. I'll readily admit he was a fucked up boy. Military brat gone to seed. And the whole frenzy marketing thing is a bit misleading. It's not really marketing. The frenzy bit was right, though. Alistair was always keen to be a killer."

"So, that's the latest rage, huh? Serial killing."

Tammy smiled, "They are media darlings aren't they?"

Harrison put on a confused face.

Bernard said, "What? That doesn't work for you, Harrison? Look at the world you live in. If you kill someone these days they are much more useful. I mean look at all the posthumous stars we've got burning up the charts. Hell, Tupac comes out with a new album every year and that mutherfucker's been dead nearly a decade. But it goes beyond the cult of personality. It goes toward the cycle of violence. The thrill of the hunt. People love a good serial killer."

"Like a nice slice of pie," Tammy said.

"You guys are royally fucked up. How much money does Ondscan sink into this deranged bullshit?"

"Millions. But it's not about money on our end, Harrison. We are the gods in the machine. The Fold isn't just some ragtag team of marketing assassins. It's a vision of the future where wars will be fought in the malls. We're entering a brave new world of terrorism and commerce, Harrison. If you're not prepared you'll be blown away."

Harrison laughed, "Right. Al Qaeda beers, Taliban swim trunks and Hamas supermarkets."

"That's right, Harrison. We've won the hearts and minds. The real battle will be terror only. Fear is the ultimate compeller. Right now, some sheik in Iran is turning over his chemical weapon stock for a share of a media conglomerate. He wants that company to do well. Whatever the costs. We will succeed even if it means bombing our own country into the Stone Age."

Harrison turned to Beth Ann, "Can we leave please?"

She shook her head, pointed to Tammy's Glock.

"Alright, Tammy, Bernard, what's the fucking deal?" Harrison said, his lips pulled back over his teeth. "You gonna kill us or what? Let's just get on with it 'cause I'm sick to death of talking."

Bernard sipped his scotch. Massaged Tammy's shoulder with his free hand. He put the tumbler down and sucked on his lower lip.

"We're not going to kill you, Harrison. Or you, Beth Ann. We're going to offer you jobs."

Harrison had an immediate gut reaction. It was akin to a gas pain. Disbelief manifest in his bowels.

"Right." Bernard read his body. "You're special. You're killers. You've got spunk. Poets at heart. Just what we're looking for. And the best thing is there is no application, no training, no bosses and every benefit in the world."

"What are you asking us to do?" Beth Ann spat.

"We're retiring. We want you to take over here. We want you to be Mother and Father. To oversee the next phase of the operation, to take Ondscan's money and do whatever you want with it."

Harrison turned to Beth Ann. Mouth agape. She put her hands on Harrison's face. Her fingers ran tickling down his cheeks. She was shaking her head and closing her eyes and tears were forming at the corners.

Bernard turned to Tammy and said, "We're thinking of going to France, Paris or maybe someplace in the south." Still looking at Tammy, Bernard smiled and said, "What do you see for these two?"

Tammy laughed, "Bouncing babies."

Beth Ann's eyes opened and stared into nothing. They were faded. Glassed over. "We don't have a choice do we?" she whispered to Harrison.

He shook his head. "I don't think so."

Bernard laughed. He stood up and offered a hand to Harrison. "Come on. You guys don't have to make this so dramatic. You're making me feel terrible."

Harrison didn't take Bernie's hand. He didn't even look at him. Kept his eyes on Beth Ann's. Bernard kneeled down beside them and he put his left hand on Harrison's knee. His right hand still on the rifle. He kneeled down there and he whispered, "There's no other option. I'm sure you're both curious. This can be a whole new life for you. You'll be on the edge of everything going on. You'll be the ones setting the rules.

"Let me just paint a picture for you here: Harrison, there would be no more scribbling dirty stories in the dark. No more obscurity. You could publish whatever, wherever. You can take your 'preoccupation' to a whole new level. Transform yourself and break out of the ghetto you've so unhappy in. Or you could cure yourself completely with the finest drugs and best shrinks money can buy. Even better you could retire from the museum and settle into a life of luxury as you define it—collect your own fossil specimens, write your uber-hot science porn and maybe settle down with Beth Ann.

"Speaking of," Bernard turned to face Beth Ann. "You could really expand the knitting scene. You could found schools, open feminist knitting stores and supply the knitting underground with all the estrogen-laced wool it so obviously needs. Or how about those eyes of yours, those slowly darkening eyes? Like your beloved here, you could have access to the latest medical advances. No questions asked. You could be at the front of the line for the latest therapies, the latest medications.

"And forget Williamsburg. You could live in Manhattan. Buy a luxury loft in the East Village. Have a private plane to shuttle your remaining friends around to concerts and dinner in Stockholm and Sydney. Everything you've ever wanted only a nod away. You just say yes and we hand it over to you."

Bernie winked.

Harrison shook his head, eyed Tammy.

"You will make the rules, Harrison. You won't be beholden to any committees, no boards. This is black ops. This is under the table. It's not talked about by the water cooler or at the gym. What you choose to do, the money you use, the people you hire and train, none of it exists in the eyes of the company. You will be accountable to no one."

"Why would you want us?" Beth Ann asked.

"Look at what you managed to do. Not only are you guys

really respected amongst your friends and peers but you're out-and-out killers. You not only found us—and really the only way to do that was to kill a few people—but you impressed everyone along the way. You did it with style and grace. Not that that's the most crucial thing but it helps. If you're going to fuck the world over you might as well look really good doing it."

Beth Ann thought back to the meaning of life according to Solange. She tried to crack a smile, something small and personal, but it wouldn't go.

"You're saying we could rob the coffers of Ondscan to fund our own gigs? That Ondscan not only doesn't care but doesn't know what's going on here and that anything we do is somehow sanctioned?" Harrison asked.

Bernard nodded. Tammy said, "Sure is."

"And if we take like five hundred grand and plaster Brooklyn with billboards linking Ondscan to the unsolved murders of Swank and Jakus and others, you're saying that would be fine?"

Bernard said, "Yes. But it'll probably cost you something like three times that."

"What if we pay someone to level Ondscan's building in midtown? What then?"

"I couldn't think of a better marketing opportunity," Bernard smiled. "Harrison, anything you think of will be approved. You need to understand that we're in the postapocalyptic age of marketing. You take this deal and anything—everything—you do will benefit Ondscan. Even if it means cursing Ondscan's name and trying to tear the company down. The sad truth is that today, the very fact that you live, breathe, and purchase means that you're a cog in the machine. You need to just decide which cog you want to be. Knowing what you know, do you want to be the blissfully unaware tool on the street or the one pulling the levers from above?"

Beth Ann squeezed Harrison's face and whispered, "We don't really have a choice."

Harrison turned to Bernard and nodded. It was a slow and

painful nod. His teeth clenched. He stood up and pulled Beth Ann up with him. "We're in this together," he whispered to her. "No matter what."

Beth Ann tried to smile. Her eyes were bloodshot. Her hands shaking.

Bernie said, "Good choice."

Tammy put down her gun and clapped. "Bravo," she said, "Bravo. Welcome to the Brave New World."

Bernard led them out of the house through the garage. The air was crisp, fresh, and the sun twinkled in the stillness. There was a limo idling in the driveway, white cotton plumes of steam puffing out of its tailpipe making smog clouds that hunkered down low to the ground. Bernard opened a passenger side door and asked Harrison and Beth Ann to get in. They did. They leaned back into the leather interior, in their shit and blood- and fur-coated jumpsuits, staring out into nothingness as the door closed and the limo pulled out. Tammy and Bernard waved from the living room window. Smiling. Perfect.

35

"*The Tarantula Screams* EP."

"Seriously?"

"You bet. Forget paying hundreds for the vinyl. We'll be re-leasing it in a re-mastered edition with all of Iron Curtain's singles as well as ten demos, six unreleased studio cuts—including my fav 'The Second Punk Wars'—and five live tracks that we've scrubbed the fuck out of and made nearly as pretty as the studio cuts. It'll be the minimal synth coup of the century."

Rad's rubber hand tapped gently against the table, beer suds glistening on its beige PVC surface. He was beaming and the two men sitting at the table with him nodded in approval.

"You've done it again, Rad," Jerry Rudnick said. He was tall and thin, a big orange afro on his bespectacled head. His sunglasses picked up all the lights in The Grande Lounge and it looked like he had disco balls on his eyes. Jerry owned a club, Ministry, a few blocks away on DeKalb. He was bipolar and spent a good part of the year in his bed, crying and whispering to his cats.

Rad sipped his beer and said, "We'll have to trot it out to the Ministry and see what your patrons think of it."

"They'll eat it up," Jerry smirked. He was on a high. "They always eat it up."

That's when two women walked in. Blanche Markham, a blonde with raccoon eyeliner and pouty lips, sat across from Jerry and said, "Evening, boys." Her British accent was thick and she spat when she spoke. Blanche was a sculptor, her work adored by Godzilla fanboys. Mostly it was ten-foot-tall plaster recreations of Toho monster melees—King Ghidora swooping down on Godzilla, Gigan jumping over Mothra, Jet Jaguar frozen in fisticuffs with Rodan—and they toured the sci-fi conventions and got center spreads in all the geek magazines. She lived alone and had non-Hodgkin lymphoma.

"Hello, Blanche." Rad waved his rubber hand. "Hello, Carla."

Carla Chan, a Chinese-American with a purple buzz cut, sat across from Rad. She was a molecular biologist at NYU and had a thing for leather bondage gear. Carla was proud to announce to anyone she met that she was what she dubbed "the antithesis of the typical Asian servant-whore." Carla was a sexual dynamo, in and out of bed with nearly everyone she knew. She'd fucked Jerry, Rad, and Blanche, and was trying to get into Dennis' pants.

The burly guy sitting next to Jerry, Dennis Grimshaw, was picking his teeth and laughing. "Wait 'til you see this shit. Rad's lost his mind."

Dennis, originally from Wyoming, was owner of Sucker Sticks. His infamous bumper stickers—the most notorious being "My high school dropout ass-fucked your honor roll student"—were all the rage in Newark and he'd recently expanded into offensive web banner ads. Dennis was a binge eater and incredibly paranoid.

"What surprise do you have for us now?" Carla asked.

Rad leaned over and pulled a green jumpsuit from the duffle bag at his feet. He stood up and held it out in front of him. Across the front, in bold black letters, were stitched the words: Clinton Hill Furies.

"Fucking awesome!" Dennis shouted. He pulled his shoes

off, grabbed the jumpsuit from Rad and slipped into it. Then he modeled the look, turning slow and striking poses before sitting down and slamming the rest of his PBR.

"I don't get it," Blanche spat. "Wha' the fuck is this shite?"

"These are our uniforms," Rad smiled. "We're a gang now. We're a team. Haven't you ever seen *The Warriors?*"

Blanche nodded. "Of course," she said.

Rad said, "That's what the fuck this is. It's called vigilante justice. Wild West. If the FBI won't stop these fuckers at least we will."

"You're not kidding," Jerry ran his fingers through his fro and grinned ear to ear. "I'm so down for this!"

"Fuck yes!" Dennis shouted.

"How?" Carla asked. "We don't even know who these people are. We only have a few photos of them scouting locations and even those are pretty sketchy. I mean, what if these guys aren't killers? What if they're just some shmucks playing a game?"

"A game?" Rad leaned in and squinted at Carla. His pale scar looked practically ominous in the half-light of the bar. "Do you even realize what we've uncovered? I mean these fuckers are plotting a massacre. It's like Columbine but twice as big. I've already laid all the details out for you. The police, the FBI, they're not going to stop this 'cause they don't think it's really going down. They can't see the threads that we see. They don't tie it all together. Besides, we've done enough illegal shit getting ready for this that if you were to go to the cops they'd lock you the fuck up."

"So how?" Jerry asked.

"That's the best part," Rad grinned. He paused as the MC5's "Rama Lama Fa Fa Fa" blared out across the bar. "These guys are coming after me next."

And Rad spun his web. It worked flawlessly. He found it so easy to convince this maladjusted team that they were indeed the only ones who could save the day. And the more they drank and the more coke they snorted and the more hash they smoked the more his plan made sense. The more the flimsy lies that hung it all together strengthened.

When he was done, Dennis, Carla, Blanche and Jerry were as wasted as they'd ever been, stumbling out of the bar and into the street in a cacophony of curses and toasts. Rad stayed behind, sipping a beer and sighing.

He slipped out of the Grande Lounge a few minutes later, looked up into the night sky at the few scattered black clouds and lit a smoke. Then he walked down Greene and took a left on Classon and walked up beside a limo double parked around the corner.

The right side door of the limo swung open and Rad got inside. The interior was dark, just the flicker of a television screen casting dim squares of light. Sitting across from Rad was a young couple. Dr. Harrison Gelden was wearing black jeans and a sweater. His face shaved clean, his brown hair grown out long and in a tight ponytail. Beth Ann Belling sat beside him, her Chelsea cut grown out and long hair died black. She wore one of her slack housedresses but it bulged around her protruding, pregnant belly.

"It's amazing how easy this has gotten," Rad said pouring a drink from the limo's small bar.

Harrison nodded, "I spoke with my contact inside Mantlo today. They've got no idea we're moving into Clinton Hill. She says the boys have assumed that their territory is secure, that the market is completely defined. It'll be quite a rude awakening when we take out their top astroturfers."

Beth Ann rubbed her belly and said, "We're reinventing this whole scene. Our boy's going to grow up in a very different world."

Rad smiled, "You guys settle on a name yet?"

"Sure," Harrison laughed. He leaned forward, ran his hand over the top of his head and tightened his ponytail, "We're thinking of Severin."

"That's a nice name," Rad nodded. "Very nice."